Not Quite Enough

Also by Catherine Bybee

Contemporary Romance

Weekday Bride Series

Wife by Wednesday

Married by Monday

Fiancé by Friday

Not Quite Series

Not Quite Dating

Not Quite Mine

Paranormal Romance

MacCoinnich Time Travels

Binding Vows

Silent Vows

Redeeming Vows

Highland Shifter

The Ritter Werewolves Series

Before the Moon Rises

Embracing the Wolf

Novellas

Soul Mate

Possessive

Erotica

Kilt Worthy

Kilt-A-Licious

CATHERINE BYBEE

Not Quite Enough

Montlake
Romance

Published by Montlake Romance, Seattle

www.apub.com

ISBN-13: 9781477809594
ISBN-10: 1477809597

Library of Congress Control Number: 2013907670

To every ER nurse and doctor I've

ever had the privilege to work beside.

You know who you are.

Chapter One

"Don't let my baby die."

Monica stared into the desperate eyes of a mother on the verge of losing her seven-year-old daughter. The little girl made the unfortunate mistake of riding her bike in the street and into the path of a passing car. A mistake that would most likely end her life.

"We'll do everything we can," Monica told the mother. Her reassuring smile was a pathetic attempt, but she had to do something to give the woman hope.

Monica ducked into the trauma room, where no fewer than fifteen people worked feverishly to save the child's life.

With the help of the ER staff, the paramedics moved the child from the stretcher to the gurney and whisked their stretcher from the room.

Dr. Chuck Meeks, the trauma surgeon on call, stood at the patient's head and listened to the report from the medic. Monica listened while she helped the emergency medical technician and another nurse remove the remainder of the child's clothing.

"The car struck her and tossed her thirty feet from the point of impact. Her friend said she was moaning after it happened but when we got there she was unconscious."

As the medic spoke, Monica ran down her own list. A, airway . . . the child was already intubated. B, breathing . . . the doctor was listening to the patient's lungs as the medic spoke. Blunt force trauma could result in a collapsed lung, internal bleeding . . . any number of injuries. But Monica was getting ahead of herself.

C, circulation. The patient's heart rate was too fast with a blood pressure of 68/50. Monica systematically moved down the child to check for pulses.

"Let's get her off the backboard," Dr. Meeks instructed. "X-ray, I need a chest film here to check this tube. Did CT clear?"

"CAT scan is ready when you are." Patricia Keller, the nursing supervisor, stood at the door and informed the doctor.

Monica cut through the child's jeans. D, disability and neuro status. A CAT scan would let them all know the extent of the head trauma, but some less life-threatening injuries could be seen with the naked eye.

"What's her name?" Monica asked the medic. Using a pronoun for her patients, instead of a name, didn't feel right.

"Bethany. Her friend called her Beth."

When removing the jeans from Beth's lower limbs, Monica noticed an obvious break above her right knee. "Dr. Meeks?"

Meeks glanced Monica's way with a nod. "Pulses?"

Monica checked for pulses distal from the injury, found a faint rapid tap to match the child's heart rate.

"Faint, but they're there."

"Get a box splint on it until we see what else is going on. I don't like the sound of her right lung. Get a chest tube ready, X-ray, push in and let's get a picture."

"Pressure's dropping, Chuck."

Valerie, the other ER nurse in the room pulled everyone's attention to the monitors at the head of the bed. Beth's blood pressure dropped dangerously low.

The chatter that had hummed over the room stopped, and everyone moved faster.

Thirty minutes later Monica walked out of the operating room where she'd given Bethany's report to the nurse taking over. Shattered femur, collapsed lung, internal bleeding, most likely spleen but the doctors would have to determine that in the OR and work to fix it. The bump on Bethany's head turned out to have no significance, which begged the question as to why the child was unconscious. It was as if God swept down and said, "Time for you to take a little nap, sweetheart." Maybe, just maybe, with the skills of the surgical staff Bethany would live to ride again.

So Monica hoped.

Back in the ER, the noise of the department swelled up inside of her until her ears rang with the energy of the room. New patients moved into the halls, while others walked, rolled, or limped their way out.

Just another day. She loved it. All of it. Well, most of it anyway. There were some things she didn't love about her job at Pomona Valley Hospital. Like the sunken eyes of a loved one when they learn that someone hadn't made it, or the politics that forced non-emergent cases into the ER on a daily basis. Understaffing . . . union battles. OK, maybe she didn't *love* all of her job.

The computerized board indicated a couple of vacant rooms and highlighted a number of patients in the waiting room. Seemed like the number of patients in need always outnumbered available space. There were two ER doctors on, a dozen nurses, and several EMTs.

Monica nodded to the clerk, Nancy, and asked, "Do we have any runs coming in?"

"Nope." Nancy had an ear to the phone and was simultaneously entering orders for the doctors into the computer system. They'd yet to go paperless. Most of the hospital was completely computerized, but so far, the ER had resisted the change. Monica couldn't wait for a shift in management to recognize the benefits of computerizing and streamlining their system. Anything to help move people through faster.

Monica grabbed a chart from the rack and moved to the lobby door to call in the patient.

She glanced at the name the triage nurse had written on the assessment, recognized the name, and cringed. *Owens!* She looked at the complaint. *Stomach pain.*

Gary Owens was a frequent flyer who didn't have a mileage card. He visited the ER no less than once a week, most of the time coming through the back door via ambulance. The man was an alcoholic who'd brushed aside death more times than Monica could count.

The man had a death wish. As much as Monica hated herself for thinking it, she wished he would just get it over with already. It was hard to feel sorry for someone who self-inflicted nearly every medical problem he ever had.

Mustering an ounce of propriety, she opened the door to the lobby and glanced over the eager faces of the waiting patients. Patients who deserved her attention. *Don't pass judgment, Mo.*

Too late.

"Owens?"

Gary sat three rows back with crying children on both sides of him. His head was dipped into his chest, his eyes were closed.

"Owens?" she said louder.

He didn't even look up.

The bastard was asleep. Probably drunk. Unable to avoid the inevitable, she moved past the door and walked over to the man, smelling him long before she shook his shoulder. "Gary?"

He startled awake, glanced around the room. His expression softened when he realized where he was and he stood with a slight waver. Monica had no desire to have him drag her to the floor, which might injure her back and put her out of work. "Do you need a wheelchair?"

He swallowed and his glassy eyes met hers. "I'm good. Fine."

After a moment, he followed her back into the busy ER where she led him into a private room. One where he'd probably sleep for the better part of the night. Abdominal pain workups often took hours and they'd likely find nothing inside they could help mend. Which meant he'd go out and drink himself back again next week.

Monica shook the thought from her head.

It wasn't easy. She thought of the child in OR fighting for her life and here this man was pissing his life away.

Without a smile, Monica walked Gary to a room and pointed toward the gurney and the hospital gown sitting on top of it. "You know the drill, Gary."

He nodded and started to undo his shirt. Monica left him to inform the ER doctor of Gary's presence.

"Walt?" Dr. Walter "Walt" Eddy would be just as *thrilled* with Gary's presence as she was.

Walt glanced up from the chart in his hands and offered a smile. "Yeah?"

"Gary Owens is in room sixteen."

Walt rolled his eyes, something she'd refrained from doing.

She grinned.

"GI bleed?"

"Not this time. Abdominal pain."

"He drunk?"

"Isn't he always?"

"Drop a line, draw labs. I'll be there in a minute."

After grabbing an IV tray, Monica turned to make her way back into Gary's room to begin the daunting task of finding a vein. She knew from experience the task wasn't easy. Gary had been in some kind of fire several years before, leaving scar tissue over both arms and half his back.

At least the man had never been toxic with her. He didn't come in cussing and fighting. He wasn't a mean drunk, just a drunk. The age on his chart said forty-three, but he looked sixty.

A woman from medical records stepped up to the desk and started piling charts. It was routine for any returning patients to have their charts pulled and brought up. Monica recognized Gary's overstuffed manila folder, which was a good four inches thick.

She picked up the chart and walked down the hall to Gary's room. Each step built frustration with the man. She cautioned herself briefly before entering the room and closing the door behind her.

Gary sat with his legs dangling off the edge of the gurney. The blue and white spotted gown covered most of him.

He wouldn't look at her.

Fine.

Monica set the IV tray down quietly on an overhead table and paused.

"Do you know what this is?" she asked him, her tone cold.

His gaze flickered to the chart in her hands. He shrugged.

"It's your chart. Your ER chart." She dropped the heavy folder on the gurney beside him.

He flinched.

"Most charts are no more than a handful of pages. Yours . . . yours is proof that you're trying to kill yourself." Anger boiled as she spoke. "People come in here every day and fight to live. You come in here nearly every day fighting to die." The image of the child she'd just left flashed in her memory.

"I'm not trying to die." His voice was flat and he never met her gaze.

"Drinking yourself to death isn't trying to live. When are you going to wake up, Gary? One of these days you're going to come in here too sick for us to do a damn thing for you."

His tired eyes hardened and he finally met her stare. "What does it matter to you?"

Good question. Why was she closed in this room reaming him a new ass? Her boss didn't like her to begin with . . . this little stunt could get her written up, or worse.

She shook her head. Did this man have kids? If so, where were they? Did they wish their father was sober? "None of us live in a bubble. Someone out there thinks about you."

His jaw twitched.

Monica swallowed, picked up his chart, and turned to leave the room. She'd find him another nurse. She wasn't objective enough at the moment to deal with him.

The nurse she'd asked to take over returned to Monica's side a few minutes later and reported that Gary had left.

Two hours later Monica sat in the break room with her aching head in her hands. The day hadn't gotten better. The only redeeming feature was when news came from the operating room that Bethany had survived surgery.

That was the most important news.

The door to the room opened, letting the noise of the department leak in.

"You OK?"

Monica glanced up at Deb, a fellow nurse and sometime nightclub friend when they both had the same day off.

"Bad day?" Deb asked.

"It's been busy."

"Maybe John will make it better."

Monica attempted a half-ass smile. *John.* She hadn't thought about him once all day. They'd dated for the better part of two months. She should have known better than to sleep with a co-worker. They'd had a good time but it wasn't working, not for her anyway. John seemed genuinely into her and that sucked.

"Oh . . . that is *not* a good look," Deb said.

"What?"

"Things aren't good with you two?"

"It's OK . . . I guess."

Deb, who always had her hair pulled back in a tight ponytail, narrowed her eyes. "You guess?"

"He's a good guy. Thinks he's more a doctor than a nurse." He was a nurse. A good one, but one with too much ego and not enough education. "He talked about moving in last week." A conversation she quickly snuffed out. She lived in a two-bedroom apartment she'd first shared with her sister, Jessie, and her nephew, Danny, before Jessie married Jack and moved to Texas. Then Jack's sister, Katie, had moved in for a brief while with her daughter. Now it was just Monica and she wanted it that way, for now anyway. "I don't want a roommate."

"John would be more than a roommate."

"I know."

Deb sat beside her on the worn-out sofa and patted Monica's knee. "If you're not into him . . . you might want to cut it off sooner than later."

"I know." She sucked at relationships. Two months was a long stint for her. She had to admit if it wasn't for the fact that John worked with her, she'd have cut it off by week four.

"I mean it, Monica. He asked me if you liked round diamonds or square ones last week."

A chill ran up Monica's spine. Her eyes snapped to Deb's. "You're kidding."

Deb sucked in her bottom lip and shook her head. "He asked me not to say anything to you."

"This is bad. Oh, so bad."

"When do you see him again?"

"I'm off tomorrow. We were going to get together for dinner." A dinner that was supposed to be a dress-up affair. Monica dropped her head in her hands again. "Am I too old to run away?"

"Yes."

"But—"

"No buts. Let him go before he pops the question. Men don't recover from that kind of rejection."

"You really think he wants to marry me?"

"Diamonds aren't for promise rings."

Monica pushed off the couch and moved to her locker. Inside she fished through her purse for aspirin. "Two months. We've only dated two months." She didn't see this coming.

"You've known him for over a year."

"So?"

"Didn't your sister agree to marry her husband in less time than that?"

"They were different." They loved each other to bits. Mutually. Monica didn't love John.

This needed to end.

Tonight. Before anyone got hurt.

———

Wearing scrubs . . . possibly the most unattractive outfit ever, Monica insisted that John meet her for a drink at a quiet bar not far from her apartment. She opted for her hospital-issue uniform in an effort to hide her curves. She swept her blonde hair up into a ponytail and rid her high cheekbones of the blush she'd had on earlier in the day. There was no hiding her light blue eyes unless she wore sunglasses in the dim bar. After sending him a brief text that they "needed to talk," she hoped her words didn't translate into anything romantic.

She'd found a quiet table in the back, away from the men walking in and searching for a good time. Her earlier conversation with Gary Owens kept her from ordering anything other than an iced tea. As much as she wanted the liquid courage, she would wait until she got home and sank into a hot tub with a glass of wine.

Three televisions lit up the space behind the bar. Two were focused on baseball games while the third was on the evening news.

She sipped her tea and checked her watch right as the door opened letting the evening sun into the room.

John was easy on the eyes. Light brown hair cut military short. Not quite six feet tall, he strode into the room and spotted her.

Monica nodded and attempted to smile.

Her earlier headache started to pound again.

"Hey." He slid into the seat opposite her. "Must have been a bad day if you're drinking Long Islands."

"We were busy." She didn't correct his assumption.

He slid his hand over the table and covered hers. "I'm glad you messaged me. I know I don't like going home alone after a bad day."

Monica flinched.

John's eyes narrowed. "Is everything OK?"

As slowly as she could, Monica removed her hand from under his. "I had a hard day, but that isn't why I wanted to meet with you."

Someone at the bar yelled at the TV, drawing her attention away for a moment. She hated this part. Not that she was an expert at it or anything, but hooking up was always easier than splitting off.

"What's up?" John tucked his hands in his lap, his gaze pinned to her face.

She glanced around the dark bar. It was quiet . . . early. She kept her voice low. She got right to the reason she'd asked him there.

"The other night, when you were talking about moving in . . . I realized that maybe we weren't looking for the same thing."

He fidgeted and sat taller. "You're not ready to move in with me. I get it. We'll slow down."

She shook her head. "I don't think slowing down is going to help. I'm . . . I'm not ready for commitment."

He sat back and crossed his arms over his chest. The defensive move wasn't lost on her. The smile on his lips fell. "What are you saying, Monica?"

She rubbed her hands on her cotton scrubs. "We've had a good time."

His mouth opened, then closed. "A good time?" He rubbed his thumb against his forefinger. "I was a good time? I thought we were getting along."

"We were. Are. This is hard, John. We work together. I don't want to mess up my job . . . your job."

"Then don't."

If only it were that easy. "I think you're into *us* more than I am. I wish I felt more, but I don't."

He ran a hand through his hair. "You're breaking up with me."

Monica sat on her hands. "I'm sorry. I'm not ready for a committed relationship. I don't even have a pet."

"Is there someone else?"

"No. Of course not. I don't want to lead you on. Make you think I want something deeper when I don't." He had to understand that . . . right?

"I really thought we had something special." Through the veil of anger was a lining of hurt behind his eyes. For that she was very sorry.

"I'm sorry." She couldn't look at him.

"Commitment is part of growing up."

Instead of saying anything, she skirted her gaze across the room.

"You have to *grow up* sometime." His words were harsh. Considering the shitty day she had . . . very harsh. She was trying to spare his feelings. Trying to let him down easy.

The noise from the bar hushed and someone turned up the volume on the news.

"Don't make this harder than it has to be, John. We were friends before. I'd like us to stay that way now." She did. Though she wasn't stupid enough to believe being *only* friends would work.

"That's it? I don't have a say?"

"You can say what you want. It isn't going to change my feelings." She met his eyes.

John stretched his neck and pushed away from the table. "Maybe in a few days I can say something nice. But right now I want a drink . . . alone."

"I'm sorry," she said to his back as he walked out the door.

That went well.

She pushed a long-suffering breath through her lips and pushed out of her chair. One dirty martini wouldn't hurt.

Monica made her way to the bar and flagged down the bartender. She ordered her drink and looked over her shoulder.

John wasn't coming back.

Monica pulled a ten dollar bill from her wallet and set it on the counter. When the bartender placed her drink in front of her he asked if she needed change.

"We're good," she told him as she lifted her drink.

"Can you believe this?" he said as he slid the ten in his palm and motioned toward the television.

"Believe what?"

"The earthquake in Jamaica."

Breaking news had interrupted the local broadcast to show amateur footage of devastation.

Waves broke on the shore . . . only it wasn't a shore. It was the inside of a small town. People were screaming, cars and entire houses were floating out to sea.

Monica's insides chilled. She set her drink down before one sip.

"Can you turn that up?"

The bartender picked up a remote and upped the volume.

" . . . three hundred years past due, this earthquake has been predicted for decades. Preliminary reports placed the quake at 7.5 on the magnitude scale. Much larger than the 1692 quake that killed over five thousand people in Port Royal."

Monica's back teeth ground together. A man stood on a porch of what looked like a beach town boardwalk holding on to a child. He grasped onto a wooden beam as a wave of water retreated from the camera, taking everything with it.

"Oh, God."

"Makes me damn happy I don't live on the beach."

Inside her purse, her cell phone buzzed.

She fished it out, staring at the broadcast.

"Yeah?" she asked without looking at the name on her phone.

"You watching the news?"

It was Walt.

"I am."

"I put in a call to BD. You in?" BD stood for Borderless Doctors. Monica helped with Borderless Nurses. The relief organization put in time and skill from trained professionals to help with aid after nature shook, flooded, or blew up an area. With Borderless Nurses, she'd go straight into the devastation, live out of a backpack for a couple of weeks . . . help.

Getting away from John and the ER for a while wouldn't suck, even though she knew she'd be walking into the soggy depths of hell.

"I'm in."

Chapter Two

"You ready for this, Mo? I know you think you're tough . . . but you lost it when you learned that Santa wasn't real." Jessie was talking to her on the cell phone before the team was about to pile into the second airplane of the day.

Monica laughed. "I survived. I'm ready. Besides . . . why did I become a nurse if not to help people?

"You can do that at home."

"But these people really need me. If no one went where would they be?"

There was a long pause. "Be safe, Mo. Watch out for you." Right about then someone was giving Monica a vaccine of some sort. She didn't even bother asking what it was for. She didn't want to know the risk. She was going . . . she had to.

"I love you, Jessie. Kiss Danny for me. I'll try and call."

"Once every couple of days."

"I'll try." She'd do more than try. Unless the lines were completely down, she'd call.

The flight from Florida to Jamaica was on a cargo plane. Less than twenty-four hours had passed since the tsunami hit the northern coast of the island, and the death toll was estimated in the thousands. There hadn't been a tsunami of this nature on the shores of the island in recorded history. Even earthquakes were rare. There had been an earthquake in the ocean hours before the shaker hit the island, causing the tsunami to hit close behind the quake. It really didn't matter how or why the devastation happened, it needed to be cleaned up and the suffering people needed help.

According to their team briefing, bodies were washing up on shore and those who survived filled the hospitals and clinics all over the island.

Earlier, Monica had attempted to sleep on the flight from LA to Miami but only managed about an hour. Even with the ear protection, the noise in the cargo plane was too difficult to think past to allow her brain to turn off and rest.

The conversation with John hummed in the back of her mind . . . but the conversation with her boss, Pat, was what really weighed on her mind.

"You're due in on Saturday." Pat never had liked Monica. Her voice and words echoed the sentiment Monica knew was there.

"It's a humanitarian effort. The hospital can release a press statement about allowing your nurses and doctors leave." This was a practiced line Walt had said to use. On top of that, Walt had spoken with the head of the doctors' group expressing his need to be there. "The hospital can always use good PR."

There had been a long pause. "Get your shifts covered, Monica. And use the part-time staff to do it. I'm not authorizing any overtime."

Monica's vacation time would keep a paycheck coming in her absence. Five to eight days was usually the limit to these efforts. What kind of vacation it would be . . . that was left to be seen.

Instead of giving Pat the snarky reply that sat on Monica's tongue, she smiled. "I'll get it covered."

Monica's ears popped as the plane began its descent. Unlike a commercial flight where a smiling attendant reminded you to stay seated and keep your seat belts on, this one was met with the head of their team attempting to yell over the noise of the plane. "Stay seated," he said before gesturing with his hands to keep the seat belts on. Not that Monica had taken hers off.

Other than the training she'd been a part of a year and a half before in Florida, this was Monica's first real test. A foreign country with multiple issues that would bring untold patients. Flood victims, earthquake survivors, patients cut off from their families. When she'd stepped on the plane, she locked away the part of her that bled for those who truly suffered.

Early in her ER career one of her mentors had told her something that stuck with her from that day forward. "You're here to help. Either get in there and get your ass to work, or step away. You won't do anyone any good crying. You can cry later."

Best advice ever. It made her a better nurse. Monica knew that. Patients didn't always understand, but her colleagues . . . they got it.

As much as Monica braced her spine for what was coming, there was no way to brace for the reality of the scale of this mass casualty incident.

The airplane met the tarmac with a jolt, the landing anything but smooth. *American Airlines has nothing to fear.*

The nurses and doctors were shuffled off the plane while search and rescue workers were helping unload the cargo. They brought with them everything they thought they'd need. Boxes of first aid supplies along with emergency medicine, antibiotics, and their own food supplies were crated out.

Dawn was just starting to spread on the horizon. The humid heat of the Caribbean felt mildly uncomfortable on Monica's back. Other than Walt, she didn't know any of the other nurses or doctors on their team. They'd met in LA before taking off. Most had their heads in their iPods or on movies on the first flight. Tina, the only newbie aside from Monica, stood beside her outside the plane as they met the Jamaican officials by the cargo doors.

"You ready for this?" Tina asked.

"Doubt it. You?"

"Until we've both said we've done this . . . exactly this . . . I doubt either of us are ready."

Tina pointed to a pallet of boxes that were painfully familiar to an ER nurse. "What are those?"

Monica's back teeth ground together. "Body bags."

Tina's face went pale. "Oh."

The medical staff was shuffled off to another part of the runway. They'd landed in Kingston. They would be helicoptered into the Ocho Rios area and spread out from there in various means of transportation that would manage to traverse the damage.

Monica had never been on a helicopter. In truth, heights and she had an understanding . . . on second thought, they didn't. She managed airplanes because there was a strange safety inside the metal tube with wings. Out in the open . . . on a ledge? No. She didn't even have a desire to see the Grand Canyon. That massive ditch did nothing for her hormones.

"This is Reynard Kiffen. Second in charge of the off-island relief effort." Their team leader, Dr. Donald Klein, introduced the Jamaican native.

Reynard offered a smile, his white teeth in direct contrast to his dark skin. The smile was brief. "Thank you. My country, my people, thank you." He spoke slowly and enunciated his words clearly through his obvious accent. "We have a temporary hospital set up in Saint Mary's province. You will set up there. Accommodations are the best we can manage under the extreme circumstances."

"We aren't expecting five-star hotels, Reynard," Dr. Klein told him.

The smile on Reynard's face fell. "Some of the resorts are operational. Not many. They are taking in those they can. Moving tourists out as quickly as possible."

Monica hadn't thought about the tourists, those visiting for the ultimate vacation only to find themselves in a war zone.

"Everyone in the north is affected. No one I've met is free of the death."

Dr. Klein patted Reynard's back when the man's eyes lost focus, the effect on him obvious.

Dr. Klein carried on with their instructions. "The choppers in use hold only four people at a time. That includes the pilot. Only the essentials are going with you onboard, the rest of our supplies will arrive after us by ground."

The mere mention of the helicopter made Monica's skin crawl. The sooner she got this part of the trip out of the way, the better.

As the group disassembled, Monica made her way to Donald's side. "Excuse me, Dr. Klein." Monica pushed into his personal space with a half smile.

"Donald, please. It's Monica, right?"

"That's right." She'd met Dr. Klein briefly in Florida but didn't have a chance to talk to him. Something told her that the next week would change all that.

"You're ER with Walt?"

Monica nodded. "I am."

"He talks highly of you. This is your first time on something like this."

Monica was impressed. She wasn't the only newbie on deck, but it seemed Donald had used the flight time to study his team.

"I think it's the first time for most of us on 'something like this.'"

Donald's smile sobered slightly. "It's something new every time. An earthquake alone can be devastating."

"I grew up in Southern California. Most earthquakes aren't bothersome enough to get out of bed in the night." And they always tended to strike before the sun rose.

Donald nodded and reached to his feet to grab his backpack when the sound of a helicopter filled her ears.

Ignoring her heightened pulse, she reached past her fears and blurted out her needs.

"Listen, Donald. I'm not ashamed to admit that heights aren't a friend to me. Can I volunteer to go first? I'd just as soon get this part over with."

He lifted an eyebrow and scratched his bald head. He appeared as if he wanted to say something, but decided against it. "No problem."

"Thanks." Monica shuffled her pack from one shoulder to the other and drew in a deep breath.

Donald looked over Monica's head and shouted. "Walt?"

Walt turned around.

"You, Monica, and Tina are up first. Everyone else group in threes. I hope everyone managed some rest on the flight over. I will be making rounds when I can to force you to rest. If the opportunity presents itself, do it! We're here to help, not make stupid mistakes because we're tired. If you have questions, ask. Weaknesses, tell me." He glanced Monica's way. "We're a team. Remember that!"

The chopper flew in behind them, cutting off the conversation. Monica turned toward the wind and gripped the strap to her backpack.

The sun had crested the horizon and the thick heat of the Caribbean started to make itself known. She stared at the "bird" as the skids planted down on the pavement. Unlike when she'd wait for a chopper on the helipad at the hospital, this time the anxiety coursing through her veins was personal.

A hand on her shoulder brought her attention to Tina, who noticed her hesitation when they boarded the plane in Florida. Instead of giving her shit about her phobias, Tina spouted off a few facts about flying being safer than driving in LA and then proceeded to tell her about the many flings she carried on in college. Soon the sexual antics of a horny twentysomething diverted Monica's attention. "It's just a smaller plane," she said close to Monica's ear.

A plane. Right. Without wings and without a jet engine. If *this* chopper was just a smaller plane then a smart car was a chip off a semitruck.

Her fingers tingled, reminding her to force slow, deep breaths into her lungs.

"C'mon, help me gather a couple of duffel bags. Don't look at it until you have to."

Monica turned away from the chopper as the giant propeller slowed to a stop. Those around her mobilized, moving in a common direction to shift their bags into some sort of order as the sound of another chopper met Monica's ears. Not able to help herself, she glanced toward the tarmac. Another chopper, about the same size as the last, hovered over the first until the tail lined up and the skids moved in a slow descent to the ground. Out of the first, someone jumped to the ground.

Monica narrowed her eyes and noticed the man spilling from the pilot's seat and running a hand through his hair. He rounded the tail of the aircraft and shoved his palm into Reynard's in greeting.

That's my ride.

Monica glanced at the sky coming to life above her and reminded herself that those who needed her help were subject to an earthquake and a tsunami. None of which happened in the sky.

Still, her fingers tingled.

A hand clasped onto her shoulder. "Ready?"

Monica's fingernails dug into her palms. Her head swiveled toward Donald. A slight lift to his lips was the only emotion on his face.

"Ready," she said with more conviction than she felt.

Lord knew she understood how to fake it. From orgasms to happiness, so faking confidence was easy.

She shoved her backpack up on her shoulder and straightened her spine. Donald moved in front of her to speak to the pilot. Monica hesitated until Tina nudged her shoulder.

"Ready?"

"Born ready."

Tina snorted and turned toward Walt.

Monica forced her feet toward the chopper as if she was born to ride in the tin box with a single propeller on top and a tiny one in the back. *How the hell did the thing actually fly?* It didn't have wings.

Donald's back was to her as he spoke to someone. He twisted when she approached, revealing a man. His dark hair was too long, his jaw held more stubble than would be considered sexy. He wore a button-up silk shirt and khaki cargo shorts. And no shoes.

Monica took in his bare feet and forced her gaze back to the man's face. Strong jaw with a firm set. No smile. His eyes were covered with dark glasses but they didn't detract from the pure masculinity of the man. He had to stand at least six feet tall, with broad shoulders and a narrow waist . . .

"Monica? Monica?"

She was checking out the man and not realizing someone spoke her name.

"Yeah?"

"This is your pilot. He thinks you should ride in front. Let Tina and Walt take the back."

Her eyes skidded from Donald's face to that of the barefoot stranger. "*He's* the pilot?"

"One of the best on the island."

The pilot dipped his head as if he were sizing her up. Then abruptly turned toward the helicopter.

"He's barefoot," she whispered. As if a lack of shoes meant he couldn't fly the helicopter. *If I take off my shoes, I'm still a nurse.*

Donald didn't hear her words. The pilot was already jumping into his seat and making the propeller above her head move.

She ducked and allowed Donald to push her toward the door. Behind her, Tina and Walt were climbing into the backseat.

Monica's hands were sweaty and at the same time cold as she allowed herself to be pushed into the small, suffocating aircraft.

"You'll be fine," Donald yelled in her ear as the noise of the chopper made it impossible to hear normal conversation.

Monica nodded. Her nephew, Danny, would be laughing at her if he could see the panic in her eyes.

She forced herself into the passenger seat and ignored the sound of the door closing her in. Shoeless and sexy shoved headgear into her lap. Monica glanced his way as he switched levers and went through some sort of series of system checks before they took off.

Behind her, Tina and Walt were buckling into their seats.

Monica shifted to her right and found her belt. She secured it and fumbled with the headgear before the noise in the chopper overcame her.

Once the earmuffs were on, the noise lessened, giving her a moment of calm.

The chopper shifted, and Monica's racing pulse lodged in her throat.

"You going to be sick?"

Soft and non-accusatory, Barefoot's voice sounded in her ears.

Her heart was racing, but she'd yet to feel her stomach churn. "I'm OK."

Far from OK, but maybe her voice would convince him otherwise.

Barefoot snorted. A full-on snort complete with a shake of his head. He reached over and pried her fingers off her backpack and placed them onto a large rod in the center of the chopper.

"Hold this," he told her. "When I say up, push it forward. When I say down, pull it back."

What? Shit. Was she some kind of copilot? "You can't fly this thing on your own?"

"You're shotgun, Blondie. And everyone licensed to fly is solo today."

Monica's stomach lodged near her thyroid. She glanced to the back of the chopper where Tina and Walt were giving her a smile.

"They can't hear us," Barefoot managed.

"Why not?"

Instead of answering, he gave a thumbs-up to someone out the window and grasped his controls with both hands.

He can't really mean he needs me to help him fly this machine.

"Up."

Monica shoved the stick forward with the command and ignored her brain telling her to get off the damn chopper and *walk* toward the needy.

The chopper lurched and within seconds, they were in the air. The tarmac disappeared with alarming speed. Those on the ground scrambled into the next chopper and Monica felt her already chilly insides grow even colder.

Barefoot's hand left his controls and kept her hand on the stick between them. "Keep pushing it up," he instructed.

"You can't fly this thing on your own?"

Instead of answering, he moved his hand away and switched a lever on his side. Monica kept her hand shoved forward, as if it were a joystick on a video game and she was close to breaking her all-time record. *This isn't happening.* The sky was streaming at her, the earth was slipping away, and she had her life in her hands. Walt's and Tina's, too. Not to mention Barefoot's. Not that she cared about him. Who brought a passenger on board and expected them to help pilot the flight?

The sun blinded her as they made it into the sky but Monica's death grip on the helicopter joystick didn't falter.

"Keep looking toward the horizon," Barefoot instructed.

"OK," she told him. Did she have a choice?

The world whizzed past with thick trees below them.

"Don't look down. I need your attention on the horizon."

Monica swallowed her stomach back. Maybe that late-night sandwich wasn't a great idea. Donald told them to eat and she'd forced herself to down a turkey and cheese and a bag of stale chips. Normally she loved salt and vinegar chips. Only now, they didn't feel good so close to the surface.

Barefoot's hand moved back to hers. She'd slacked off.

Monica gripped the joystick again and forced her eyes on the sky. Good thing the pilot was watching her.

The chopper sliced through the sky at a speed that defied nature.

"First time on a chopper?"

Monica swallowed.

"Yeah." She dared a glance to her left. Barefoot was looking below them. Monica attempted a look down and gulped.

"The horizon, Blondie. Look out there."

She swallowed. "It's Monica."

He chuckled and squeezed her hand still under his. "We'll be landing soon."

Thank God.

He squeezed her hand again as if he read her thoughts.

The chopper shook and pitched down a few feet.

"Just the morning wind. Ease back a little." Barefoot moved the joystick with her until it was centered. Monica kept her hand as steady as she could, even when he moved his hand away.

At second glance, Barefoot appeared a little more together than at first glance. His shorts were tailored and his button-up shirt might seem like a typical island floral, but she knew Tommy Bahama silk when she saw it. His Ray-Ban sunglasses weren't dime-store quality and he obviously knew how to fly his chopper.

Is it his helicopter?

"Is this your chopper?" she asked.

He glanced her way and his lips turned into a smile.

He didn't answer.

Monica glanced behind her to see Walt and Tina staring at something below them. Without thinking, Monica glanced down as well. The trees of the Jamaican forest abruptly thinned out and large lakes appeared in the center of the landscape. Only on closer inspection they weren't lakes . . . they were collections of ocean water brought in by the tsunami. In its wake were fallen trees and debris miles wide. Homes . . . or what Monica thought were homes, were nothing more than stacks of wood, branches, and garbage brought in by the surf.

She was miles above it.

"Oh, God." Her stomach pitched.

"Pull back a little," Barefoot instructed.

She did. At the same time, she forced her eyes on the sky. The ocean streamed out beyond the devastated shoreline.

Barefoot pitched the chopper to the right and Monica leaned into the craft as if her slight weight was going to make a difference in a proper landing.

"Down . . . slowly."

Unlike the tarmac where they'd landed the first time, the spot in which Barefoot was planning on placing the chopper was a postage stamp of a yard. It reminded Monica of the yards behind the tract houses springing up all over Southern California.

Below them, someone waved an orange light.

Barefoot placed his hand over hers and pushed the lever back as the chopper slowly made its way to the ground.

As the skids came to rest on the ground, Monica released a shuddering breath. *I made it. Without puking.* The last part was the most impressive. Smelling up this small cabin wouldn't bode well for future passengers.

Barefoot tapped her fingers before he pried them off the lever she'd gripped with all her life. "This is your stop," he said with laughter in his voice.

"Right. Right." She shook her head and unclenched her fist.

Under the sunglasses and headgear, Barefoot sent her a hundred-watt smile. Or maybe he was laughing at her. She forced her lips into a smile. "Ah, thanks for not killing me."

Barefoot chuckled. "Be safe, Blondie. It's a mess out there."

Someone opened her door. The noise of the propellers along with the wind they created removed the smile from her face. Walt was standing there gesturing for her to exit the chopper. She placed a foot outside the craft and then remembered the headgear.

Barefoot's attention was on her as she pulled the earphones off and gave a slight wave. She'd barely made it away from the aircraft and Barefoot was flying away.

Without a copilot.

Chapter Three

Trent accepted the bottle of water Reynard shoved in his hands and downed it in one continuous swallow. The beverage quenched his thirst but what he really needed was a bolt of caffeine. Maybe even a mainline IV full of the stuff. And food. Damn . . . when was the last time he'd eaten? Outside of a few protein bars and similar open-the-package-and-consume-the-food products, it had been almost two days.

He'd been asleep when the earthquake hit. Knocked his ass out of bed and had him ducking into the doorframe of his house. He knew the moment the shaking stopped that he was going to be one of the lucky ones. He'd overseen the construction of his home personally. Unlike most homes in the region, his was made with standards spelled out to pass US inspections even though he could have paid off the locals to have his needs met. Trent didn't work that way. Not with a home he'd planned on living in for a time. He had planned on staying for a year, maybe longer, then using the home for holidays.

As it turned out he stayed longer than a year, and spent his holidays in the upper forty-eight.

"Have you eaten, mon?"

"I'm good," Trent lied to Reynard. Reynard's own home had partially crumbled during the quake. His children, all four of them, were at their school, which sat on higher ground. It too suffered major damage but the tsunami hadn't washed it away. That was a blessing. Reynard's wife, Kiki, had been home while Reynard himself had already gone to work.

Mrs. Kiffen hadn't yet been found.

The weight of her absence sat behind Reynard's eyes.

"Any word on Kiki?" Trent asked.

A swift shake of Reynard's head gave Trent his answer.

"I'll check the list of patients on my next run. Make sure the Americans are keeping an eye open for her."

Reynard blinked several times. "My Kiki is a strong woman. We'll find her."

Trent squeezed the man's hand as he shook it. He'd make sure the doctors and nurses he'd flown into the zone had Kiki's description and name. She'd turn up . . . the question was, in what condition?

The sun lay directly overhead. Its rays blistered the tarmac under Trent's feet.

He needed his shoes, some decent food, and a couple hours' sleep. He removed his sunglasses and rubbed his eyes.

"The next group will be here in four hours. Go home . . . rest," Reynard told him.

"There's too much to do." And there was. Between transporting the relief help from the airport to the zone, Trent flew medical supplies from one clinic to another. Military helicopters and medevacs were busy transporting the most critical off the island altogether. More help was on the way, but they weren't coming fast enough.

"At least put on some shoes, mon. Cutting your feet now isn't wise. The hospital is lacking antibiotics. The dead are going to fester in this heat . . . disease—"

"Got it." He knew he couldn't add to the burden. "Make sure she's fueled. I'll be back in an hour for another run."

"Go. Eat."

Trent walked off the tarmac, dodging those who rushed in all directions. Most of the islanders were dressed like him. Two-day-old clothes, dirt covered much of their legs and arms. Some were scraped and bruised. But those he dodged on the way to his Jeep were nothing like those on sea level.

After fishing the keys from his pocket, Trent shoved the 4x4 in gear and turned his car toward home. Thank God help had come. His fleet of four helicopters, all designed to entertain tourists on sightseeing rides over the island, had instantly become the only way to move around after the quake. So much for a quiet existence on a tropical island.

He thought of calling in, to make sure his brothers knew he was safe. Landlines were down everywhere and he'd left his cell at home . . . not that cells were working when he'd left there. They would worry. Trent knew he would if the shoe were on the other foot. He glanced at his bare feet.

Natives walked along the side of the road without their normal wave and smile. Trent didn't find a smile on his face either. For once, the frown wasn't placed there by his own life, but because of the plight of others. He turned onto his private drive, drove around several boulders that had tumbled onto the road after the quake, and proceeded to his roundabout drive.

Ginger, his two-year-old Irish setter, bounded off the steps of his porch and greeted him with two paws mid-chest.

"Hey, girl." He found his lips pulling into a grin. "It's good to see you, too."

Ginger wagged her tail and barked three times in response.

Trent pushed her off with a pet and encouraged her to follow him.

He stepped over a broken ceramic vase the earthquake shook to the ground. He should probably clean up anything that could cause damage to Ginger before he left again. Trent tried the light in the bathroom, it didn't turn on. Power was probably the least of the island's concerns . . . at least for where his home sat. He considered firing up the generator, but thought better of it. He wouldn't be there long. No need to waste the gas.

He finished in the bathroom and washed his face and hands. "At least the water is still on," he said to himself.

The kitchen was a minefield of broken glass. Ginger trotted in beside him.

"Out!"

Ginger sat on her hindquarters, her tongue lolling to one side. Ten minutes later the kitchen was safe enough for the dog to enter. Trent topped off Ginger's food bowl with kibble and filled up a cooking pot with more dog food. Luckily Ginger ate when she was hungry and didn't mow down the whole lot in one sitting.

After eating two raw hot dogs and an apple, he moved into his bedroom. His cell phone sat in its dock, the blinking red light letting him know he had a message. There were five missed calls from Jason and two from Glen.

Trent rang Jason's cell phone. His brother would be at the office, but he knew the call would go through. Trent lay out on top of his covers. Damn it felt good to put his feet up.

The phone rang twice before Jason picked up the call. His brother's words were rushed. "Trent? Jesus, Trent, is it you?" Worry laced the question, making Trent feel all kinds of sick for not trying to call sooner.

"It's me, Jase. I'm fine."

"Dammit. We thought . . . we heard . . ." Jason took a deep breath and started over. "You scared the fuck out of us, Trent."

"You've been here. My house isn't on sea level. She handled the quake. I've been flying supplies and people. I haven't been home since it hit."

Trent imagined his brother looking out over the city in his three-piece suit and running his hand through his hair.

"The media footage shows total carnage. Is it as bad as it looks?"

The memory of bodies floated in Trent's mind. "Worse."

"Thank God you're OK. Can I do anything?"

Ginger jumped up on his bed and set her head in his lap. "Call Glen. My phone has a charge, but I'm not sure for how long. Power's out over much of the island."

"We can be there in a few hours."

Trent smiled. "I know . . . but hold that thought. What we need is doctors, nurses, and search and rescue. Not suit-wearing businessmen."

Jason huffed into the phone at Trent's dig. "What about another pilot?"

Their father had made sure each of the brothers had his pilot's license before a driver's license. "The birds are on the ground at night. The military is bringing in more power."

"I feel helpless."

"If you came here you'd feel worse."

There was a pause on the phone. "You shouldn't be there."

Trent shook his head. He wasn't about to go into *that* argument again. "I've got to go."

"Take care of yourself."

"I will. Don't worry." Trent ended the call and tossed the phone next to his side. He leaned against the headboard and closed his eyes. His brother's life . . . his old life, wasn't anything like existing in Jamaica.

Existing. Make that *living*, he corrected himself.

Thirty minutes later, he shook himself awake and forced himself off the bed. He took five minutes to shower and change clothes.

This time he grabbed a pair of shoes and filled a sack with food and energy drinks before he headed back out.

————•————

Monica ran the back of her hand over her forehead to keep the sweat from dripping in her eyes. She'd stepped off Barefoot's chopper and straight into hell.

Her scrubs stuck to her skin, her blonde hair was pulled back into a crude bun. Patients were everywhere and on every possible surface. The hospital, which wouldn't pass as a clinic back home, was only two stories. It withstood the earthquake, which apparently was offshore. The tsunami hit the island quickly. The locals told her the quake had been impossible to sleep through and when the wave came they ran.

Monica's station was a second level of triage. The first wasn't even manned by someone with a medical degree. A receptionist of the hospital had been elevated to triage nurse in one day. She separated those with lacerations that could wait outside. Broken bones, so long as they weren't open fractures or cutting off circulation, were sent to the same holding area. There were thousands of them.

"Help . . . please. Someone?" The voice rose above the chaos of the room; moans and desperation filtered thick in the air.

Monica twisted toward the voice.

Two Jamaican men rushed in a twentysomething man on the back of what looked like a plank door. A woman stood over the man screaming for help.

Their desperation alone made Monica's legs move. Behind the band of newcomers was the poor receptionist-made-nurse. "You said to let through cold feet."

Monica shook her head. "Cold feet?" Her eyes moved over the man on his back. His head shook from side to side. His ebony skin was ashen.

"His leg. It's cold."

Monica moved closer.

"You a doctor?" the woman by the patient's side asked.

"A nurse." Monica was reaching for her trauma shears. "Do you speak English?" she asked the man on the door.

He nodded, but didn't say anything.

"He needs a doctor!" the woman screamed.

Monica felt herself folding into the woman's drama.

"The doctors are busy. Tell me what's wrong." Monica started at the feet since that was where the receptionist said the problem was. The man's right leg, above the knee, was bent in an awkward position. It didn't take an X-ray to tell it was broken.

Monica cut from the bottom until she exposed the entirety of the problem.

"He was under the rubble. Two days my boy." The woman hovered over the patient.

"He's your son?" Monica asked in attempt to get information and calm the woman.

"Yes, just seventeen. Help him."

He looked much older. "What's your name?"

"D-Deon," he said through chattering teeth.

Airway . . . Breathing . . . Circulation . . . Monica placed her fingers on a pulse point below his injury.

Weak. And cool.

She looked around and hoped her poker face was intact.

The kid was pale, his pulse rate at his wrist too fast.

Femur fractures could bleed. Excessively. And what other damage could the rubble have caused? If she didn't try to correct the fracture and restore this kid's circulation soon he could lose his leg.

Monica had never had to do this on her own. In fact, she'd only assisted doctors and only in extreme circumstances. Yet paramedics were often put to the task in the field. Life or limb and all that.

"Help him!" the mother cried.

Walt was in surgery and Tina was two rooms away with just as many severe cases as Monica.

"Deon? Does anything else hurt other than your leg?"

He shook his head.

Monica ushered the men holding Deon to a nearby desk and pushed everything on top of it to the floor.

The men holding the door Deon lay on were older, too old to help Monica with what she needed. The mom was hysterical and virtually useless.

Ignoring the mother, Monica positioned herself over Deon's face. "Deon, listen. I need to straighten your leg."

His eyes grew wide, his nostrils flared. "It's going to hurt. You're going to want to fight me." He would fight her . . . he wouldn't be able to stop himself. Although he may only be a teenager he outweighed Monica by a good forty pounds.

How the hell am I going to do this?

She looked up and frantically swept the room with her eyes.

Dark hair, Ray-Bans . . . "Barefoot?" she yelled at the pilot who'd delivered her to hell.

He shifted his gaze toward hers.

"You. Come here!"

Barefoot glanced behind him then back.

"Yes, you. I need your help." His strong shoulders and lack of relationship with the patient were exactly what Monica needed.

Monica found a towel and wrapped it around Deon's leg while Barefoot moved to her side.

"I need to straighten his leg." She gathered the edges of the towel and handed the ends to him. "You," she looked at the men who had carried Deon in. "Hold his shoulders down. Mom . . . talk to him."

The mother nodded. "You know what you're doing?"

"Yes." *No.* Monica hated the self-doubt. But she knew this boy could lose his leg if she did nothing.

Monica lifted her gaze to Barefoot. He'd taken off his sunglasses and she met his dark, piercing gaze. He saw her doubt. She knew it.

"What can I do?" Barefoot asked. His voice was a rough timbre and the opposite of all the panicked calls inside the room. It grounded her.

"Hold this. I need traction so he doesn't slip."

Monica crawled up on the table with Deon and wiped the moisture from her palms before grasping his leg.

Just touching him caused pain. Normally, in an ER, this wouldn't be done without heavy sedation, but that wasn't going to happen here. Not only did they lack cardiac monitoring, they didn't have the drugs to accomplish the job. Besides, they didn't have time for that. As it was, there was no guarantee what Monica was about to do would save his leg.

Because it wasn't completely cold or mottled she knew he had a chance of saving it.

"Ready?" Barefoot asked, bringing her attention back around.

Monica nodded. "Hold him," she told the others.

Deon tensed, waiting.

Monica grasped him above his leg, supported his calf on her thigh. She waited until Deon took a few deep breaths. She glanced at Barefoot and mouthed the words, *three, two . . . one.*

It wasn't a jolt, but more of a pull. Even though Deon screamed out Monica kept pulling his leg, feeling as best she could through his skin as the bone attempted to move back into place.

Her arms shook as she fought the patient and the displaced fracture.

Barefoot held traction and watched her as she struggled to keep her grip on Deon's leg. Monica shifted her position, attempting to pull the bone through muscles and tendons.

This is just as hard as it looks when the doctors do it.

Deon screamed when the bone moved, but it still wasn't in place.

"Hold up." Monica instructed Barefoot as she lost her grip. The femur was closer to being in place, but not right.

Deon was moving on the makeshift gurney, making it even harder to set his leg.

Monica rubbed her hands on the towel and leaned into Barefoot so only he could hear her. "Pull harder."

He nodded once.

She leveraged one leg on the table and sat taller.

Monica counted down again. *Three . . . two . . . one.*

Deon filled the room with his cry.

Monica pulled with every muscle she owned. Her hands started to slide, she repositioned again and felt his leg move.

Monica ground her back teeth together. Her arms started to shudder under the strain. Finally, Deon's leg shifted and she manipulated it into line.

"Thank God," she said.

Barefoot eased his pressure off and she set Deon's leg on the table. She located a pulse behind his knee, felt a beat. Lower, his pulses in his foot were still faint, but better. Much better.

"We need to splint this to keep it in place."

The receptionist who'd watched the entire procedure left the room.

Deon was already more comfortable.

"I'm sorry I had to do that," Monica told him once she jumped off the table. The swelling and bruising were evident. She couldn't rule out a critical bleed. She removed a permanent marker from her pocket and flexible ruler. She marked Deon's leg in two places and measured the circumference. There wasn't a chart to write on so she did the next best thing . . . she wrote the numbers right on the boy's leg. Then at least she would have a starting point when she checked on him again.

He attempted a smile.

"Wait with him," she told the mother. "We'll splint his leg and have a doctor look at him as soon as we can."

Soon could be the next day if his pulses held and the leg didn't swell, but Monica didn't want to tell the mother that.

"I'll try and get him something for pain. Is he allergic to anything?"

"No."

Monica added the letters NKA to Deon's leg in pen. No known allergies . . . such a simple fact written on a chart. Here it could be life or death.

Monica turned away from the patient, her shoulders slumped slightly. The room was packed. If she could split into five people, she still wouldn't be able to manage what all of them needed.

A strong hand rested on her shoulder. "Good job back there."

She glanced over her shoulder and up. Barefoot was tall and surprisingly broad. Unlike anyone else, he smelled good. Sandalwood and man. Such a relief from blood, sweat, and dirt. "Thank you for helping."

"You did all the work. Have you done that before?"

"No."

"You made it look easy." He smiled and for a brief moment, the room slid away. Something curled in the pit of her stomach and heated. Was it desire or was it hunger?

The weight of his hand never left her shoulder. It would have been too easy to lean on him.

She shook off the yearning and moved out of Barefoot's reach. Unable to stop herself, she glanced at his feet. He wore a pair of running shoes.

"I've got to keep moving. Thanks for your help."

Monica took a few steps away only to hear her name. "Monica?"

He remembered?

"The name's Trent. Not Barefoot." He lifted a leg and wiggled his foot.

Monica felt her face heat. "Good to know," she said with a rare smile before turning away.

Chapter Four

"I need a volunteer." Donald pulled Monica aside twelve hours after she'd set foot in the blazing inferno.

She rubbed a clean hand over her face and blinked a few times. "Volunteer? Isn't that what I'm doing here?"

Donald offered a half smile. "I need a nurse to go over one county to the east, it's a fishing village, Port Lucia. The clinic there is bursting. The local doctor hasn't been seen since the quake."

Monica shook her head. "There isn't a doctor?"

"No. There's a couple of nurses . . . aides." He glanced around them. As organized as chaos could go, the room had some order. "Your triage skills kick ass."

As much as she'd like to bask in the compliment, she couldn't get over what he was asking. "You want me to go to a clinic where there isn't a doctor? How does that work? My license . . ."

"Your license is safe here. There are people suffering and I need to send someone to triage the worst back here. We have standing orders you'll take with you, and a two-way radio to ask questions if needed. The last thing we need is more walking wounded filling these rooms."

Monica couldn't argue with that. "You're *asking* for a volunteer?" The way his eyes looked through her said he was more than asking.

"Tina's good . . . but you're better. If I put the best nurse there, I won't worry that careless mistakes are happening. Either Walt or I will come up every twenty-four hours to lend a hand."

"A lot can go wrong in twenty-four hours. I'll need to sleep."

"Like I said. There are aides. They've been sending most of the wounded here. Half of them didn't need to come."

Like a bad flu season in California, when the ER would fill with patients, bottlenecking the entire department and eventually the hospital, which made it next to impossible to treat anyone in a timely manner. Here the numbers of critical patients were too great to let sit.

"So . . . can I count on you?"

The inside of Monica's stomach twisted. She liked to think she had some autonomy as a critical care trauma nurse. The bottom line, however, was there was always a doctor around. She followed a doctor's orders.

A cry from a patient three beds away had Monica glancing around the room. All day she'd treated people, tended their needs . . . directed them to the next level of care if need be and she could count on one hand how often Donald or Walt had made it past her side.

"How far away is Port Lucia?"

———

There was an excited hum in his veins Trent had forgotten existed. For the first time in what felt like ever, he woke with a sense of real purpose. He tried to convince himself the reason for his overzealous sense of self was due to the state of emergency the island had been under since the quake. That was part of it, but the itchy, hot exhilaration came from something much baser.

Blonde hair and cool blue eyes found him while he slept. Even there, her sassy tongue and knowing eyes found a moment to mock his bare feet.

Before leaving his chopper on the tarmac the night before, he'd been asked to arrive early to pick up one of the American nurses and deliver her to Port Lucia. Because Trent's home resided between the short runway and Port Lucia, Reynard asked him to deliver the nurse personally. There wasn't anywhere to land the chopper close to the clinic so a short drive would be in the travel plans.

Trent wanted to ask which nurse was taking the new assignment, but didn't. He'd find out soon enough. He didn't hold too much hope that Monica would be that nurse. He knew she didn't take to flying and probably wouldn't volunteer.

Either way, he'd have an excuse to see her again briefly, if only to find out who he was escorting around the island.

After a short shower and a cup of god-awful instant coffee, Trent filled Ginger's dog bowl and pulled his Jeep out of his driveway.

Clouds blocked the morning rays of the sun and threatened more than a few drops of rain. The last thing the island needed was bad weather.

The closer he made his way toward the airstrip, the more concerned with the clouds Trent became. Visibility was everything in a helicopter. If the ceiling of clouds wasn't high enough, he'd be grounded until the thick layers lifted.

Alex, one of his pilots, met him outside of the air traffic tower. Alex was a good thirty years older than Trent. He and his wife, Betty, both flew for Blue Paradise Helicopter Tours, an offshoot of Fairchild Vacation and Charter Tours, which Trent and his brothers owned. Unlike Jason and Glen, Trent decided to run one exclusive leg of the worldwide company. A decision that still provoked arguments between the three of them.

He and Alex shook hands. "You look like you finally slept," Alex told him.

"A good six hours. You?"

"More like four. Betty had a hard time falling asleep."

"It's hard to close your eyes and see anything other than destruction." Trent almost felt guilty for dreaming of a blonde nurse.

"She told me to come pick her up if we really needed her. Otherwise she needed a break."

Trent shook his head. "No worries. Outside of some jockeying, I think the officials will take over most of the runs. I'm doing an early run," Trent told him. "If you're not needed go home."

Alex shook his head. "I need to do something."

Trent knew how his friend felt. Everywhere they looked there was a need for help. Even if it lay in the packing of water bottles . . . or body bags.

He squeezed his eyes shut and pushed away the thoughts of lifeless people . . . of the despair that took him by the throat every time he landed his helicopter.

Above their heads, the clouds were breaking up. "I'll be on the radio when I'm onboard. I have an angel to deliver to Port Lucia. Call me if you need anything."

Alex nodded and leaned against the building.

Trent walked around his aircraft and performed his visual inspection of the chopper before climbing inside. He signaled air traffic and awaited their approval before taking to the air.

A sputtering of rain graced his short ride and heated the air. This, exactly this, might not be quite what it was he imagined when he decided to live on the island. But life wasn't always what he thought it should be.

Hell, his own parents had expected so much more and yet their lives had been cut short . . . so painfully short.

Trent's jaw ached and he forcefully managed to stop grinding his teeth. Temporary lights blinked where his intended target lay. He flipped the chopper into the onshore wind and set the skids on the ground. Unlike any time in the past, there wasn't an extra hand standing by when he powered down the chopper and exited his aircraft.

People lined the outside walls of the hospital, some waiting on loved ones . . . others simply waiting. Trent kept his sunglasses in place . . . and his mask. The air smelled of humidity, death, and despair. Such a far cry from the happy-go-lucky tourist and sightseer that had been in his life only a few short days earlier.

Even though the island had experienced nothing short of an apocalypse, the world still slept during these early hours. The stairwell was filled with people. Some slumped in sleep beside the walls, others were awake beside them. Trent moved past them in search of the director.

Past the room where he'd witnessed Monica help fix the boy's fracture the day before, he moved into the next room. There lay two dozen patients. Some with IV bags of fluid hanging over them giving some semblance of normalcy of a hospital. Trent knew better. There was nothing normal about people stacked this high or thick in what used to be a waiting room.

He glanced around and found a nurse he recognized from the flight over slumped against the wall. She'd fallen asleep. He considered waking her, but realized that no one in the room was screaming for assistance, so he moved on. Up the stairs he found a smaller room with an attendant . . . or maybe it was a nurse . . . with a half dozen patients.

Trent swallowed. The patients rested on gurneys in a line. Used to seeing the dark umber skin tone of the residents, it shocked him to see so many gray faces.

Pushing past his unease, Trent stepped up next to the attendant. "Excuse me. I'm looking for the American, Dr. Klein?"

The woman behind the workstation nodded toward the closed door beyond the patients. "He's in surgery."

Trent ran a hand over his neck and glanced around the room. "I'm supposed to be escorting a nurse to Port Lucia."

The woman shrugged and returned to the work.

Disturbing the doctor didn't seem wise so Trent twisted around and moved back through the hospital. He found the sleeping nurse and stood over her.

As he debated waking the woman, someone behind him beat him to it.

Hearing a patient's groan, the nurse shot to attention, her gaze disconnected from the world. Her eyes moved around the room, panic clouded her face before she realized he stood over her.

"Oh, God . . . I fell asleep."

He couldn't imagine the exhaustion she must be experiencing. "It was quiet when I walked through a moment ago."

She moved to her feet and the clipboard in her lap fell to the floor. Trent moved to pick it up for her. A coy smile passed her lips.

"Thanks."

"S'OK. Listen. I'm supposed to pick up a nurse to take to Port Lucia. Do you know who she is?"

The brunette shook her head. "Not me. Monica ducked out a few hours ago. Said she was being moved somewhere east."

Trent felt his lips pulling into a smile. "Where will I find her?"

The nurse pointed in the opposite direction. "They set up a small room for us to rest. Go through four sets of doors, up a stairway one flight, and take a left. There's a doctors' lounge. Girls on the right, boys on the left."

"Thanks," Trent uttered as he turned and walked away.

Four sets of doors opened to rooms filled with misery. He kept his sunglasses on, though the sun wasn't out and it certainly didn't filter into the rooms. If he could block out all the images around him he would.

The stairway up to the lounge was quiet and void of anyone. He stood outside the door and wondered if he should knock. If there were nurses sleeping, he might wake all of them instead of the only one. He took a gamble, inched the door open, and peeked inside.

Sure enough, there were a few cots in the small space, all of them filled. A quick assessment brought his gaze to Monica. She'd fallen asleep fully clothed with a hand tossed over her head. Her blonde hair hung loose around her shoulders, the tight lines in her face from the day before were erased while she slept.

Trent stepped over a duffel bag and avoided a cot before he stood over his passenger. He had no idea how long she'd slept and felt awful for waking her.

He knelt down to her level and whispered her name. "Monica?"

Nothing.

"Monica?" he said a little louder.

Her hand drifted off her forehead.

The other women in the room hadn't stirred.

"Monica?" He placed his hand on her shoulder and gave a gentle shake.

She shot up so fast Trent didn't have time to move back. Her head collided with his bringing gasps from both of them.

"Ouch!" she yelled, waking everyone in the room. She blinked several times while staring at him. "What the . . ."

Trent stood and rubbed his head. "I was trying to wake you without disturbing everyone."

"Too late," someone said before rolling over and going back to sleep.

"Sorry," he mumbled.

"What time is it?" Her voice was rough with sleep.

"Almost seven."

Monica flopped back down to her cot. "You're driving me to Port Lucia?"

"Yeah."

She rubbed both hands over her face and pushed her legs off the bed. "I'll be ready in a minute."

Trent took her words as his cue to leave the room. His wait in the hall took less than ten minutes. Monica emerged with her hair pulled back in the same ponytail he'd seen the day before. He liked her hair down, he decided. Why his mind would travel to how this woman wore her hair, he didn't know.

But he did. He was attracted. The curling in his gut wasn't something he could ignore.

She hid a yawn behind her hand and closed the door quietly behind her.

As she started to hike her bag onto her shoulder, Trent moved forward and reached for it. "Let me," he said.

"I got it." She pulled the strap higher on her arm.

He reached for her bag again. "I wasn't raised to let a woman carry a bag while I'm empty-handed."

She cocked her head to the side as if she'd argue with him. Instead, she shrugged the bag down her arm and handed it to him.

"I wouldn't want to be responsible for blowing your mother's good intentions."

The memory of his mother repeatedly telling him to grab a bag or hold a door for a woman filtered past his mind. "My mother would thank you."

He took her surprisingly heavy bag in one hand and encouraged her to walk in front of him down the stairs.

The gentle sway of her ass caught his attention as he followed her. She wore scrubs, and loose cotton hid most of her petite figure. Most, but not all of it. The cotton shirt covered her slim waist, but there was no mistaking her delicate neck and full breasts.

Monica turned when she opened the door at the bottom of the stairs. Good thing his sunglasses disguised his eyes. He held the door and let her pass. She waited for him to walk beside her as she spoke.

"So, Trent. It is Trent, right?"

"As much as I liked Barefoot, my name is Trent."

She smiled. "Sorry about that. I didn't catch your name on the flight over."

"I've been called worse." He stepped around a man sleeping on the floor and urged Monica out the door.

Monica glanced up at the gray skies and frowned. "So, Trent," she began again. "Are you the only one shuffling the foreign medical staff around the island?"

He shook his head. "There are a few others. Why?"

He kept his eyes on where he walked and avoided her questioning gaze.

"Just wondering."

He didn't buy that. "Just wondering?"

"Seems like *anyone* could drive me to the clinic."

He walked her behind the hospital and up a short path to where his helicopter waited. "Anyone could *drive* you."

She hesitated when she saw her ride. "I thought you said you were *driving* me."

"I am. After a short flight to where my car is parked."

She turned a full circle. "Can't we just drive?"

Trent moved in front of her and removed his sunglasses. "It's a short flight back to the airport, then a thirty-minute drive. That's if the roads are cleared."

"Can't we just—" Her ice blue eyes never left his.

"I didn't kill you the first time, Monica. I won't this time either."

She swallowed.

"It was better thinking you *volunteered* to take me instead of being the only person *capable* of it."

Actual fear hid behind her eyes. "Why's that?"

"I prefer flirting to flying."

A slow easy smile met his lips. He knew then, irrevocably, that Monica thought about him at some point during her short stint on the island.

He replaced his sunglasses and reached for her hand. "How about a little of both?"

"Damn," she mumbled as she let him drag her to the aircraft. He opened the door on the passenger side and quickly shoved her bag in the back.

Inside, he reached across her body and latched the passenger door. "I could have done that," she said.

He caught her eyes over the rim of his sunglasses and winked. "That would be the flirting portion of our flight."

She laughed then. A nervous laugh that seemed to surprise her as the sound escaped.

He handed her the extra headset and buckled in.

Once her ears were in place he could hear the quickening of her breath. He powered up and switched his radio to air traffic control.

"This is Bravo Papa one."

"I hear you, Bravo Papa one, over."

"I'm en route to you. Can I get a weather reading? Over."

Trent listened to the wind report and received an all clear of the fog lifting.

The hum of the helicopter wrapped around him with a warm welcome. He glanced over to see Monica's fists clenched in her lap.

"Do you want to copilot?"

She rolled her eyes at him. "I fell for that once, Barefoot. I'm not that gullible twice."

So he was Barefoot again. "Took your mind off the flight the first time." He removed a stick of gum from its pack and handed it to her.

"And what, gum is going to do it this time?" She took the gum and unwrapped it.

"No, but it helps the ear popping."

She placed the gum in her mouth and took a deep breath.

"Ready?"

She shook her head. "You sure we can't drive?"

He patted her knee as he would a child. "If it makes you feel better, I've been flying since I was fourteen. Two solid years longer than I've been driving."

"I'm not sure that helps."

He smiled, and lifted the aircraft off the ground. Once he was above the trees, he turned the chopper around and headed toward the airport.

Her white knuckles were not a sign of his flying, he reminded himself. "How long have you been a nurse?" he asked, hoping to calm her down.

"Three years . . . almost four."

He would have thought it was much longer based on what he'd witnessed the day before.

"Did you follow in your mother's footsteps?"

She sputtered a laugh. "Not hardly."

That's a loaded answer. "She's not a nurse?"

"She's not anything. Go nowhere jobs. Go nowhere husbands."

As in plural.

"What about you? Is your dad a pilot?"

"He was one of the best."

"He doesn't fly anymore?"

"He passed away."

Trent felt her eyes on him. "I'm sorry."

He shrugged. "Some dads teach their kids how to ride a bike or throw a ball. My dad taught us how to fly."

"I'll bet your friends were insane with jealousy."

Trent had always been thankful for his parents' desire for him and his brothers to fly. He glanced over and noticed Monica's hands resting loosely in her lap. Their conversation was distracting her. Trent did something he almost never did. He talked about his past. "On my eighteenth birthday a buddy of mine convinced me to go for a joyride."

"A joyride? In one of these?" Her voice rose with alarm.

"We took a couple of girls up. I thought I'd show off my skills."

"Strut for the ladies?"

"Some guys show off their cars. I showed off my dad's helicopter."

She glanced out the window as if noticing that she was still in the air. "Did you stay this close to the ground on the joyride?"

"No. It was a clear fall day."

"Clear fall days allow you to fly higher? Or are you staying close to the ground to keep me from freaking out?"

"Is staying low keeping you from freaking?"

"No," she said laughing.

"Staying low is necessary today." He didn't want to worry her about flying conditions and kept his explanations simple. "Not on my eighteenth birthday."

"So what happened? Did your skills get you lucky?"

There was an innocence about discussing one's youth with a virtual stranger. "It almost landed me in jail."

"Seriously?"

"Security at the private airstrip notified my father that his bird was missing. After he found and quizzed my older brothers, he assumed someone had stolen it. It never occurred to him that I'd take it."

"You weren't a wild child?"

Oh, he was wild. His parents had very little idea of how wild. "I wasn't bad."

"Why don't I believe you?" Her tone teased and when he looked over he noticed her slow steady breaths pushing her breasts against her clothing.

"Anyway. When we landed, the police were there and put us all in handcuffs. My parents were livid," he told her, taking his eyes off her chest.

"I can't imagine why. Did you ever see the girl again?"

The lights of the airstrip appeared in the distance. "Her parents forbid it."

"That doesn't usually stop teens from anything."

Trent banked the chopper in a wide turn. "I think it was the handcuffs that turned her off."

Monica smiled. "Handcuffs wouldn't bode well for a second date. Unless the girl is into that sort of thing."

Trent turned to stare at her and had to erase the thought of Monica in handcuffs . . . the fuzzy kind, in order to swallow.

Chapter Five

Shameless flirt! Monica shook her head and chastised herself as she exited Trent's helicopter for the second time. She had to admit, this flight had been much better than the first. Maybe the key to kicking her fear of heights was sexual tension. That and talk of handcuffs. Oh, she'd read her share of *those* books, but never once *acted* on them. The penetrating stare coming from the pilot's seat had been worth the snark and innuendo. The stress of the past thirty hours didn't weigh on her nearly as much as it had before she'd gone to sleep the night before, well, the morning before. She hadn't fallen into her cot until after one.

She followed Trent off the helicopter pad and toward a parking lot. His confident strides and sexy li'l smile made her wish she knew what was going on inside his head.

Monica matched his stride and kept up her side of the conversation. "So after your joyriding youth you decided to fly helicopters for a living?"

"You could say that."

His two-door Jeep had one of those half tops on it that covered your head but left the back open to the air. Trent tossed her bag in the backseat and opened her door.

He waited for her to climb in before shutting her in. *Yeah, his mother taught him well.* "Did you ever consider a different line of work?" she asked once he was inside.

"I worked in business administration for a while."

"I can't see you wearing a suit, tie, and dress shoes."

His shoulders buckled in with a laugh.

"What's so funny?"

"My older brother, Jason, says he has a hard time picturing me wearing shorts and flip-flops every day." He started the engine and put the car in gear with the same finesse as he did his helicopter. He waved at a group of people standing by what looked like a guard shack before pulling onto the road.

"Are you and your brother close?"

"We watch out for each other."

Monica thought of Jessie. She and her sister had been inseparable before Jessie married Jack. Jessie lived in Texas but still flew out all the time to visit. Easily accomplished when your husband owned his own plane.

Except Jack didn't fly it. He had pilots to do that.

"What about you? Siblings?"

"My sister, Jessie. She was worried when I told her I was coming here."

The small road leading from the airport was hardly large enough for one car, let alone two. Yet a few compact models hugged the edges as they passed.

"It takes a lot of courage to dive into this mess."

Monica shrugged. "Sometimes leaving your personal life behind for a heavy dose of reality reminds us of the important things." *Damn, where had that come from?* She settled into the words that had come from her lips and realized how true they were.

"Most people come to the island to escape their lives."

Was that him? Was Trent hiding from *real life*?

"Not this week."

Another small car passed them. "Good God this is a narrow road."

"You get used to it."

Where they were on the island was free of any flood damage left behind from the tsunami. A few rocks had obviously come loose and Trent swerved between them. "How was the damage from the quake here?"

"Many lost their homes. I think once everyone is accounted for, the reality of what it's going to take to rebuild will be enormous."

"What about your home? Did it fall?"

He shook his head. "New construction. Almost makes me feel guilty for having a home when so many don't."

She watched the passing trees while rain started to fall again. "A version of survivor's guilt. That's normal."

"So, what? You're a psychiatrist and a nurse?" The question could have been sarcastic, but it sounded a lot like admiration.

"Half my job is psychological, calming patients, families. Keeping a cool head when everything is going bat-shit crazy." Some of the staff back home called her the Ice Queen, or Queenie. At first, it had to do with how she'd turned down the guys in the department when they asked her out. But now she liked to think it was because she kept an icy grip on her emotions when everything exploded.

Monica noticed Trent watching her from behind his glasses. "Do you ever lose it?"

"No." Her answer was quick. After a deep breath, she said, "But this place is already testing me."

"Oh?"

She considered what she was driving into. It would be worse than the day before. At least in the main hospital there were other doctors and nurses she could grab to help. Donald had asked her to go into a war zone virtually empty-handed. "I don't know what I'm headed into and I'm doing it without coffee on board or even a shower. The lack of sleep doesn't even need to be mentioned."

"Isn't there a doctor following you out here?"

"Not right away."

"Damn."

"I know, right? I have two hands and one brain. I can only do so much." The more she thought about it the less she liked the idea of being at Port Lucia without a doctor.

Trent pulled off the main road and wound his way through an even narrower street. This one was better maintained but didn't leave any room at all for passing cars.

Trent slowed the Jeep as they rounded a curve, and out the window Monica saw a sprawling single story home.

"Where are we?"

Trent pulled the car to a stop and shoved his sunglasses into the center compartment. "Twenty minutes will take care of your need for coffee and a shower."

"But Port Lucia?"

"Can wait twenty minutes. They may not even have running water there. I do. I'll fire up the generator and make us coffee."

Monica sat staring at him with her mouth half-open. "This is your home?"

He nodded and opened his door. "C'mon, Monica. I have a feeling this will be your last shower for a few days. Might as well grab it while you can."

She swung her gaze to his house again. An open beamed porch wrapped around the outside. Beyond the roof, she could see a glimpse of the ocean. The thought of a shower . . . coffee . . . heaven. "I don't even know you."

Trent chuckled. "I didn't kill you in the air, and I don't own a pair of handcuffs."

Monica squeezed her eyes shut and tried to ignore the heat filling her cheeks. "Oh, what the hell."

Trent stepped out of the car and from nowhere sprang a large red dog. "Ginger, down," he yelled when the dog jumped up in greeting. "Say hello to our guest."

Ginger barked with a happy wag of her tail.

"Her manners aren't the best, but she won't bite."

Monica put her hand out for Ginger to sniff. "She's beautiful."

"Spoiled, too. C'mon in. The shower has a point-of-use water heater. It should take less than five minutes to heat up once I turn over the generator."

Monica followed Trent inside. The front door wasn't locked. Inside there were several household items scattered on the floor. She stepped over a pile of glass.

"I haven't had time to clean up since the quake hit." He clicked a light switch and nothing happened.

"I take it the power's been off since, too."

Ginger nudged her hand asking for a pet.

Monica obliged.

"I don't know why I bother checking. Lines are down everywhere."

She followed him into a great room that opened to his kitchen. Bay windows framed a breathtaking view of the ocean. Lucky for Trent, the water was well below his home. In fact, from where she stood, Monica didn't see the damage of the tsunami, just endless vistas of turquoise blue and green. Well, gray at this point, but on a clear day she imagined the view would provide hours of serenity. "What an amazing view."

"We like it. Don't we, Ginger?"

Hearing her name, Ginger barked again.

"You can stay here. I'll get the generator going." Trent opened the French doors to the back patio.

"Trent?"

"Yeah?"

"Thanks."

He shrugged. "No problem."

———

The road to good intentions was apparently paved in rubble; at least it was this week in Jamaica.

With a cup of strong coffee in hand, Monica relaxed in the passenger seat of Trent's Jeep feeling a slight bit of guilt for taking the twenty-minute refresher. Only slightly. Even Donald said to take her breaks when she could manage them.

"The main road around the island was severely damaged from the water. It's only a twenty-minute drive down the hill," Trent told her as they hit yet another pothole in the road.

"I can see why you own a four-wheel drive," she said. "Are all the roads on the island this messed up?"

"Those around the tourist areas are nice. Well, most anyway. Up here, and in the backcountry, they're awful."

"I guess if you're flying over them all the time it doesn't matter." One plus on the side of being the pilot.

The Jeep lurched to the right again, and then abruptly to the left. When Monica peered out the window, the road didn't look to be the cause of the bumpy ride. "Slow down," she told him.

"My driving scaring you?"

She shook her head. She'd grown up in Southern California, earthquake central in the States. When an earthquake rattles you in your home, or in a building, you often hear the buildings move long before the earth bumps you around. When you're driving a car, it's silent and feels like you've got a flat tire. "No, stop the car."

Trent lowered his speed while Monica glanced out the window. They were surrounded by trees and a power line that followed the road. There wasn't a high-rise to crumble on top of them.

Sure enough, when Trent stopped the car it still felt like they were moving. Monica held her coffee in front of her to avoid it spilling. The rolling lasted only a few seconds longer, but it reminded her why she was there. "That was probably in the fours," she said.

Trent looked out his window before narrowing his eyes on her. "That doesn't bother you at all?"

"The earthquake?"

"Yeah."

"No. That was a baby quake, not even enough to make me get out of bed in the middle of the night."

He visibly shivered and started down the road again.

"So, you can guess the magnitude? No need for a seismograph?"

She chuckled. "You really don't feel anything under a three. Well, unless it's close to the surface and you're right on top of it. Then maybe . . ." She sipped her coffee and went on. "Upper threes and lower fours . . . you roll over and go back to sleep. Now when you start getting up into the fives you start to wonder if it's going to get worse. The sixes, the jolty ones, those make you move . . . if it's a rolly one you still move, but not as fast. Over six and a half, you're moving. And look at all the damage after a seven and a half. Makes you wonder what a nine, or God forbid, a ten, would do."

"You've given this some thought."

She shrugged. "I'm a Southern California native. Goes with the territory."

They rounded a corner and found the road blocked by a landslide. There were a couple of cars ahead of them with the passengers already out and attempting to remove the debris.

"Well I guess I can stop feeling guilty for taking the twenty-minute breather at your house," she said.

Trent rolled to a stop and cut the engine. "You stay here. I'll help."

Monica finished her coffee and leaned her seat back. Trent and a half dozen locals pushed, kicked, and carried rocks to the side of the road for nearly an hour. At one point Trent removed his shirt to beat the heat. Taut muscles stretched over his broad chest and tapered to a slim waist and tight butt. Monica couldn't help but enjoy the attraction.

The fact that any mutual attraction would have to be temporary didn't push her away.

Monica Mann was used to temporary. Less messy that way. No one to depend on, and no one depending on her.

Perfect.

Chapter Six

The clinic, or what was left of it, resembled nothing of its former glory. Trent maneuvered his car as close to the main structure as he could. He didn't ask if Monica wanted him to accompany her inside, he simply grabbed her bag and led the way. The main hospital at least had some semblance of order. Not here.

"Are you sure this is right?" Monica asked as they approached the structure. Several locals watched their approach, their gazes speculative.

Trent noticed a few sets of eyes linger on Monica and he moved closer to her side.

What the hell was the doctor in charge thinking sending her here alone? Even the local tourist authority warned visitors to keep their valuables locked up and to avoid wandering the streets alone. Monica, with her fair skin and blonde hair, didn't blend in with the locals. And she was more valuable than a purse or camera bag.

The clouds had broken, leaving heat in their wake. On both sides of the clinic, brick buildings had collapsed making the path inside an obstacle course.

Trent captured Monica's hand and helped her over a pile of rubble. She started to question him again when he heard the unmistakable sound of human suffering.

People were piled up outside of the clinic, three rows thick.

A couple of pickup trucks had people in the back of them, there were stretchers lining the outside wall of the building.

Trent glanced over at Monica. Her eyes had grown wide and any hint of a smile was now gone.

"Holy hell."

"Do you know who's in charge here?"

Monica shook her head. "Apparently the clinic doctor hasn't been seen since the quake."

Trent pulled her along behind him, weaving in between people as he went.

"Help me." The person speaking leaned against the wall closest to the door. "Doctor?"

Monica offered the patient a smile. "I'm a nurse. Hold on, OK?"

"I'm here two days. Please, ma'am."

"C'mon, Monica. Let's find who's in charge."

They walked past the man and inside. More people spilled from every corner of the room.

"Is there a nurse here?" Trent called out.

Several heads turned, a few pointed to another door.

"It doesn't even look as if anyone has even been triaged," Monica said almost to herself.

They found a woman in the middle of a room bandaging a woman's chest. Trent had to swallow hard to keep his coffee down from the rancid smell inside the room.

"Hi," Monica said as she approached the woman.

The lady glanced over her shoulder, looked them both over quickly, and returned to her task. "You here to help?"

She was Jamaican, but her accent wasn't as thick as most.

"I'm the nurse from the States."

"Thank the gods. What about you? You a doctor?"

Trent assumed she meant him. "I'm just her ride."

She grunted. "You're walking. You're standing. You can help."

Trent swept the room with his gaze. Even if he could get past the stench in the room, he'd have to take in the blood, this misery.

Monica moved around the patient and glanced at the bag of fluids hanging over the patient's head. "Are you a nurse?"

The woman huffed. "I'm a secretary. The nurse, she's with the *sick* patients."

Monica's hand dropped to her side. "One nurse?"

"Two . . . but the other one, she had to rest. Hand me that gauze." The secretary pointed to the table separating two make-shift beds.

Monica's hands hesitated over the dirty bandages. "Don't you have clean ones?"

"Not enough. Those will do."

Trent could see the argument on Monica's lips. Instead of saying anything, she handed the gauze over and attempted to smile at the patient. "What's your name?"

"Freya."

"I'm Monica and this is Trent."

Freya finished her task and turned away from the patient. "Come. I'll show you where everything is."

"Wait," Monica said, stopping her. "Who's in charge here?"

Freya stuck her ample hip out and laid a heavy hand on it. "Right now, in this room, I am. There are only a few of us and none of us were trained for this."

"Who's triaging the patients? Making the decisions?" Monica's voice was elevating and at the same time, Freya's jaw drew tighter.

"I'm doing my best."

Monica took a deep breath. "I'm sure you are. Without a doctor or skilled help, this can't be easy. I'm just trying to figure out what has been done so far."

From the looks of the room, not a lot. Some patients were sitting up, but on a gurney or some kind of flat surface. Others rocked back and forth, moaning. Trent was way out of his league and he knew it.

"Maybe it's time for me to go," he suggested.

Monica whipped her head around so fast Trent thought it might spin in a complete circle. "Don't you dare."

He held up his hands in surrender. *Couldn't be that easy.* "I'm not a nurse, doctor, or even a secretary in a clinic."

Freya and Monica were both glaring now.

Monica's eyes narrowed. "Where's the nurse with the *sick* patients?"

"In the clinic."

"This isn't the clinic?" Monica's eyes never left Trent's. It was as if she knew if she turned away, he'd slip out.

"This is the waiting room."

"Show me. And you," she pointed a finger into his chest. "You're coming with me."

"But—"

She stopped his words with a hand in the air. Monica blinked a few times before she said, "A couple of hours. That way you can tell my help back at the main hospital exactly what we need."

"A couple of hours?"

She held up two fingers.

"Two, tops."

————

Tauni, the nurse with the sick patients, went from pleased to see Monica to pissed that she couldn't leave the clinic immediately to sleep.

Monica tested every skill she owned in mass casualty incidents and rearranged patients according to severity. The immediate need patients were in the clinic's red room. There was a generator running lights and the oxygen tanks were still full. For how long, Monica didn't want to guess.

Tauni was a young nurse, much like Monica, but the entirety of her work was in the clinic. Her license was that of a vocational nurse back home. Shandee, the other nurse, returned to the clinic four hours after Monica had arrived. Though Shandee was happy for the help, she didn't like Monica taking over.

"This is what I'm trained for," Monica had said to her.

"This is where I work for twenty years." Shandee was in her fifties; gray hair peppered the dark strands. "I've been a nurse longer than you've been alive."

"Age does not dictate my abilities."

Shandee's eyes swept over Monica's frame as if to say she could sit on her to keep her from taking over. "I know these people."

Shandee had her there. Monica tried not to get any more defensive than she already was. She needed every hand, even a disgruntled nurse who would love it if Monica were anything but a young, petite blonde from the States.

Monica lowered her voice and took a deep breath and started over. "Look, Shandee, we need to make this work for the minimal people we have helping here. You need to take the red room, Tauni in the yellow room, Freya in the green room. Once we have the sickest inside the building we can manage this better." Though Monica had her doubts. Two critical patients were already in the red room dropping their vitals. There wasn't enough power to run the X-ray machine and there certainly wasn't a CAT scan available. Not that there was a surgeon to operate if they knew the severity of the patients' injuries.

"The red room?" Shandee glanced around and noticed several people watching them.

It was time to put on a smile and tell Shandee what she needed to hear. "I'm told you're a gifted nurse. These people need your help. I'll focus on triage."

Shandee twisted on her heel and walked to the red room.

Monica blew out a frustrated breath. *It's going to be a long-ass day.*

Trent followed her around for the next couple of hours while she dime-store triaged as many patients as she could. After about fifteen patients, two teenage boys—Jerrick, who was Tauni's brother, and Arcus, Shandee's son—understood enough of the basics of triage to help.

"If they're breathing too fast, find me. If their skin is pale below their injury, find me. If they're not making any sense or are unconscious, take them to Shandee."

Jerrick led a couple of his friends to help move patients around. Arcus moved in a different direction to look over the wounded opposite Monica and Trent.

Monica crawled up into the back of one of the trucks where a patient lay. She placed a hand on his shoulder and found it stiff and unmoving. One look confirmed what she already knew. "Damn," she whispered to herself.

How long had this patient been out here? Was he alive when he arrived? Where was his family? Who owned the truck? She started to shiver despite the heat.

Trent was returning from inside the clinic when she jumped out of the back of the truck. "Inside, or out?" Trent asked.

Monica stiffened her spine. "He—he's gone."

Trent looked behind her, his half grin faded. "Oh."

She brought a hand to her forehead and noticed it tremble.

"Are you OK?"

"Fine. We, ah . . . we need to find a place for him." She swallowed. There were probably others. Maybe Shandee had already placed the dead in a certain spot . . . somewhere.

Monica clenched her fists, trying like hell to stop the shaking. Exhaustion nipped at the edges of her sanity. Now was not the time to lose it.

"Hey?" He placed a warm hand on her shoulder. "It's OK. You can't save everyone."

His soothing voice and comforting hand would undo her if she let it. Monica pulled away. "I know that. He's cold. Probably gone before we even got here."

Trent stepped back as if stung.

Way to go, Ice Queen. "I'm sorry. Listen, I know you're trying to help me, but I can't think about all this right now. I have to stay focused. OK? Do you get that?"

She needed his help, but didn't want his compassion. Not yet anyway.

"Got it."

"Good." She nodded and realized a tear had fallen. She wiped it away, frustrated by its existence. "Maybe Shandee knows where they're keeping the deceased."

The hours lumbered by in the heat and misery. Using the protocols given to her, Monica started IVs on the sickest patients, and administered antibiotics in hopes that the minimum of infection-fighting medicine would help until Walt, Donald . . . or any doctor at all could come. The patients in the red room were simply too sick to send to the hospital. Monica knew they wouldn't survive the trip on the Jamaican back roads.

Tauni had gone home to sleep and Trent was still roaming the clinic . . . somewhere. Trent opted to stay, and had the locals transfer the patients in trucks to the main hospital. All Monica had to do was wait for help. And pray their supplies held up.

Shortly after noon the next day two small miracles shed light in Monica's world. Walt arrived in an ambulance, a real equipped medical transport, complete with a portable monitor and supplies. The second miracle was power. Real power, not the flaky kind that was knocked out with the wind. Monica would have been giddy if she'd managed anything other than a catnap beside the red room wall.

Like a zombie, she led Walt from patient to patient, explaining everything she'd done. "The antibiotics are dangerously low. We've managed a gram of Ancef on the worst of them, and a secondary dose on these four," she said pointing to those in the room. "We ran out of tetanus last night. Our gauze, antibiotic cream, splints . . . everything is nearly gone. There's not quite enough of anything to fill everyone's needs."

Walt shook his head and pulled her aside. "We need to get Mari to the main hospital." Mari was a thirty-two-year-old woman who'd come in with a penetrating wound to her abdomen. Every hour her vital signs grew graver.

"I didn't think she'd make the trip in the back of a truck."

Walt patted her on the back, as if assuring her for her decisions. "She might not make it anyway. I can't operate here. It's worse than Donald thought. No one told him half the building crumbled."

"Shandee assured me the only thing under the debris was a storage room."

Monica hid a yawn behind her hand.

"When was the last time you slept?"

She was fading, and knew it. "It's been a while."

Walt tilted his head to the side in question.

"Back at the main hospital. But I've managed a few winks against the wall."

"Is there any place you can go here? A quiet room?"

"Are you kidding me? The people are roaming the streets. Most have lost their homes. You saw it out there. If it wasn't for Trent, I wouldn't have managed even a shower since we arrived."

"Who's Trent?"

Monica glanced around the room searching for him. He'd left during the night for a few hours, and returned with coffee. Thank the heavens.

"The pilot. He's around here somewhere."

As if Trent heard his name being called, he emerged in the doorway.

Monica waved him over.

"Trent, do you remember Dr. Eddy?"

"Walt," her colleague corrected her.

The men shook hands.

"Thanks for stepping in," Walt said.

"There's not a lot I can do."

Walt glanced between them. "Can I ask a favor of you?"

"Sure."

"Can you get Monica out of here for a while? She needs some sleep."

She wanted to argue. She'd already put Trent out enough. The poor guy didn't have much of a choice. As it was, Monica recruited any able-bodied person to some task or another. But Trent had something none of the rest of them did. He had a house that still stood . . . and a shower. "You don't have to," she offered but knew her lame voice gave away her desire for a little downtime.

"Don't be ridiculous. I keep waiting for you to drop."

Walt laughed. "Not our Monica. She's the embodiment of the Energizer Bunny." He nudged Monica with his shoulder. "Get out of here. I don't want to see you for at least ten hours."

Monica's eyes grew wide. "But—"

"Another group of medical relief arrived. I'll have Donald send more help." He made shooing motions with his hands.

"If you're sure."

"Go."

Monica caught Trent's smile as they turned around.

"Oh, and Monica?"

"Yeah?"

"You did great."

Chapter Seven

Trent shot out of bed, his heart racing, sweat dampened his sheets.

He didn't remember his dream. He didn't need to. His body recognized the uncomfortable burn of memories . . . lost dreams. It had been two years since a dream forced him from his bed.

Why now?

But he knew. A woman slept in his home, a beautiful, intelligent, and smart-ass woman who sparked memories.

With his sleep patterns completely screwed up, Trent pushed back the covers, encountered Ginger who had taken to the bed since the earthquake, and padded barefoot around his room. The moon shed some light inside the house, and kept him from running into walls. He slipped on a pair of sweatpants and walked quietly past his guest's bedroom and out onto his back deck.

The warm Caribbean air was a welcome relief. Up here, on his perch that overlooked the ocean, he could forget the world literally crumbling around him. Here he could listen to the gentle waves far below and the crickets calling in the night.

Here he could forget.

Here he could heal.

Ginger walked in a circle at his feet and curled up in a ball before settling to sleep in a different spot.

Jamaica had been his sanctuary, a sabbatical that was no doubt coming to an end. It would take years for the island to regain its legs, for tourists to have a desire to return.

He could relocate Alex and Betty . . . if they wanted to leave. Blue Paradise Helicopter Tours could return when the island rebuilt.

Without work, without something occupying his mind, Trent would likely feel guilty and he'd avoided that pesky emotion for a long-ass time.

The past five days he'd felt plenty.

Has it only been five days?

Five long, grueling days that would all fold into themselves for some time to come if he stayed on the island.

Ginger whined at his feet and jumped up. The crickets grew quiet, and the night seemed to pause.

The earth rolled, a small shock that stopped nearly as soon as it began. Trent wondered if it woke his guest. Did Monica open her eyes and roll back over? Ginger was already curling back into a fuzzy ball to sleep. *Ah, to be a dog . . .*

A noise from inside the house, and Ginger lifting her head, answered his questions about Monica.

He sensed her eyes on him before she stepped beside the open French doors. "So was that a four?" he asked.

She chuckled. "Hardly. I just can't sleep."

Trent looked over and caught his breath. Her hair was ruffled from sleep, her eyes still half-open, or maybe half-asleep would be a better description. She wore tiny sleeping shorts and a soft pink T-shirt that said "Classy" over her breasts. Breasts that were not held up by a bra. He noticed her pert nipples through the thin fabric at the exact moment he realized he was staring.

After shifting his gaze to the landscape, and not that of the beautiful woman standing in his home, he said, "It's a nice night not to sleep."

She walked around him to the other cushioned chair and curled her legs under her as she sat. "It's nice out here," she said just above a whisper.

"In about thirty minutes it's going to be even better."

"Oh?"

"Sunrise."

Monica leaned her head back with a sigh. "I don't think I've watched a sunrise. Plenty of sunsets on the West Coast."

"Do you live by the ocean?"

"No. I'm an hour and a half from the shore. I wouldn't mind moving closer, but coastal living is so expensive."

They sat in silence for a while. Monica was alone in whatever thoughts were running through her mind, and Trent was stealing a glance at her bare legs and comfortable presence. It dawned on him that if she wasn't with him at that moment, he'd wonder where she was . . . what she was doing.

He pinched the bridge of his nose and wished the thought away. His skin heated just thinking of her. *It's chemistry.* Nothing more, he told himself. The brief affairs he'd had while living on the island were always with a tourist visiting for a week, maybe two. Mutual sexual satisfaction that never ended up with the woman sitting across from him watching a sunrise in his home.

Monica might not be a tourist, and she certainly wasn't there on a pleasure trip, but she was *just* as temporary.

"I was thinking—" Monica interrupted his thoughts. "You fly the helicopter for tourists, right?"

"Yeah."

"Does this mess mean you're out of a job?"

Not hardly. But he understood her question. "In a way. Tourists won't return anytime soon."

"Are you going to stay here? Will you lose your home?" There was real distress in her voice.

"Nothing so dire. Blue Paradise has other locations."

"Oh, so you think they'll transfer you?"

He chuckled.

"What's funny?"

"I'm part owner of Blue Paradise."

Her lips formed a perfect *o*. She shifted her gaze back to the ocean. "Will you stay here and help rebuild?"

He shrugged. "Probably not. Getting groceries is going to be a problem and living on a generator long-term is a lot like camping."

"It sucks that you'll have to leave your home."

And his sanctuary. "I'll be all right."

Now she laughed softly. "You'll find another place for shorts and flip-flops?"

"Maybe."

The dark sky started its slow dance toward light. The faint glow of blue stretched out on the horizon and grew steadily until orange and red rays filtered through the distant clouds. He glanced over and saw the wonder on Monica's face. Her bright ice blue eyes never left nature's opening act. Even the crickets seem to hold their breath, and the birds held off their morning song, as the sun rose.

"Wow," she whispered.

He shivered. Just watching her sent a different sort of chemistry through him.

She caught him staring and offered her smile.

He knew then that messing with Monica wouldn't be a simple exercise in sexual relief. No, it would get complicated . . . very complicated.

"I'll make some coffee," he said suddenly, pulling himself out of the tractor beams of her gaze as he left the patio and escaped into the house.

—————

Monica watched as Trent fled the patio as if she were the head "pregnant" cheerleader walking into the high school football team's locker room, and he was the quarterback.

Even Ginger popped her head out of her paws to watch him leave.

"What's with him?" Monica asked the dog.

Ginger released a deep sigh and settled back down.

Monica returned her attention to the sunrise and smiled. It really was spectacular. For a brief moment, she forgot why she was in Jamaica and just enjoyed the sky.

Noise from the back of the house indicated that Trent fired up the generator so he could brew the coffee.

Her mouth salivated with the thought.

Her limbs started to twitch with a need to move. Letting Trent do all the work didn't feel right. Monica unfolded from the chair and walked inside. Trent stood over the sink, one hand poised on each side. He was staring out the window lost in his own thoughts.

He was a million miles away . . . and Monica was disturbing him.

She started inching her way back outside when Ginger took that moment to bark from behind Monica.

Trent's eyes traveled to her and narrowed before they slid down her frame.

Monica wasn't sure if it was admiration or discontent, but she knew something about the man had changed from the moment she stepped outside to watch the sunrise. She crossed her arms over her chest, aware for the first time that she wasn't dressed for mixed company . . . especially with whom she wasn't intimate. "Did you need some help?"

Trent shook his head and turned away, opened a cabinet. "I got it." His tone was gruff.

She suddenly felt very exposed and extremely unwanted. "I'll shower then," she said just as quickly.

"The water's not warm yet."

"It's OK, a cold shower will wake me up." Besides, this room was cold enough to chill her. Being alone with cold water would feel better.

She started toward the guest bathroom when Trent's voice stopped her. "Monica?"

A rush of unwanted and unexpected tears filled her eyes. She hesitated and felt her throat clog. "On second thought," she said with only a slight tremor in her voice. "A quick run will give me the jolt I need for today."

He called her name again, but she fled to the room she'd slept in and closed the door behind her. She wasn't sure what had changed . . . changed before either of them could act on the sparks that were obvious between them, but she was glad for it. She didn't do tears and heartache. *Disappoint them first.* Leave before either of them could care was even better.

Apparently she and Trent would be a "leave him with only a thought," which was better.

He'd probably be terrible in bed. A sloppy kisser. All wet with no meat.

Two minutes later, she pushed out of her room, her running shoes on and the one pair of running shorts donned. She'd seen the stairs that led down the steep cliff below Trent's home and let the early morning light lead the way. She didn't hear anything in the house as she snuck away.

Not long after her shoes hit the beach, she heard a bark behind her.

Ginger.

Thankfully Trent wasn't behind the dog. The tightening in her chest was relief and not disappointment, or so she told herself. A quick run would clear her head; bring her back to her own level of homeostasis. A word she didn't know existed before she went to nursing school. Her state of normalcy had always included a void of some sort in her life.

Even those years when she lived with Jessie and Danny, life had never been truly complete.

Monica called the dog and took off at a fast run.

Just thinking of Jessie reminded Monica of home. Home being nothing more than an empty apartment in an inland suburb of California surrounded by other people just trying to make a buck and pay the rent. The apartment was empty now that Jessie had moved to Texas, and it appeared that Katie and Dean would be moving back to Texas as well since Dean's construction company was expanding. The move made sense. Both Katie's and Dean's families lived in the big state and they couldn't get enough of their daughter, Savannah.

For Monica, however, not having Katie nearby, and with Jessie spending less and less time in California, made her feel strangely empty.

Where did that leave her?

In a go nowhere place, way too close to her mother.

If there was one person on the face of the earth that didn't get her it was Renee. Her mother shacked up with whoever the latest guy was, and moved on when the sex grew stale.

Monica didn't even know her dad. He left when she was hardly out of diapers and she certainly didn't remember him. He was an enigma. A useless mystery, but a giant question mark in Monica's life nonetheless.

In short . . . everyone that should mean something to her had moved on.

Monica leapt over debris swept up by the tsunami and kept running. Ginger thought it was a game and ran ahead only to stop, pant, and keep going when Monica caught up.

People moved on.

Just like Monica would do with the people she'd come in contact with here on the island.

Just like with Trent.

She'd known him for what, three days? Why did she care that he'd seemed desperate for her to leave his space?

Because rejection sucked.

I should be used to it by now.

Monica pushed her body harder, dodged the foamy sea as it rushed her way, and kept going.

The sea stopped her progression with an outcropping of rocks, forcing her to turn back.

She wasn't ready, but unless she wanted to go for a swim, she'd have to run back to Trent's home and suffer his indifference through a stiff coffee and a ride back to the clinic.

She'd find a way to avoid him after that.

And she'd be all right. The Ice Queen didn't crack.

Trent sat on the steps leading to his home. Waiting for her.

Monica slowed as she approached him, but was ready to blow past him with the need for a shower ready as her excuse to avoid him.

She knew he saw her, but he kept his eye on the sea. He glanced at her feet when she wasn't two yards from him. There was a cup in his hand. "It's probably cold by now," he said.

She took it from him anyway. "Iced coffee is the thing back home." She tried to laugh off his gesture.

One sip and she knew he paid attention. There was a slight taste of sugar mixed with a strong, albeit cold, java. "Thanks," she said.

Turning her back to him, she took another swallow of the coffee.

"You left," he finally said.

"I needed to clear my head. Get ready for a crazy day." *Starting with you and ending with God knows what.*

After an obscene amount of silence, Monica needed to break free.

"I'll shower and then . . . can you take me back to the clinic?" Last night she didn't feel the need to even ask, but for some reason she did now. The lack of control in her life made her shake. It wasn't as if she could call a cab . . . or anyone. She had Walt's number, but there was no guarantee he was still at the clinic, or that he could retrieve her.

"Of course," he said as he stood.

Her throat tightened again. *So much for the run clearing my head.*

He stood rooted on the step so she attempted to move around him. His hand caught her forearm. His touch felt like fire. Hot with a current of its own.

"Monica?"

She stopped and felt the air around her disappear. He stood close, too close to breathe. The pull of his gaze wasn't avoidable. When she looked, his eyes were focused on her.

Something behind his eyes spoke of sorrow.

He loosened his hold and lightly traced the inside of her arm.

She shivered and felt her breath catch again. In a bar, or a local hangout, the feeling swimming inside her and settling deep in her core would have been welcome. But here, on the beach with the sunrise a recent memory, with more life and death than anyone could ever imagine filling every corner of her world, Monica didn't welcome it.

It scared her more than being in a helicopter with a barefoot pilot en route to the end of the world.

It scared her more than living life alone. She closed her eyes.

Trent's warm hand traveled up her arm and he stepped closer.

"This is a bad idea," she whispered. There was no reason to deny the sparks. She hoped he wouldn't make a fool of her by saying he didn't know what she meant.

She couldn't look in his eyes. His chocolate brown eyes would see through her and call her out.

When his hand dropped, she released a breath she didn't realize she held, and fled up the stairs.

Chapter Eight

Silence came in two categories, quiet and painful, or quiet and comfortable. How she and Trent had gone from comfortably quiet to get-me-the-hell-out-of-this-car quiet, Monica would never know. The way Trent gripped the steering wheel told her he was just as ready to have her out of his space.

Monica reduced herself to closing her eyes and acting as if she was trying to rest the final miles to the clinic. Her heart started to skip as they rounded the last corner and the now familiar town came into view. More people were milling about and there were Jamaican police combing the rubble with dogs. The chances of finding anyone alive at this point would be minimal, but that didn't stop the collective effort of those still searching for their loved ones.

Trent slowed the Jeep and Monica unhooked her seat belt in hopes of a quick getaway.

"I really appreciate the bed and ability to duck out of here last night." She did, despite how uncomfortable she was now.

"No problem." He stopped his car, put it in park.

She reached for the handle to open the door, and gathered her backpack in the other hand. "Thanks for everything, Trent. It's been a pleasure knowing you."

A wave of confusion marred his brow. "I'll come by later—"

Monica forced a smile to her lips. "No, it's not necessary. Walt said there was more help coming today." *And if you come back I might not push you away next time.* "But thanks . . . for everything."

Then she fled, not willing to hear him say good-bye.

Monica congratulated herself for not running. Still, she made it inside the clinic, stowed her backpack, and went in search of a familiar face.

Dr. Eddy had gone back to the main hospital with a critical patient, and in his place, Tina came to help. She'd driven with the medics, using the time to sleep.

Monica rushed into the job, and pushed Trent from her mind. What was done was done. Thinking about him, or what might have been, would be a waste of energy.

The day reached temperatures into the high eighties and the humidity was unbearable, but the misery was in the smell. Monica placed a mask over her face and encouraged the patients and family members alike to wear one. Between the dead that were too many to count, and the lack of sanitation in most of the structures, disease was going to be the next immediate problem.

Dr. Eddy had left her orders to start taking antibiotics as a preventative measure. Monica had had her share of scares after treating patients back home, but this felt different.

Several hours into her day, Monica managed a few minutes of a break. She slipped out the back and found the shade of a tree.

When her mind started to picture Trent, she cursed herself and picked up her phone.

Jessie answered on the second ring. "Mo?"

"Hey, Jessie."

"Oh, God . . . I've been so worried. The news is showing . . . oh hell, I don't have to tell you. How are you? Is it awful?"

Monica listened to her sister ramble and understood her concerns. "I'm fine," she lied. "And it's worse than awful. These poor people have lost nearly everything. They're filling the streets and sleeping next to the ruins of their homes. It's chaos."

"I can't believe you're there."

"Someone has to be."

There was an audible sigh on the other end of the line. "I'm proud of you, Mo."

"Oh, stop."

"No, really. You've done something with your life and really made a difference. I don't tell you enough how proud I am of you."

Monica stared at her feet and felt her cheeks heat. "Thanks, Jessie. So, how is everything there? How's Danny?"

Jessie bent her ear for several minutes about a mother-and-son dance Danny had taken her to. Complete with cowboy hats and boots. His attire of choice since Jessie married.

Monica attempted to laugh at her sister's antics with her son, but as much as she loved hearing her sister, Monica was having a hard time concentrating. She kept wondering where Trent was. Was he thinking about her? Would she see him again?

"Mo?"

Was he flying? Was he sitting on his porch watching the waves with Ginger?

"Monica?"

"Yeah?"

Jessie paused. "Are you OK? You don't sound yourself."

"I'm fine. A little tired, but fine."

Maybe it was the distance, or maybe Monica was a better actress than she gave herself credit, but Jessie accepted her excuse and continued for a little while.

" . . . oh, and Jack should be there tomorrow. Do you have any idea how much longer you'll be there?"

"Wait? What? Jack's coming?"

"Haven't you heard a thing I've said? There is a Morrison on the island. He'll only be there overnight, to show support and offer the hotel's help to those affected."

Monica didn't even consider that Jack and his family would own one of the hotels on the island. But they were the Morrisons, for God's sake. Of course they owned a hotel on the island.

"I don't know how much longer we'll be here. It seems like there's more than enough work to keep me busy for a month."

"You're not staying that long, are you?"

"I wouldn't have a job to go back to if I did that. But we haven't even discussed when we're pulling out yet." It would be a few more days at least. Even Monica knew that a relief effort was exactly that . . . an effort. She couldn't stay on permanently. Already the locals were coming in asking her what she could do about their homeless status. As if Monica could help with that.

"You can always fly home with Jack if you wanted to."

"Don't be ridiculous. I'll pull out when the team pulls out."

Jessie sighed again. "Be careful, Mo."

"Aren't I always?" In fact, Monica had always been the most careful person in their collective lives. Oh, she would advocate a reckless act, but she never once truly jumped off any metaphoric cliff.

Sensible Monica. She set her mind on a goal and achieved it.

Always.

Like making sure Trent knew he wasn't needed.

Done.

And now . . . where was he?

"I love you, Monica."

"Love you too, Jessie."

After she hung up, Monica sat staring at two birds building a nest. Numbness seeped into her veins and made her back teeth grind.

Maybe the Ice Queen was starting to live up to her reputation. Maybe she didn't care if she ever built a nest . . . or had someone to build it with.

Tauni called her from inside the clinic, ending Monica's thoughts.

———

"You need to find her, Jack." Jessie pointed a finger at her husband as if he'd told her no already. Not that he denied her anything. "I could hear it in her voice. She's not OK. I don't care what she said."

"Darlin', I'm sure she's just stressed—"

"Oh, it's more than stress. I know Monica, and she's not OK. Something's going on."

Jack shook his head. His brown hair, wet from his shower, shook rivulets of water down his chest. "There's a huge disaster over there, Jessie. Of course something is going on."

It wasn't often that Jessie argued with her husband but she was ready to take him by the shoulder and shake him. "It's more than that. She's . . . off. Really off. I only remember one time she sounded like this. It was right before I moved out of Mom's. She moved in with me a few months later."

"Wasn't Monica still in high school?"

Jessie had Danny at that point and needed to get out from under her mother's roof. When Monica had shown up with a suitcase Jessie couldn't turn her away. It wasn't that Renee had kicked her out, it was simply that Monica couldn't live with the uncertainty of their mother's life. With the men, the instability. Today both Monica and Jessie had a relationship with their mother. Not the best of relationships, but something they could build on so long as they didn't live together.

"And she was desperate to move in with me. That's how she sounded . . . desperate."

Jack shrugged. "It's probably just stress."

"It's more than stress!" Was the man not listening to her?

Jack offered his dimpled smile and walked over with his Texan swagger he wore like a badge of honor. He pulled her into his arms.

She tried pulling away.

He wouldn't let go. "Darlin', don't worry. I'll check on Monica if it will make you feel better."

She settled.

"You will?" A rush of emotion started to well inside.

"Did you tell her?"

"I couldn't. She sounded so sad."

Jack ran his hands down her back and to her waist. "It might have cheered her up."

"It wasn't the right time. And don't you dare tell her about the baby unless I say."

Jack rubbed noses with her and sealed his lips with hers. They'd just passed her second month of pregnancy and were waiting for the perfect time to tell the family.

"I'm good with secrets," he told her.

Jessie rolled her eyes. "You should have been an actor."

Jack had spent the first months of their relationship disguised as a broke dreamer who didn't keep a steady job, when in reality he was heir and part owner of the Morrison empire of hotels and resorts. All because he wanted to know if Jessie loved him for who he was and not the dollars in his bank account.

Jessie knew he could keep a secret.

"Just find her and check for yourself. And if something is wrong you bring her home."

"Yes ma'am," he said with a wink.

"I mean it." She knew her hormones were doing the talking. Thankfully, Jack didn't do anything else but relent with a kiss and a smile.

I don't care.

Three little words that filtered through Trent's head for hours were easy to repeat, but hard to hear.

After he'd dropped Monica off at the clinic, he'd returned to the airstrip and poured himself into the relief effort. Although the military and several helping agencies had larger cargo-holding helicopters to shuttle supplies around the island, Trent found a reason to get in the air. More than one actually. He flew tourists back to the airport so they could leave the island behind even though there were now buses of people fleeing.

Even with all the back and forth, eventually there wasn't a need for Trent to be in the air.

His sanctuary at home felt more like a holding cell. Instead of returning, he called Alex and Betty and suggested they meet. Although they hadn't spoken of the future of Blue Paradise, Trent wanted to assure the couple they'd be taken care of.

There was a private pilots' lounge, where Trent met with his employees.

He hugged Betty and shook Alex's hand. "How are you two doing?"

Alex spoke first. "Better." Alex took hold of his wife's hand. "We consider ourselves lucky."

"Almost guilty," Betty added.

Trent understood that emotion. "We are the lucky ones. I know it's soon, but have you thought about what you might want to do?"

Betty glanced at her husband then back to Trent.

"We were hoping you'd tell us our options," Alex said.

Trent smiled and did his best to ease their minds. "I can't even guess how long it will take to rebuild, or bring tourists in. You know how many locations we have and I'm sure I can find a place for you if you want to leave. If you want to stay here, we can work out something while things rebuild. It's going to be your call."

"Our daughter's in Florida. We were thinking of visiting her for a while. At least until the basics are restored to the island. We don't even have power at the house." Alex ran a hand over his bald head. "Our food stores are nearly gone. Betty's worried about disease."

"It feels like we're abandoning ship," Betty uttered.

"It isn't as if you've lived here all your lives," Trent reminded them. They'd moved to the island a little over a year prior to the quake and had made it clear that they wanted to work through a "long vacation." Alex was retired military and Betty had been a flight instructor. Between the two of them, they worked one full-time job . . . most of which Alex flew. "You tell me what you want to do, and I'll help you do it. If you want to go to Florida to consider your options and get back to me, that's fine too. None of us saw this coming and no one knows how long it's going to take for normalcy to return."

There were tears in Betty's eyes when she said, "Thank you."

"What are you going to do?" Alex sat back in his chair and sipped his coffee.

"I'm not entirely sure myself."

"You have that beautiful house," Betty reminded him.

"And like you, I feel guilty being the only one walking around in it." For the first time since he'd had it built it felt too big and too empty. Trent pushed out of his chair. "You two talk it over and let me know what you decide. I'll have Jason make a couple of calls about changing locations if you want. Just say the word."

They said their good-byes and Trent made his way to his car. His stomach reminded him that he hadn't eaten since late morning. He had a few more reserves than most, but he too would run out of food eventually. The government had set up soup kitchens for the locals, but as much as Trent liked to call Jamaica home, he wasn't a local, and he wasn't without means.

He didn't have to stay.

Ginger greeted him and followed him around the house.

He set out to make a sandwich for a simple dinner. One sniff of the bread had it in the trash. "Looks like a can of chili and crackers," he told the dog.

Ginger ate her food with a wag of her tail.

He ate on the back patio and kept looking at the empty chair to his side.

He'd blown it. He could be easing at least one person's suffering while they gave of themselves, but no, Trent let memories swallow him and shut him down.

Monica had made it clear that she didn't want him to return.

What was she eating?

Was she eating?

He'd heard of at least one nurse returning to the States with a critical patient. Was it Monica?

The chili sat in Trent's stomach like a stone.

"I don't know her last name." How would he know if she returned home safe?

His cell phone rang, interrupting his thoughts.

Caller ID told him Jason was on the line.

"Hey, Jason." Trent tried to sound upbeat.

"I thought you were going to call, keep us up to date."

"I'm fine," Trent interrupted his oldest brother's rant. "Thanks for asking."

"Dammit, Trent. Mom and Dad aren't around to worry about you, which leaves me to do the job."

Trent shivered picturing his parents. "I'm good. Things are—" Things were completely FUBAR. "Messy. But I'm glad you called."

Jason released a long breath. "Finally come to your senses and ready to come home?"

The words "I am home" sat at the top of his lips but didn't slip out. "I needed to talk to you about Alex and Betty," he said instead. He went on to ask Jason to look into options for his faithful employees.

"It sounds like you'll be leaving soon after."

"I haven't packed my bags," Trent told him. "The clinics are full and people need help."

"And what? You're playing nursemaid to them?"

Well actually . . .

He thought of the day before when he walked beside Monica as she called out orders as if he was her personal aide. He hadn't minded. She knew what she was doing and couldn't possibly do it all alone.

"It's obvious you can't stay there much longer," Jason continued with a softer voice. "Living the hermit life isn't going to bring them back, Trent."

Trent's skin heated, his gaze turned red. "Is that what you think I've been doing here?"

"What do you want me to think? Right after the crash you left. We barely said good-bye to our parents and you left, too. It's like Glen and I lost our brother as well as our parents."

Old hurt settled in his chest. He hadn't thought about that. "They would never have been in the air if I didn't push Dad to take her home."

It was supposed to be the weekend when Connie could get to know his family. She was a flight attendant for a commercial airline. They'd met in an airport when bad weather had grounded air traffic and the two of them were waiting for a cab during a snowstorm in New York. They'd shared a cab, a late dinner, and a bed. She lived in Chicago and Trent lived in a Connecticut suburb.

When he thought of her now, years after her death, he saw who she really was as clear as the moon in the night sky. At the time he only saw her laughing smile and zest for life.

They met in exotic locations, or stopovers in nowhere places. They talked about their futures, and after a short time, Trent wanted to find a way to combine their lives.

He'd surprised her by flying his father's midsize Lear 60 to pick her up for the weekend. When they landed in Connecticut, she thought it would be a cozy weekend with just the two of them. But his parents, Beverly and Marcus, wanted to meet the woman Trent wanted to make a permanent fixture in his life.

Connie didn't hide her surprise or discontent when Trent took her to a restaurant and met his parents inside. Dinner had been strained. Halfway through Connie excused herself and Trent followed.

She turned so fast he hadn't seen it coming.

What the hell was he doing?

They were just having a good time and why did he have to go and make it complicated?

She'd always left his side saying how much she'd miss him and how much she'd like their relationship to be different. But when pushed to the wall, she didn't want a relationship at all. Then she broadsided him with another half truth.

There was someone else in Chicago.

Trent was numb.

They'd returned to the table and shortly after Trent asked his father to fly Connie home.

Marcus, being the man he was, was happy to help, and Beverly didn't want him flying back alone so she went along.

The plane never made it to Chicago.

And Connie's *someone* was her husband.

So yeah, Trent was hiding from life. Licking his wounds and what of it? He'd lost two of the most important people in his life because of his inability to see the truth.

Jason was talking and it took a minute for Trent to focus on his brother's words. "They wouldn't want you to piss your life away. And they sure as hell wouldn't have blamed you."

He hated that his brother was right.

Somewhere between the last time he'd talked to his brother about all this and now, something had changed. Something inside Trent had thawed.

"Come home," Jason encouraged him.

"I don't know if that's home anymore."

"Maybe it's not. But you won't know if you stay there."

Maybe it was time to move on. But he couldn't abandon Jamaica . . . not yet. "I'll think about it."

"Really?" Jason sounded hopeful.

"Yeah." They said their good-byes and Trent tried to relax.

It didn't last long.

He took a last look at the empty chair next to him and jumped to his feet. "Come on, Ginger. Let's take a drive."

Chapter Nine

A child laughed, and the happy sound caught Monica by surprise. There had been so little laughter in her life in the past few days. She glanced up and noticed Ginger licking the hand of a small girl sitting beside her mother's bed.

Trent?

He stood in the doorway, his attention directed at her, his eyes hidden behind his sunglasses.

Why is he here?

He walked toward her, leaving Ginger to entertain the child and another teenager who slid off his chair to pet the dog.

As Trent drew closer, Monica looked around to see if anyone else noticed his direct stance. The thin line of his lips. She couldn't tell if he was pissed or happy. She shifted in her chair as he approached.

"Hey?" she managed when he was close enough to hear her.

"Can I talk to you for a minute?"

She sighed, not trusting herself. "Uhm."

"Just for a minute."

Monica swallowed and stood. She dropped the chart on the table and wrapped her stethoscope around her neck.

Trent turned toward his dog. "Stay!"

Ginger sat on her haunches and watched them as Monica led him out the back door.

The light outside was growing dim. Before they cleared the door, Monica tried to put distance between them. "I thought I said you didn't need to come back."

The door closed behind him and Monica turned around. He removed his sunglasses, hung them on his shirt. "I had to come back," he said.

He stood over her, looming with a hint of a smile playing on his lips.

"Why?"

He moved forward, and before she could step back, his arm was around her waist and he was pulling her close. Monica couldn't breathe and Trent didn't give her time to think.

His lips took hers so swiftly and so completely, Monica's world exploded. She'd thought of him all day. About his body close to hers, the soft touch of his fingers on her arm, and how much she wished she'd at least sampled his kiss, and here he was folding her into his arms. There was no hesitation on his part. He acted as if he'd kissed her a hundred times and had a right to do so whenever, wherever he pleased. Trent's confident possession of her lips, his tongue mating with hers, wasn't sloppy or poorly executed.

It was heaven.

Monica closed her eyes, reached up, and touched his shoulders, his neck, before she fanned her fingers in his hair. She was alive, whole, and completely aware of every cell in her body reaching for the man in her arms.

His sunglasses bit into her chest. Before she could protest about their barrier, Trent slid a hand between the two of them and tossed the glasses to his feet.

She giggled under his kiss and attempted to get closer.

He kissed her breathless, until her breasts felt heavy with need and her body softened. Until he hardened.

It was Trent who started this madness and Trent who eased his lips from hers minutes later.

She sighed as he kissed her softly then moved his lips to her temples.

They stood there, holding each other and catching their breath.

"I couldn't let you leave without tasting you," he whispered in her ear.

She heard the pain in his voice. "I'm not leaving yet."

He didn't offer a comment about that. Instead, he asked, "What's your last name?"

His hand was rubbing up and down her back. "Mann. Monica Mann."

"When are they sending you back home?"

"I don't know yet."

He leaned back, placed one hand on each side of her face, and kissed her again, briefly. "Can you get away?"

She shook her head. "No." There was too much to do and only one other nurse there.

His eyes searched hers. "Don't leave without telling me."

"One kiss and you're telling me what to do?" she asked with a smile on her face.

"Please."

Her skin broke out in gooseflesh, despite the warm temperature.

His thumb traced her lips and slid from her face, down her neck, and off her shoulder. He stepped away as if it was painful for him to do. Trent opened the back door and whistled. Ginger bounded to her feet and followed him to his car.

All Monica could do was watch him go.

She lifted her fingers to her lips and felt the sting of his kiss linger long after he sped away.

Trent winced at the taste of the coffee in the pilots' lounge the next morning.

"That bad?" The pilot who asked the question was off a private jet that had landed thirty minutes earlier. His hand hovered over the carafe filled with coffee.

"It needs CPR," Trent told him.

The pilot let his hand drop.

"You wouldn't happen to know who flies the chopper, would you?" the pilot asked.

Trent pushed his coffee away. "You're looking at him."

"My boss needs to get around the island. We're told the roads are passable but slow."

Trent eyed the jet on the runway. "Do you have coffee on board?"

The pilot laughed. "Yeah. We have everything."

Trent stood, put out his hand. "I'm Trent."

"Roy. C'mon, I'll introduce you to my boss."

Trent followed Roy across the tarmac and up the steps into the luxury jet. He knew money when he saw it, and this Gulfstream was dripping in money. Leather seats, a couch, a door leading to what Trent assumed was a bedroom. *Nice!*

At a table sat a man close in age to Trent and wearing a cowboy hat and jeans.

"Jack?" Roy called as they stepped inside. "I found your pilot."

Jack stood and offered a hand to Trent. "Jack Morrison."

"Trent Fairchild."

Jack's handshake was firm, confident. You could tell a lot from a man's handshake. "I'm not sure what Roy told you."

Trent rocked back on his heels. "All I heard was coffee."

Jack's Texan accent laced his words. "That we can do." He slid behind the bar, found a cup, and poured what smelled like nirvana. "How do you take it?"

"Black or maybe intravenously at this point."

Jack laughed. "You sound like someone I know."

"Coffee is worth more than gold here these days."

Roy stepped around his boss and poured his own cup. Obviously, the employee/boss relationship wasn't set with unnecessary pretense.

Jack handed him the coffee and Roy left the plane.

The first taste of good java hit his tongue and he felt the jolt hit his system. "Perfect." He hadn't slept much the night before. Thoughts of Monica leaving in the middle of the night haunted his dreams. Alternately, her kiss sparked his fantasies.

"I can pay you for your help."

Trent shook his head. "Not necessary. I assume you're not here on a pleasure trip."

Jack offered the seat opposite him and sat down again. "The Morrison was hit hard. I'm told the bungalows on sea level are wiped out, but the main hotel is solid."

"You're *that* Morrison?"

Jack laughed. "One of them anyway."

Trent thought of his brothers, wondered if they'd met the man in front of him. "I think we might know some of the same people," he said. "Fairchild Vacation and Charter Tours works with many of your resorts." The contract had been a reason to celebrate when his father was still alive.

Jack's eyes lit up. "You're *that* Fairchild?"

It was Trent's turn to laugh. "My brothers run the business."

"Well, hell. It's a small-ass world isn't it?"

"Sure is. Made smaller when you have your own wings." It was safe to assume the man in front of him had had access to private planes since he was in diapers.

"So are you here checking on your business, too?" Jack asked.

"I live here."

"Oh. Then you're the one I need to know. Is there a place to land close to the hotel?"

Trent noticed the map of the island sitting on the table and pulled it over. He went over the options for landing and talked about the condition of the roads.

"And where's the hospital?"

"Here." He pointed. "I hope it's not serious." It hadn't dawned on Trent that Jack might have lost someone on the island.

"I need to check on someone. Are there other hospitals, clinics?"

"Several, but this is the only one really operating on this side of the island. There's a functioning clinic in Port Lucia."

Jack shook his head. "Well then, looks like we have some flying to do. You sure you're able?"

Trent finished his coffee and set the cup down. "It's what I've been doing for a week. Bring your own food and water. There isn't any to spare anywhere."

Chapter Ten

Trent flew Jack to a clearing used for landing close to his hotel. Trent could see the horror on Jack's face as the devastation became more than an image on the TV set.

The beach in front of the hotel was yards of debris, washed-away roads, downed trees, and the occasional boat piled above what used to be outbuildings of the hotel.

"How the hell are you dealing with this?" Jack asked Trent before The Morrison Hotel's management descended upon them.

Trent looked around, thought that everything that wasn't a body was fixable. "Broken buildings are the easy part. It's the people that didn't make it . . . or only half made it, that are difficult to deal with."

Jack Morrison was the kind of man Trent would hang out with back home. The occasional friend here on the island had always been a temporary entity. He had his colleagues, and a few friends, but no one he knew understood the world he grew up in. A world where multimillion-dollar airplanes were bought, flown, and enjoyed. Although the Fairchilds had their share of the American pie they didn't flaunt it.

His mother, Beverly, had always kept their own home, cooked their meals, and driven them to school growing up. His father, Marcus, worked hard, created Fairchild Vacation and Charter Tours to combine the two things he loved in life . . . flying and travel. He capitalized on his vision using money from investors and his own life savings. When the company took off, he involved Trent and his brothers as much as they would allow.

Outside of the business his parents were always there for him . . . for all of them. There was nothing any of them could ask that would have been denied. They'd been a close family. Laughing and playing all over the world. God did Trent miss his father's booming laughter, missed his mother's sound advice. His parents were insanely happy in their marriage, their life. Trent missed them. Blamed himself for their loss.

Jack had spent a couple of hours at the hotel, talking with those who remained and offering his own personal support to make sure the employees were taken care of. He made notes, and shook hands . . . and let more than one woman cry on his shoulder.

Trent stood by, watched.

While Jack walked through the hospital, Trent worked his way to where Monica had been when she was at this location. He was pleased to see a few familiar faces from their flights over, assuring him that the relief staff hadn't yet started their exit from the island.

Trent heard his name through the throngs of people.

He searched for the source of his name and found Kiki lying on a bed.

His heart flipped. "Kiki?"

She reached her hand toward him. Her ever-present smile on her lips. "Trent, my friend."

He moved to her side, and swept her frame with his eyes, and clasped her hand. "Kiki, my God, are you all right?"

"I'm better."

Trent hadn't seen Reynard in days. "Does Reynard know you're here?"

She nodded. "He found me yesterday." She lifted a hand to her head. "Out cold I was. The American doctor said I'll be fine."

Her left leg was in a splint and she appeared in a bit of a daze. "Reynard told me you were tough," he said with a wink.

"You flirt."

"I try." He made her smile. "Where's your husband now?"

Her brow pinched together. "The last of the house fell yesterday. He's looking for shelter. The kids are too many for my mother."

Trent knew their home was small, and could only imagine Kiki's mother's house held less space.

"Perfect," he said with a smile. He knew he had to play this right or Reynard's pride would keep him from saying yes.

"What?"

"I need someone to stay in my home when I leave. You, Reynard, and the kids can stay there. Keep an eye on it for me."

Kiki angled her head, as much as she could while lying flat on a bed. "Trenton! That is not—"

He placed a finger to her lips, silencing her. "My brothers need me back home. I'll be back . . . eventually. If I leave it without someone inside the jungle will take it back."

Kiki shook her head, but her eyes softened as if a heavy weight had been lifted.

"When will you leave?"

"When I'm no longer needed here. One, two weeks at the most."

Saying this aloud made it real. He had been hiding from life and it was past time to start living it again.

"You tell your husband to take you there when you get out of here. You don't want the kids to get sick." Trent knew how to push a mother's buttons. "I'm home only to sleep right now."

He stood ready to make his exit.

Kiki held his hand, tears swam in her eyes. "Your mother would be proud."

Yeah . . . she would have been.

Trent found Jack waiting outside. "Did you find who you were looking for?"

Jack shook his head. "I was told she's at the other hospital."

"Let's go then."

"What?" Monica took a call from Deb, who was still in California and taking a break from her day job.

"Pat's on a warpath. Said you didn't clear your schedule before you left and that it was your responsibility."

Monica's jaw ached from grinding her teeth. "I had the shifts covered."

"Someone called in sick."

"How the hell was I going to fix that? Staffing said they'd take care of any issues."

"That's not how Pat's spinning it. We've had two short shifts when you were supposed to be on."

"Ah, fuck." Losing her job was not supposed to be part of a relief effort.

"There's more."

"What?"

"Word has it that one of the patients there died because of a nursing mistake."

"Here?" Monica's insides started to boil.

Deb went on to tell her about a reporter somewhere on the island that was following a story of a rich tourist who didn't make it and how the family was holding the Borderless Nurses and Doctors responsible for their death.

"That's ridiculous," Monica told her friend. "We're all doing our best with toothpicks and duct tape. I'm out of tape, bandages, most of the antibiotics. It's a freaking war zone, Deb."

"Either way, Pat's gunning for you, and not in a good way."

Monica couldn't think about this now. "What the hell am I supposed to do about that now?"

"I just don't want you to stress about getting back."

"I'm on the schedule next week." Monica's stay was self-limited.

"Not anymore."

"What?"

"Pat took you off."

That bitch.

Her job was her independence. Her life.

"I'm sorry, Monica."

"Not your fault. I'll take care of it when I get back."

"Be careful."

Monica disconnected the call and leaned against the back of the building where she'd taken herself for privacy. A legal team worked with the doctors and nurses in the program. Walt and Donald would vouch for her, raise hell if the hospital, or Pat, fired her for being in Jamaica.

But it sucked that she even had to think about any of that here. Sucked!

———

Monica ran from patient to patient, hour to hour. Tents had been set up outside in an open field for those who were ready to go home, but didn't have a home to go to. There were children in another tent who had yet to have a parent or family member collect them. The despair started to weigh on Monica.

She'd heard Walt mumbling about their leaving. Already four members were slated to depart within twenty-four hours. "But there's still so much to do."

"I know," Walt had said.

"How long are you staying?"

"Another week."

Monica had thought she couldn't be in Jamaica, but without a job to go home to, what was her hurry? Wouldn't it just be like Pat to force her to come home just to throw her job out the window.

She needed to talk to Walt about her options but he'd already returned to the main hospital. The poor guy was being dragged around more than she was.

Tauni held a teenage girl's leg as Monica wrapped it in a bandage. "Do we have any more four-by-fours?" The square bandage material was in extremely short supply.

Tauni moved her hand to give Monica room to tie off the bandage. "Less than half a box."

"I'll call Walt and ask if he can spare more when he comes back tomorrow."

"The government says we'll get more soon."

The government, as Tauni called them, promised all kinds of things *soon*. Yet *soon* had yet to come. They brought food with armed guards and had no problem pushing people away from the trucks with excessive force. It was downright scary. Hunger was becoming the next national disaster.

People were becoming short with each other, the goodwill effort was bending to the basic human needs. Goodwill was in the toilet when your family was hungry.

Monica released the girl's leg and offered a smile. "It's looking good. Healing perfectly," she told the mother who sat at the girl's side.

"Thank you."

Tauni nudged Monica's shoulder and nodded toward the door. "Looks like you have a visitor."

Monica glanced up and saw Trent. Beside him was an even more familiar face.

She squealed and all but ran to hug her brother-in-law.

"Hey?"

She felt a hand on her arm, pulling her away from Jack.

"Hey?" Trent's frown was lethal. He kept looking between the two of them. "You two know each other?"

"Yeah, he's—"

Trent threw his hands in the air, stopping her words. "I don't want to know." He turned and started to storm away.

"Wait up." Monica grabbed Trent's arm and spun him around. What the hell was his problem? "What's wrong with you?"

"Me?" Trent glared at Jack and returned his glare to Monica. "What about you? I wouldn't have kissed you if I'd known there was someone waiting for you at home."

Monica's jaw dropped.

"Kissed you?" She heard Jack say.

She poked a finger in the middle of Trent's chest. "You might wanna check your testosterone at the door, buddy. Jack is my brother-in-law. As in married to my sister."

It was Trent's turn to drop his jaw.

"Oh."

"Yeah, oh! You thought I'd . . ." God, what he must think of her. Never, even in all her Ice Queen days, did she fool around with more than one guy at a time. She couldn't even date different guys. She turned her back on Trent and placed all her attention on Jack. "Hi."

Jack winked. "Hey, darlin'. You look . . . well, you look like crap."

She laughed, despite the turmoil in her belly placed there by the man whose stare was boring holes in her back.

"Only *family* would say that. Even if it's true." She made sure the word *family* could be heard by anyone within ten feet. "Speaking of family, how's Jessie . . . you know my *sister*? Your *wife*?"

Jack glanced over Monica's shoulder and offered a pained look at Trent. "You're in so much trouble. Monica's like a burr in a saddle when she's mad." Jack glanced back at Monica. "And she's pissed."

Monica didn't even turn toward Trent. She grabbed Jack's arm and pulled him out of the room and out the back door. Maybe Mr. Testosterone would get the hint and leave them alone.

Jerk.

She dragged Jack to the shade tree she'd dubbed her break room and pulled up a patch of grass. "Jessie told me you were coming. You didn't have to search me out."

"Jessie would skin me alive if I hadn't checked on you personally."

Monica smiled. Jack would do anything for her sister. "Well, I'd say it wasn't necessary, but I'm so happy to see a familiar face I can't tell you."

"I don't know how you do it, darlin'. Your sister is so proud of you. We all are. Katie wanted me to tell you there's a spa day planned the minute you get home."

Katie was Jack's sister, and although not truly Monica's sister-in-law, she might as well be. "Tell her I'm counting on it. Looks like I may have all kinds of time on my hands when I get home."

"Oh . . . why's that?"

"It's complicated. My boss took me off the schedule. She's always looked for a reason to fire me."

Jack's dimpled smile fell. "She what?"

Monica waved off his concern. "I'm sure it will be fixed when I get back." She wasn't sure of anything.

"Who would fire a nurse who rips apart their life to do this?" He tossed his hand in the air and indicated all the people, the tents, the destruction.

"It will be fine."

"I have lawyers—"

"And I'll let you sic them on her if she tries to make my termination stick. Let me try it my way first." Good lord what a switch in her life. In Jessie's life. Neither of them could count on a man for anything growing up. Monica knew that Jack didn't offer empty promises and if his father, Gaylord Morrison, got word of Monica's problem, the whole damn hospital would have lawyers crawling all over it.

"Just say the word."

Monica had liked Jack from the minute she met him. He was perfect for her sister. "I will."

Jack leaned back on his arms and nodded toward the clinic. "So, what's with you and Fairchild?"

"Fairchild?"

"Trent."

"Oh, is that his last name?"

Jack's eyes narrowed. "You're kissing the man and don't know his name?"

She kicked his leg. "One kiss. And names are . . . useless here." Yet Trent had driven back yesterday just to learn hers.

"Still think you should know his name first. Makes a man feel used otherwise."

Monica busted out in a belly laugh. "Men love being used for kissing."

"Not that one. He didn't seem happy to think you might have someone else."

"Yeah, well . . . it's not like he has a right to own a jealousy card. We just met."

Jack flicked off an insect that had crawled up on his leg. "That doesn't always matter. Just thinking of Jessie looking at another man was an issue the day after we met."

"That was different."

"Oh, why?"

"I don't know. It just was." Jack and Jessie were meant to be forever. Monica didn't think that was out there for her. She had serious trust issues and was the first to admit it. "Enough about him. Tell me about Danny. Is he riding that colt yet?"

Her nephew was a constant source of chatter in the family. The kid loved life and was happier on a ranch than any kid could be.

They talked about home for a while longer and then Jack started to stand. "I told my pilot we'd get out of here before dark."

She stood and hugged him again. "Send my love. And tell Jessie I looked great or she'll worry."

"You look tired."

"I'm exhausted. But it won't last forever. I'll get some sleep soon. Don't worry."

He looked around at the people that were everywhere and in every state of dress. No shoes, clothes that looked as if they'd been worn for days. "If you need a fast exit, I'll send a plane."

"Thanks, Jack. It makes me feel better about being here knowing someone's watching my back."

"You can be just as big of a pain in the ass as Katie. Might as well treat you both the same."

He didn't mean a word of it, and Monica knew it. He draped his arm around her and walked her back inside the clinic.

Trent had pulled up a chair and was sitting by the door, waiting. Monica hesitated.

"I'll wait for you at your car," Jack said. He kissed Monica's cheek. "Bye darlin'. You be careful."

"I will."

Jack swaggered out the door.

Trent stood and shoved his hands in his pockets. "I guess I owe you an apology."

She leveled her eyes with his. "I guess you do."

"I'm taking your brother-in-law back to the airport. I'll be back to get you out of here."

"I'm busy—"

"According to Tauni, they have enough help tonight so you can get out of here. You'll get sick yourself at this pace."

"Fine." She was too tired to argue. "Now, about that apology . . ."

His eyes walked a slow dance down her frame and back up. Her skin stood on end as if he'd touched her. He leaned forward, placed his lips close to her ear. "My apology needs privacy."

He walked away . . . again . . . with her rooted in one spot staring. Anticipation shivered up her spine.

Chapter Eleven

"I feel I need to say something here," Jack said as Trent shook his hand for the last time.

"How about *thank you?*"

Jack lifted a brow and tilted his Stetson back an inch. "Monica's like a sister to me."

Ahh, Jack is taking on the role of big brother.

"Most people think I'm a nice guy."

Jack let his hand drop, fished a business card out of his back pocket, and handed it to Trent. "If she needs anything, and I mean anything, call me. It sounds like her job is giving her a hard time back home. I'd like to know the name of whoever is in charge of the operation here."

"Her job, really?" Trent asked.

"Not everyone is a nice guy."

Trent tucked the card into his front pocket. "I'll see what I can find out."

"Appreciate it. Thanks for the lift." Jack stood taller and nod-ded. "Take care of her."

"Not a problem."

Jack jogged up the steps to his private plane and disappeared inside.

Nice guy. Good thing I don't have to hate him. Mr. Testosterone, as Monica had called him, had jumped the assumption level and nearly blown a good thing. Testosterone in his veins, caffeine was needed intravenously, and his coffee needed CPR. Yeah, he had Monica on his brain.

It wasn't like Trent to care one way or another about what a woman had back home. In fact, Trent assumed most of the women he'd met and spent horizontal time with on the island had something else going. Made it easier.

But not with Monica.

He'd have to consider the why of that later. Thinking about it now gave him a headache. Or maybe that was hunger.

His apology to the woman in question would have to be more basic than flowers and chocolate . . . none of which were available. Unless he wanted to skip through the freaking woods and pick them himself. Trent drew the line there.

Back in his Jeep, he headed down the hill again. This time to bring her to his home . . . at least for a little while.

———•———

Hormones were awful things, crazy little buggers that nudged into your good sense and often made a fool out of you.

Jessie pushed back tears when she realized Jack was calling her from twenty thousand feet.

"Hey, darlin', how're you doing?" His voice was soothing, rich, and so Jack.

"I miss you."

"I'll be crawling into your bed before you wake up," he told her.

That helped. "How is it there?"

Jack hesitated. "Horrific."

"How can we help?"

"I'm contacting community outreach through our cooperate headquarters, setting up a relief fund. They need shelter, tents, clothing, food. All the basics."

"I want to help with something," Jessie told him.

"We'll figure something out when I get home. Monica sends her love," he said.

Hearing her sister's name brought a smile to her face. "You did manage to find her."

"Sure did."

"Did she seem off to you?"

Static came through the line as Jack mumbled something that sounded like *there's a guy*, but Jessie wasn't sure. "What was that?"

"Trent Fairchild. Nice guy. Got all hot under the collar when he assumed I was someone other than her brother-in-law."

Jessie closed her eyes and shook her head. "Wait. What? Back up . . . Monica met a guy?"

"That's what I said. She was either worked up over him or the fact that the hospital isn't cooperating with her leaving."

Now Jessie was confused. She had Jack explain everything again. Slowly.

"So let me get this right," she said a few minutes later after Jack explained what he'd learned. "She was fired and she's kissing some helicopter pilot named Trent?"

Jack laughed. "Yeah, well, she wasn't fired, but close enough. And get this, the Fairchilds own a charter company we use at the Morrisons all over the country. I'll have to ask my dad about them."

Jessie grabbed a piece of paper and jotted down the name. "Oh, that's OK, I can take care of the digging. Serves Monica right for all the *nosy sister behavior* when you and I were dating."

"We never dated," he reminded her.

She chuckled. He was right . . . they hadn't dated. She hadn't allowed it.

"Hurry home."

"I love you, darlin'."

"Love you, too."

Jessie hung up the phone, held it to her chest. After a long sigh, she punched in Katie's phone number.

Katie answered on the first ring.

They exchanged hellos and how ya doings, and then Jessie got right to the point.

"We need to find out everything we can about a guy named Trent Fairchild."

"We do?" Katie asked.

"Yep. We really do." Jessie smiled at the thought of some guy twisting Monica up.

For all the years Monica had dated anyone, Jessie never knew her to go crazy over any of them. *Must be a sign.*

———

She wasn't sure what kind of apology Trent was planning, but it had better include food and a bed . . . and a shower.

Make that a shower first, food, and a bed minus a partner, at least until some zzz's had been obtained. Monica had a new respect for doctors that went through medical school and their internships where they could count the hours of sleep in thirty-six hours on one hand.

Her feet ached, her back was screaming, and her eyeballs burned. Seriously, Monica couldn't remember ever feeling so exhausted.

She left a message on Walt's phone letting him know that she was away from the clinic for at least twelve hours. Ten of which she planned to sleep through.

Monica propped herself beside the building and waited for Trent. She didn't even have the energy to smile when he pulled up.

"Do you need me to carry you?" he asked when he rounded the front of his car and opened her door.

"I'd even take your helicopter for a ride if it would get me to a shower faster."

"That's a serious need."

He pulled out onto the road, avoided a pothole the size of Nebraska, and kept going. Monica leaned her head back and closed her eyes. "You'll forgive me if I'm less than a party."

"I won't even try talking to you," Trent said.

She was already fading. "Good, cuz I need more than two brain cells to discuss your reaction to Jack."

Monica dozed all the way up the hill, and barely realized they were at his place when he helped her out of the car. Only part of her plan kicked into place. The shower was hot but she didn't even manage to dry her hair before she fell into bed. Food would have to wait.

Sunshine, bright and piercing, pounded on the back of her eyelids, waking her. Monica stretched, felt at least four different muscles she didn't realize she had, and rolled back over. The soft pillow cushioned her head and left her in a cloud for a little while longer. It felt so damn good to be horizontal, to not have anyone calling out for her help.

She blinked a few times, and remembered where she was. She'd managed to toss a pajama T-shirt over her shoulders, but never dragged on the bottoms. The night before she'd wrapped her hair in a towel and rested her head on the pillow. That was her last memory. The towel sat folded on a chair by the door to her room. She'd fallen asleep on top of the covers, yet there was a light cotton blanket thrown over her. Her legs were bare, and only a thin pair of panties covered her girly parts.

Indebted to Trent for the best night's sleep she'd had in over a week, Monica didn't mind that he'd gotten an eyeful when he'd tucked her in.

The noise coming from her stomach reminded her of the time between meals and forced her from bed.

Inside the bathroom, she clicked on the light and miracle of miracles, the power was on. Leaning her ear toward the door, she realized there wasn't the sound of a noisy generator running.

She emerged from her room a few minutes later, wearing her running shorts and shirt. All her clothes could use a good wash. Maybe if Trent's power was on she could bug him for yet one more basic need.

He was in his living room with a large big-screen television tuned in to a newscast.

"G'morning," she said, bringing his attention to her presence.

His face softened and he lifted his strong frame from the couch. "I was starting to wonder if you were going for another twelve hours."

"Twelve hours?"

"You dropped around eight." He tapped his watch and said, "It's almost ten."

"You're kidding."

"Nope."

Her heart skipped. Fourteen hours. "I've got to get back." She turned around to go change clothes. Smelly awful clothes.

"Hold up. I spoke with a Dr. Klein."

That stopped her.

"I heard your cell phone ringing in your room just after six this morning. You didn't budge."

"So you answered it?" She wasn't sure if she should be grateful or angry.

Anger took energy. Although she felt rested, she wanted nothing to do with being pissed.

"Yeah. Anyway when I told him you were one step away from comatose he suggested you return to the clinic tonight. He asked for you to call him or Walt when you woke."

"OK then. Tonight?" As in she had a good six or eight hours to call her own?

"Tonight," he confirmed. "How about some coffee?"

"I'd kill for coffee."

"No need for violence," he said with a laugh. "The power flickered shortly after you crashed. No more instant. Why don't you sit, I'll get another pot going."

"Before I get comfortable, do you have a washer and dryer? My clothes . . ."

He pointed back toward the hall leading to the bedrooms. "Back of the hall there's a door to a mud room."

"A mud room in Jamaica?"

"I grew up in the Northeast. I couldn't build a house without a mud room. Washer and dryer are in there."

Five minutes later, she joined Trent in his kitchen with all smiles. "Clean clothes and a good night's sleep. I feel guilty." She knew her colleagues weren't faring so well.

"Guilty?"

"If Donald hadn't sweet-talked his way into getting me to go to the clinic on my own, I would still be sleeping on those bunks at the hospital." She wouldn't have gotten to know Trent either. She left that unsaid.

"Remind me to thank Donald." Trent lifted an eyebrow her way before he poured her coffee, added a little sugar, and handed it to her.

"Thank you." She moaned . . . a throaty, bedroom moan, as the coffee slid down her throat. "You have some serious coffee skills, Trent."

He leaned against the counter and watched her over the rim of his cup. "Good coffee is part of my apology."

She lifted her cup in salute. "Good show." She sipped again, felt some of the strain from the past few days dissipate. "Have you always been the jealous type?"

Trent closed his eyes and wrinkled his face. "Do we have to talk about that?"

She laughed in the face of his discomfort. "If you knew just how crazy Jack is about my sister you'd laugh at your mistake."

"He was determined to find you."

"Probably because Jessie wouldn't let him hear the end of it if he hadn't. She worries like a mother."

"Is she older than you?"

"Only a couple of years. We depend on each other. Well, she has Jack now, but before . . . when I was in nursing school and she was raising her son, Danny, by herself, we helped each other out."

"What about your parents?"

Monica stared into her cup. "Dad ran off early on. I don't even remember him. My mom is wrapped up in her own life." She didn't want to talk about them. "Anyway. Jessie probably threatened bodily harm if he didn't find me."

"He seemed like a nice guy."

"He is. The whole family is so down-to-earth it's hard to believe they're filthy rich. Did you see his jet?"

He grinned. "Classy. Have you flown in it?"

"Hell yeah."

"And that doesn't bother you? I thought you were afraid of heights."

She found the bottom of her cup. "I don't have to look out the window in his plane. Your helicopter requires blinders over my eyes to avoid the outside."

"So it's not the flying, it's the visual?"

"Exactly."

He refilled her cup and pushed the sugar toward her. "Are you hungry?"

A loud gurgle erupted from her stomach right as he asked. "I guess that answers that," he said.

She moved from her perch and joined him in the kitchen. "Tell me you have something other than an energy bar."

"The fresh foods are gone. I have a decent supply of canned goods." He opened his pantry and she peered inside. "Many of the locals have chickens, so I managed to snag a few eggs."

Monica eyed a can of chicken, a sealed jar of salsa. She started taking handfuls of ingredients from the cupboard and set them on the counter. "I can make this work," she told him.

"You sure you don't want me to figure something out?"

"No, no. It's nice to have my hands in something less toxic than what I find with my patients."

He moved to her recently deserted chair to watch. She felt his eyes on her as she took over his kitchen. "Most bachelors don't have anything other than steaks, beer, and microwave meals."

"I had my share of those days. Gets old after a while. My mom taught us all the basics."

"Good for her," Monica said with a smile. "Have you talked to her since the quake?"

His silence had her glancing over his way.

"My parents passed a few years ago."

"Oh. I'm sorry. Were they young?" From the look on his face, the memory of their passing still hurt.

"Yeah."

Monica pushed on to another topic. He obviously didn't talk about his parents any more than she did hers. She got that. "Jessie was the cook in our family. We were so broke most of the time eating out wasn't an option."

Trent laughed. "And now she's married to a Morrison."

Monica opened the can of chicken and dumped it into a pan over the stove. "That's a crazy story."

"What is?"

"How she and Jack met. She thought he was a temporary waiter at The Morrison, just passing through. He didn't tell her he owned the damn hotel."

"And that mattered?"

"Well yeah. She had Danny to think about. A bad high school decision made her a single mom early on. She always seemed to attract the biggest losers. Then comes Jack pretending to be a bum . . . well, actually, he didn't really pose as a bum, but he knew she wanted to find someone who had it together, which in his head meant she wanted someone with money."

"Jack has money," Trent said.

"No guy wants to think a woman is with him for the money. So he lied."

"He told her he was broke?" There was laughter in Trent's voice.

"He omitted the truth. He didn't say he was broke." Monica stirred the chicken and added spices she found above the stove. "Jack was determined to make her fall for him. She was determined to ignore him."

"I take it that didn't work."

"Not for long." She poked her head back into the cupboard and found a package of tortillas. "You're holding out on me, Barefoot."

He smiled. "Forgot those were in there."

She glanced on the package for an expiration date. *Still a few days off.* Fresh eggs were cracked and sizzling in the pan as she finished her sister's story. "Eventually she and Jack hooked up and she found out about who he really was. Ticked her off at first, too."

"No one likes to be lied to."

"No. I get why he did, though. The guy has some serious cash. I think there was more than one woman in his life who wanted to marry him just for the money. That has to be hard on a guy."

"That's very forgiving of you." Trent had rested his chin in his hands as he watched her in his kitchen. He had this silly grin on his face that made her wonder exactly what was going on inside his head.

She pulled two plates off a shelf and scooped her chicken omelets onto them.

"They are crazy about each other. I knew he was the right guy for her long before she did. It's easy to forgive him." Monica turned off the stove and brought the plates over to him. She topped off their coffee before taking the seat to his side.

"Were you a short-order cook before you became a nurse?"

"I waited tables a little when I was going to school." She poured salsa on her eggs and took the first bite. "Hmmm."

Trent approved with a quick thumbs-up when his mouth was full. "Good," he mumbled around the food.

"Everything's good when you're starving. It needs cheese." But it was still the best meal she'd had in forever.

"It's perfect."

Not perfect, but it was nice he approved. "Did you have any crappy jobs growing up?"

He shook his head. "Not really. Went to college after high school, then straight into the family business."

"The helicopters?"

He took another bite and finished swallowing before he elaborated. "I floated around the office first. Marketing, public relations, that sort of thing."

"Doesn't sound like you had much of a choice. Was it a foregone conclusion that you'd work for the family?" She wasn't sure if that was better or worse than having no direction from your parents.

"Seemed a waste of time to look for work somewhere else. Besides, if the corporate side wasn't for me, I could always fly."

"So you took to flying."

He finished his breakfast and pushed his plate away. "I've always loved flying. Helicopters, jets . . . prop jobs. Doesn't matter."

"Ever worry you'll crash?" It scared the hell out of her just thinking of spending so much time in the air.

"Ever think you're going to bite it when you're driving a car?" he asked instead of answering her question.

"No, not really."

"Same thing applies with flying. The only day I thought about crashing was the first day I was up there. After that, it didn't cross my mind. The best way to dispose of that fear is taking the controls."

"Oh, I don't know."

"Suit yourself. But you seem like the kind of girl who likes to take control. Might cure that height fear you have."

"If God wanted us to fly, he'd have given us wings."

Trent laughed. "Or pilots."

Monica relaxed in her chair and stretched her arms over her head.

The movement caught Trent's attention and his appreciative smile spread over his lips. He wore a T-shirt and shorts, his normal attire since she'd met him. His hair could use a trim, but he didn't carry the surfer look from back home. "Well, Mr. Testosterone, what does one do on this island when they're not flying tourists at death-defying heights, or cleaning up nature's mess?"

She wasn't sure if he had a desire to pick up where their kiss had left off the day before. He hadn't so much as touched her since helping her into his home the night before. Of course, she was doing her best zombie interpretation at the time, and wouldn't have been able to do much more than snore in the poor guy's arms.

He rubbed his chin as if in thought. "There's usually plenty of steel band music and rum concoctions to entertain on a free day."

"Not a lot of that going on," she said.

He swiveled in his chair, his knee nudged against hers. The contact was about as innocent as it could get, but her breath caught anyway. When his hand dropped to her thigh, she knew he hadn't forgotten their kiss or his promise to make up for his mistake about Jack. "If you come up with some cheesy line about making our own music . . ."

He slid his hand down the back of her thigh, gripped her chair, and slid it closer.

She caught herself against his legs, and met his sudden stare.

"How about we skip the lines?" he said.

The heat in the room shot up ten degrees. Both of his palms were against her thighs but they had yet to do anything but sit there.

"Lines are for people who don't know what they want," she told him.

A smirk played on his lips.

"That doesn't define us."

No. She'd pictured him close since he told her his name. Monica slid her hands over his and moved them up her legs. She didn't like lines or games. "Do we have a definition?"

He took her lead, moving his hands along her bare skin, sending tendrils of anticipation over every nerve in her body. A squeal escaped her lips when he gripped her hips and plucked her off the chair and into his lap as if she weighed nothing. She gripped his shoulders for balance and enjoyed the feel of his hands holding her ass.

His clever move had her straddling him and terribly needy without even a kiss. "We don't need a definition." Trent's heated breath blew across her lips, his stare so charged she couldn't look away.

Monica leaned forward, not wanting to wait for whatever made him hesitate.

Trent, the big tease, leaned back. "Are you sure?"

She didn't answer. Her lips met his, all heat and tongue and it was Trent's turn to moan.

Everywhere he touched was on fire. His hand found skin under her T-shirt and skimmed up her waist, burning a path to her breasts and through her bra.

"You feel amazing," he managed to say as his lips left hers to kiss her jaw, her neck.

The hard pack of his muscles met her palms.

"So soft," he uttered.

Monica wiggled closer; the chair quickly became an obstacle to the pleasure of pressing her body closer to his.

His lips found the sensitive spot behind her ear and the quivering that was hovering low in her belly turned into something palpable. "Oh," she whispered.

Trent released a soft chuckle and repeated the kiss to her neck.

Somewhere in the back of her head, Monica heard Ginger bark. Trent was lifting her off his lap and placing her on the kitchen counter. She reached for his shirt, to help rid him of the barrier.

Ginger barked again.

Damn dog.

One second Trent was reaching to remove her shirt, her only thought was how quickly they could cover each other skin to skin, the next Trent was pulling her shirt back down and pulling her from the counter.

That's when Monica heard the noise.

People. Kids . . . Ginger barking.

Monica met Trent's smoky gaze. He was breathing as hard as she was.

"Trent?" someone called from the hall leading to the front door.

"Company?" Monica whispered.

He ran a hand over her hair and pulled his own shirt down. They didn't have time to recover much in the way of composure before a family piled into the room.

Ginger ran around the room, a playful bark in her throat. A man Monica recognized was half carrying a woman into Trent's home.

"Reynard, Kiki?"

One look from Reynard to Trent and Monica knew the man understood exactly what they'd interrupted.

Color rose to the cheeks of the woman Trent called Kiki. "We're too early," she said.

"No. No." Trent flashed a sympathetic glance toward Monica and grasped her hand. "It's fine."

Monica forced a smile to her face and felt her libido cool as if ice water had been dropped on her from the sky. One of the children, not five, ran up and hugged Trent's knees. "Uncle Trent."

Clearly, the family wasn't related. Yet this child had some affection toward her would-be lover. "Micha. This is my friend Monica." The boy smiled up at her.

"Monica you remember Reynard from your first day on the island." Trent continued the introductions.

Oh, now she remembered. "Nice to see you again," she managed.

"We've come too early," Kiki said again. "We should go."

Trent tugged Monica's hand. "No. Please . . . I told you to come." Trent turned toward Monica and explained. "Their home was destroyed by the earthquake. I asked Kiki and Reynard to stay here."

"Oh," Monica said.

Micha had engaged Ginger in a game of fetch with a plastic bone. The other children were all smiles and completely oblivious to any tension in the room.

Kiki leaned on her husband for another couple of steps. Monica took notice of her pale skin and obvious discomfort and promptly dismissed her own sexual frustration. "Are you OK?"

"Just out of the hospital," Reynard told them. "The doctor said she needs a bed and rest."

Monica passed a half smile to Trent. The same frustration inside her swam behind his eyes. "Guest room?" she asked him.

He nodded.

"Come with me." She walked Reynard and his wife to the room she previously occupied.

So much for their private oasis and alone time. The population in the house quadrupled in minutes and all thoughts of intimacy were now on hold.

Dammit!

Chapter Twelve

Trent helped Reynard unload his family's possessions from the truck and into the house.

"Are you sure it's OK we're here?"

Trent hoisted one strap over his shoulder and picked up another sack. "I won't hear another word about it, Reynard. Like I told your wife, I'm going to be leaving soon. I have little to worry about here if the house is taken care of while I'm gone."

The stress behind Reynard's eyes started to fade. "I will pay you."

Trent shook his head. "You'll save your money and rebuild your home." However, Trent wasn't sure how possible that would be or how long it would take. The economy on the island had never been great. It would be even worse now.

He turned to walk back into the house. Reynard's hand grasped his shoulder. "Thank you."

"I'll keep my room until I leave," Trent said as they walked into the house. "And keep you informed about my plans while I'm away."

"When will you go?"

Trent thought of Monica and shook his head. "I'm not sure. Week or two at most." He'd told Jack Morrison he'd keep an eye out for his sister-in-law and Trent didn't go back on his word. He'd be lying to himself if he said he was sticking around *only* for his promise to a virtual stranger. The fact was, he wasn't ready to see the last of his nurse.

Not yet anyway.

Back in the house, Monica was in the kitchen again, this time heating up soup from a can. Reynard's children were sitting up at the counter talking obsessively about living in such a big house and how theirs had fallen down. It was as if their duty in life was to relay a play-by-play of their life to Monica as she cooked their lunch.

"A house this big is going to take your help to keep clean," she told the kids. "Your mom has to be in bed for a few days."

Micha puffed out his chest. "We'll help," he said.

Monica removed bowls from the cupboard and ladled in the soup. Reynard carried the bags into the second guest room while Trent watched the kids and Monica talk. Tanya, the oldest daughter, was ten and she held the youngest in her lap. "Mother needs to sleep so we need to keep quiet," Tanya told the kids.

Trent moved behind the brood and offered his advice. "There's lots of room outside to play. Just keep an eye on each other."

Monica offered Trent a smile, her eyes lighting up.

In short order, she had the kids eating lunch and worked her way to Kiki's bedside to make sure she had something to eat as well.

Trent felt guilty for the work Monica was doing on what was supposed to be her afternoon off. Within a half an hour, she was removing clothes from the dryer and folding them into her backpack. It appeared as if she was packing to leave.

He wasn't sure they'd ever have another opportunity to get away, so instead of staying in his house, which had been overrun with kids and excitement, Trent packed a few bottles of water and an attempt at a picnic into a bag. He grabbed a beach blanket and a couple of towels as he passed his linen closet.

Monica cornered him in the hall. "Maybe you should just take me back to the clinic. I might as well—"

He silenced her with a finger to her lips. "It's your day off," he reminded her. "We still have half of it left." He slid his hand to her shoulder and down to her arm. "How about I show you a quiet place on the beach where tourists don't play and the waves hardly touched?"

She leaned against the wall and sighed. "Sightseeing?"

No, more like procuring a secluded spot away from kids and chaos so they could pick up where they left off. "Sure, we'll call it sightseeing."

"All right."

Trent loaded their day's provisions in the Jeep and encouraged Ginger to stay at the house. The last thing he wanted was another interrupting bark.

He informed Reynard that he'd be back later that night after dropping Monica off at the clinic and then the two of them drove away.

"You surprise me, Barefoot," Monica said as they turned out of the driveway.

"Oh, why's that?"

"One minute I think maybe your personal walls are high since you live here alone, and then you invite an entire family to move in with you."

"I have other options. Reynard and his family don't."

Her window was rolled down and the warm air rushing past them blew her hair in different directions. Most of the time he'd spent with her, those blonde locks were bound into a ponytail or some kind of clip. He liked what he saw. It gave Monica a wild look that made him think of warm nights and hot passion.

"You're really going to leave the island?" she asked.

"For a while anyway."

"Will you go back home? The East Coast?"

He shrugged. "I haven't seen my brothers in a while. I'll proba-bly start there."

Monica gripped the edges of her hair and stared out the window. "I can't imagine not having any ties and the whole world open to explore."

"What ties do you have?"

"My job, for one. Although that might not be the case when I get home."

He pulled off the main road and onto a dirt one. The locals knew of the secluded beach and even more private cave within, but the road wasn't often traveled. The overgrowth told Trent there hadn't been a car there in a while. Not since the last rain anyway. "Jack said something about your job being in trouble. What's up with that?"

"My boss is a bitch. I'm not being catty about that either. She'd always looked for a reason to write me up or in some way move me on. I don't get it either. It's not like I've ever done a thing to her. A friend from work called me the other day to tell me she took me off the schedule. Said I didn't fill the holes my coming here left. Claimed I abandoned my patients." Monica air quoted the last words and her smile fell into a thin frown line.

"How can you abandon anyone you've not taken care of?"

"I have no idea. Walt will raise holy hell when we get back. But the truth is, the doctors on staff don't work for the hospital. They work either for themselves, or in the case of the emergency room, they work with a doctors' group. The rules for Walt don't apply to me. I work for the hospital and they don't have to grant time off. I had vacation time coming and arranged for someone to take my shifts."

"Then what's the problem?"

"My replacement called in sick and staffing didn't fix it."

It sounded to Trent like Walt was the name he needed to pass on to Jack.

"Nurses are needed everywhere," he said, hoping to put her at ease. Her hand on the edge of the door had gripped the side as she spoke. "What else is waiting for you in California?"

"My apartment." She laughed as the word came out of her mouth. "I guess that doesn't count. My friend Katie and her husband, Dean, are there . . . although they talked about moving back to Texas."

"Your sister's in Texas, right?"

Monica grew silent. "Yeah. I guess that would just leave me and my mom." She shivered.

The conversation faded. He'd obviously made her think a little harder about where she was living and why she stayed.

The road came to an end with barely enough room to turn the car around. Trent rolled to a stop and pulled the parking brake under the shade of trees.

Monica sent him a confused look.

"We're here?"

He lifted his sunglasses enough for her to see the gleam in his eye. "We walk from here."

She jumped out of the car and grabbed her backpack. "You're going to make me work for a day at the beach?" she teased.

"It's worth it," he told her.

Monica patted her back pocket and removed her phone. "Mind if I charge this while we're gone? It's running out of juice."

He leaned over the seat, pulled the charger from the center console, and plugged it in. Then he led her down the overgrown path, his feet sinking into the damp soil left behind from the rain. He'd flown over this spot after the tsunami and was happy to see that it hadn't been destroyed by the wave. The cove was on the opposite side of the island from where the wave hit, and had some protection from the walls of rock on both sides.

"We're in the middle of nowhere," Monica said as they picked their way through the path. "How did you find it?"

"One of the locals pointed out the trail. I saw it from the air but couldn't find the road." Large ferns brushed against his legs. He pulled a few aside to give Monica room to pass. He glanced at a banana tree and saw a bundle of green fruit hanging from the stalk. "Hold up." He stepped into the brush and removed a pocketknife from his pack.

"Bananas?"

"Yeah. Look on the ground for any that are yellow. I'll pull these down and take them back with us when we leave."

Monica scouted the forest floor and managed a few pieces of fruit that were ripe enough to eat. He left the green ones on the trail to gather on the way back.

Trent took Monica's hand in his as he started down the steep trail. Halfway to the sand the view opened up and Monica hesitated. "Wow."

Yeah, he got that. Small white-capped foam sat atop bright blue water that turned turquoise green and then dark blue. The sand in the cove was pristine white with some debris left over from the small wave that hit this shore. But it wasn't enough to take away from the beauty.

"Worth the walk?" he asked.

Monica's smile caught him in the gut. "Finally. I see something here that helps me understand why anyone would live here."

"There's more," he promised.

They reached the sand and Monica dropped her pack to the ground. She kicked off her shoes and ran toward the water. "It's so warm."

"I thought you knew it was."

"I've only seen the airport and the clinic. When I ran on your beach I never touched the water." She leaned down and picked something from the ocean. "We should swim."

He picked up her pack and waved her down the beach. "Let me show you something else first."

Trent heard her run up behind him. "What is it?"

"It's a cave," he told her when they stood before the entrance. The opening was about five feet tall and six feet wide. He kicked away a log that had washed up next to the opening. He could feel the air rushing out from inside.

"This is so cool," she said as she ducked inside. He followed behind her. The wall above them opened up after a few feet and light filtered through a break in the ceiling of the cave a good thirty feet above their heads.

"How far does it go back?"

"Not far. There's a tunnel off to the left, but it narrows to the point where I couldn't get through."

Monica walked over to a small pool of water that dripped from above. She brought the liquid to her lips. "It's fresh."

"It's probably runoff from the rain. I've searched above and couldn't find a lake or even a stream." His voice echoed inside the cave.

The air inside the cave was ten degrees cooler than the air outside. It was a perfect refuge on a hot day after a cool swim.

And it was private. More so than his house at the current time.

"This is amazing. I'm glad the wave didn't destroy it."

The light from above lit up half her body. His angel nurse. A smile found his lips and she grinned back.

"What are you up to, Barefoot?"

He walked toward her and dropped their things in the sand. "Bad things," he warned her with a laugh. "Really sweaty things."

Monica caught her lip in her teeth and held her ground as he approached.

"Sweaty, huh?"

He took her around her waist and pulled her close. "Steamy, sweaty . . ." He kissed the side of her neck. "Hot."

He felt the moment she melted in his arms and he placed his lips on hers. She could have her swim, but not until he dove into her.

Trent pushed his tongue alongside hers and lost himself in their kiss. Her lithe body pressed against him, her pert breasts felt soft against his hard chest. She accepted his kiss, his touch, without hesitation. Her hands traveled down his back and over his ass. He groaned. His shorts were already confining, but now they needed to go altogether.

Monica squeezed his ass again and laughed when he growled. She tugged at his shirt until it was off his back and in the sand. Her tiny fingers spread over his chest as she leaned in for another kiss. Hot, wet kisses that promised more steam as they grew.

"Tell me you brought a blanket," Monica said when she pulled away. "Sex in the sand is overrated."

He wanted to ask her how she knew, but thought better of it. He peeled himself away from her long enough to remove the beach blanket he'd packed. He spread it beyond the light reflecting off the pool and farther away from the entrance of the cave. The ground was solid there without copious amounts of sand to interfere.

Monica helped him finish spreading the blanket out and sat in the center. "I'm starting to think you planned this," she said.

He dropped to his knees, placing a hand on each side of her. "I did." He leaned over, kissing her again, and pushed her back onto the blanket. He lapped up her kisses and pulled her shirt over her head. Creamy white breasts peeked out from under a pink bra. He liked the pink, he decided, and wondered if her panties matched. Something about a woman's lingerie made his blood boil. The way a woman cared for clothes so few actually saw made it that much sweeter when he had the opportunity to peel them away. His lips trailed down her throat and his tongue dipped beneath the fabric of her bra to find a tight nipple waiting.

She wiggled beneath him, sending shock waves straight to his cock. He pushed her bra away and lapped her nipple in soothing strokes. He caught the tip in his teeth and she squealed. "Do that again."

He smiled and complied. Her hips came off the ground and pushed against him.

Trent reached behind her, rid her breasts of her bra, and continued to explore his Caribbean present. He'd always wondered what it would be like to make love to a beautiful woman inside the cave. Her moans vibrated off the walls and filled his head with satisfaction.

She whispered his name and arched into him when he moved away enough to pluck at the fastening of her shorts. Her trim frame wasn't from a lack of food, but a fit body with enough curves to make his mouth water.

Damn if her panties didn't match her bra. The scent of her sun-kissed skin, the slight taste of salt on his tongue, made him want even more of her.

Monica kicked her shorts free and leaned up on her elbows. "Your turn, Barefoot. Those shorts look very uncomfortable."

He liked the nickname, found it endearing.

She helped his shorts down his hips and smiled. "Commando?"

"Panties are for girls."

She giggled and traced a fingernail down his hip.

His entire body shivered and his sex reached for her.

Monica hesitated. "Condom?"

He reached for his shorts, removed his wallet.

She released a breath and traced his skin to the tip of his cock. When her hand gripped him fully, his head tipped back and he closed his eyes. So good. She felt so fucking right.

Monica sat up. Before he knew what she was about, the tip of her tongue sought him. "Christ." His hand caught the back of her head. He should be more of a gentleman, this being their first time, but he couldn't push her away. The warm cavern of her mouth took him in. He pushed back the instant desire to release and focused on the pleasure of her touch.

He hadn't been this ready to go since he was a high school kid with his first girl behind the bleachers at the school.

"Hold up, Monica." He was panting.

She released him with a slight pop and smiled up into his eyes.

"What's the matter, Barefoot? Too much for you?"

He eased her back to the ground and wedged his knee between her thighs. The moist center of her body rode his thigh. "I'm not going without you."

His finger caught the edge of her panty and dipped inside. His angel, his white light, was more than ready for his touch. Pink underwear skidded across the cave floor and Monica was reaching for his wallet.

He laughed and helped her find the condom. He rolled it on and nestled between her legs. "Please, Trent," she begged when he leaned close but didn't move within her. He met her lips again instead and kissed her until she squirmed. When her hand moved between them, placing him where she wanted, he held his breath as he sank into her.

The soft blue of her eyes, which always seemed cold, now melted into the dim light of the cave. She gave him more room and sighed when she took every inch of him.

"So good," she murmured.

It was. She was.

Her hands moved over his hips, his ass, guiding him closer. There was no slow pace, no easy dance. This was where passion removed all thought except the ultimate goal. He kissed her hard and felt her legs crawl up onto his back and wedge him in. The fast staccato of their breaths matched their pace. Her body squeezed him inside, out, long before he heard the change in her breathing.

He forced back the wave of release again, waiting, moving inside her so deep he wanted to crawl inside and never leave.

When she called his name and her body gripped him hard, he released the wave and allowed the warmth to rush over him.

This was what heaven tasted like.

Chapter 13

Monica remembered the long conversations filled with talk about sex she'd had with her sister and her friends in her early years. She'd anticipated nothing but greatness for her first time. They did mention that intercourse would hurt the first time . . . but with the right partner that pain would be minimal and pleasure would soon follow.

What a crock of shit. Pain, serious get-the-fuck-off-of-me pain, didn't evolve into anything other than a mess the first time. Andrew, her first lover, wasn't all that experienced in the art of making love. It was damn near over before they got started. It happened the summer after her senior year in high school. Unlike most of her friends who'd lost their virginity somewhere between tenth and eleventh grade, Monica wasn't in a hurry to give it up. It helped that Jessie had gotten pregnant in school and constantly told Monica that it wasn't worth it. Jessie may have loved Danny from the very first moment she saw him, but being a single parent had always been a struggle. Monica figured she needed to finish school and have a life plan before complicating anything with sex.

Andrew didn't stick around, big shock there . . . and another opportunity didn't present itself for months. She'd gone on the pill long before Andrew, and after one semester in nursing school she never, not once, made love without a condom. Her next experience was with an intern. Monica knew going into the affair he was a player. That didn't bother her in the least. She was determined to find out what the big fuss was about sex. Who better to show her than someone who made women's panties weep with want after just a look. He had been sexy, suave, and skilled enough between the sheets to keep Monica coming back.

Eventually her intern moved on . . . or maybe that was her. She kept her lovers at a distance, didn't see them very much outside of the bedroom . . . why should men be the ones with reputations as players?

Even through all her exploits, never once did she roll away from her lover and think to herself, "now *that* is what everyone is talking about."

Until now.

The orgasm Trent delivered ricocheted her body somewhere into the stratosphere and it was going to take NASA to bring it back.

"Good God, Barefoot, we have to do *that* again."

Trent hadn't caught his breath yet and lifted his face, which was buried into her neck, to look at her. A self-satisfied smile radiated all the way to his eyes.

Something inside the Ice Queen started to thaw.

"Right now?" he teased.

She clawed his back and felt sand beneath her fingertips. "I'll let you rest. Maybe after a swim."

"How nice of you," he said with a laugh. He rolled to his side and pulled her with him. He blew out a breath as if saying *damn that was amazing.*

"I know, huh?"

He kissed the top of her head in response.

"I didn't even mind the sand . . . much." It was everywhere. Sticking to her skin wherever Trent touched.

"The sand sucks."

She kissed his jaw and moved away from him a few inches. Her body buzzed with energy and a need to move. "How about that swim? Wash off?"

He placed his hands behind his head and watched as she reached for her underwear. The smile on his face never fell. "You're beautiful," he told her, making her pause. His stare was a little unnerving. It seemed there was something else he wanted to say but didn't.

She dropped her hand to his leg. "You're all kinds of sexy yourself, Barefoot."

He reached for her then, and kissed her. When he pulled away he took the bra from her fingertips and tossed it to the side. "No need for this." He stood and brought her with him. "When will you have the opportunity to skinny-dip on a beach again?"

She didn't consider herself an exhibitionist, but she wasn't shy either. With a smile she said, "That ground is hard on the back. Last one in is on bottom the next time." Then she turned and ran.

Trent caught her at the water's edge and picked her up around the waist. Together they fell into the water.

She emerged shaking water from her hair and smiling. Trent held her and pulled her deeper. "That's not fair. We hit the water at the same time."

"Not exactly. My feet were in first."

Monica splashed water in his face. "Brat."

When they were waist deep, he turned her around to face him. She wrapped her legs around his waist and let her body float. The water caressed her skin as she let her arms fall to the side and she leaned back. Trent held her, his eyes gazed down at her naked frame. His thumbs found the swell of her breasts and teased them.

"This is the life. I finally get why you like it here."

"Warm Caribbean water, a beautiful woman."

He spun her around to keep the sun from glaring in her eyes. "Do you bring women here often?"

"Would you believe me if I told you you're the first?"

Oh, yeah . . . the ice was melting. "You don't strike me as the kind who lies."

"I never lie."

"Not even little white lies? You know, the ones where you tell someone you're fine when you're really not?"

"Well . . ."

"Or the ones where you say you'll call when you know you won't?" She was fishing now, and cursing herself for doing it. Theirs was a temporary fling. They lived in different places, different lives.

Those warm eyes that melted when he held her hardened a little. "If I tell someone I'll call, I call. I don't like games."

A wave caught them both, and washed over her head. Trent pulled her face from the water. Monica unlocked her legs from his waist and stood beside him. "I don't care for games either," she told him. "We both know what we're doing here . . . now—"

"Is right here and right now," he finished for her. It saddened her to think on that.

A shadow passed over his eyes before the salt from his lips met hers with a brief kiss. At least she knew where she stood. No use pretending they could be anything more than what they were right then.

"Well, California, how about I give you a second shot for that top position?" He set her from him with a smile that wasn't quite as bright as she liked.

"California?"

"You keep calling me Barefoot. I have to have something."

She liked it. "I'm listening."

He gave a quick nod toward a rock in the center of the lagoon. "First one to the rock and back wins."

She cocked her head to the side. "You said you didn't like games."

"Friendly competition, not games. I'll even give you a head start."

"How much of a head start?"

"I don't know. Ten . . . nine . . . eight."

Monica dove into the water and kicked her feet. She reached the rock first, but Trent was fast on her heels. It was useless. He was a stronger swimmer and a faster runner. When she reached the beach, he was there and didn't even appear winded. "Not fair. Home court advantage." She felt like a kid . . . a naked kid without a care in the world.

He reached for her and she dodged his hand. The chase was on. Sand kicked up from their feet as Monica managed to escape him with quick unexpected moves. He cornered her toward the cave. She ducked inside, laughing.

The chase was fun, but the catching was so much better. They circled the pool of water inside the cave. Monica considered a dash back outside but thought maybe staying inside would hold a better reward. If her time with Trent was limited, there wasn't a need to swim it away.

She paused at the exit of the cave and sucked in a deep breath. "A gentleman wouldn't make me take the bottom twice."

Trent lifted both hands in the air. "I give up. You can have the top."

She took a step toward him. "You're so easy."

They were both laughing when the world started to shake.

———•———

The jolt knocked them both to the ground.

It took a nanosecond for Trent to realize what was happening. This wasn't a roll-over-and-go-back-to-sleep quake, this was a loud, plane-crashing-into-a-building quake. The sound inside the cave jolted him to his feet. Something was falling, somewhere. He caught sight of Monica who had been standing next to the entrance. She was now on the ground and rocks were falling.

She screamed. He found his feet and rushed to her side. The earth kept moving.

The light from the outside faded with a loud crash. All he could see was Monica being crushed by the falling rock.

When he reached her, he attempted to bring her to her feet to escape the falling rock. She grabbed his shoulders with terror in her eyes. Trent pulled her and she screamed.

Her right leg was pinned under a rock.

The earth grew quiet.

"It's OK," he told her. "I'm here." Above her, the rock still crumbled. One small shake . . .

Trent peered through the now darkened cave, the only light came from the opening at the top, and he reached for the rock holding Monica in place. "I can't move," she cried.

He looked past the blood under the rock and grasped her leg with both hands. He pulled against it and more rock came down a few feet away.

Monica covered her face with her hands. Trent leaned over her to keep more rock from hitting her.

The dust settled and he pulled her hands away. "Listen. I'm going to dig. You're going to have to push out when I lift the rock." If he could lift the rock.

Her eyes were moist with unshed tears. "That was a big one, Trent. An aftershock . . ."

Was inevitable. He knew.

He dug around her leg like a madman. When he felt her leg shift in the sand, he wedged the rock to keep it from collapsing again.

"OK, I'm going to try the rock again. You ready?"

She nodded and rose up on her elbows and bent her good leg.

"One . . . two . . . three." Trent heaved the rock. His back protested, his arms were on fire, and the rock wasn't moving.

He kept trying, sweat poured off his brow.

Monica's hand stopped him. "That's not going to move. We need to dig."

She sat up as best she could and helped him dig the sand away from her leg. He didn't even want to think of the pain she must be in. There was blood dripping down her calf, he couldn't see the rest of her foot under the rock.

As they dug, the rock sank into her leg and the hole. Monica cried out twice as the rock shifted. Trent kept digging. Just as he felt they were getting her loose, the aftershock hit.

Terror took the place of reason and Trent shoved her leg to the space he'd dug out as the rocks started to move again. He saw her toes and reached for her shoulders to pull her away.

Monica screamed.

Several feet from the cave opening, he collapsed with Monica in his lap.

Rock filled the space where she had been trapped.

His arms surrounded her, both of them too shocked to move.

Only when she whimpered did he release the vise grip he had on her.

"It's OK. You're safe." Only again, he wasn't sure of that either. They were in a cave and a ton of rock separated them from the outside world. The steep walls of the cave didn't give him a means to climb out from the top and Monica wasn't in any shape to walk, let alone climb.

"Save the white lies for someone who's good at them, Barefoot."

He hugged her again and felt her shiver. They were both caked with sand and dirt and he hadn't even assessed her leg yet. After scurrying out from under her, he attempted to look at the damage.

"It's broken," she said before he even looked.

"Are you sure?" It wasn't obvious to him looking at it. There was a gash where the rock had fallen on it and it was swelling rapidly. But there wasn't a bone sticking out where it shouldn't be . . . that had to be a good thing.

Monica glanced behind them to the pool of water. "I need to get the dirt out of there."

He lifted her as gently as he could and settled her next to the pool. He found the bag he packed for their day, thankful it wasn't on the outside of the cave, and removed the towels from inside. With painstaking slowness, he helped Monica take the surface dirt off her wound. They both had scrapes but other than the one on her leg, none were terribly deep. At one point she shoved the towel in his hand and leaned back. "You're going to have to do the rest."

"Do the rest?"

She swallowed. "Scrub the rest out." Her color went white just saying it.

"That's going to hurt."

"Has to be done."

"You sure?"

"I won't scream if you don't." She attempted to joke, but he knew she was hurting.

I can do this. He cleaned the edge of the towel with the water from the pool. "Hold on."

She gripped his shoulder.

By the time he was done, there were nail marks in his skin and Monica was ghost white. It took some time, but he soon managed to clean her off and get her dressed. She had a small roll of tape and exactly three gauze pads in her backpack. "Never leave home without it," she told him.

She'd been taking prophylactic antibiotics since she arrived on the island, so that was one less worry.

One less.

Neither of them spoke the obvious until after Trent managed to arrange Monica on the beach blanket.

"Now what?"

Trent removed his cell phone from his pack.

"No service."

The expression on Monica's face didn't change. "I didn't think there would be in here. Did you tell Reynard where we were going?"

Trent shook his head. "He'll know something's wrong when we don't come home."

"The clinic staff will call Walt."

Trent wedged himself between her and the wall and gave her someone to lean on. "We have some food. Water."

Monica nodded.

"Someone will find us."

Someone would. The question not asked was when.

Chapter Fourteen

If I don't move . . . if I don't breathe. It didn't matter what she did, her leg hurt like a bitch and there was no escaping it. She had six ibuprofen and antibiotics, though probably not the ones she needed, to last for a couple of days. The water in the pool was fresh but neither she nor Trent thought it was a good idea to drink from it. Not right away in any account.

"You know those little white lies you're against telling?" she asked Trent as night fell and the light from above started to fade.

"Yeah?"

"I need you to tell me we're going to be OK even if you think we're not." There weren't many times in her life when Monica had been scared. This was one of them. What if no one found them? What would they do when they ran out of food?

"My car is on the road. Someone will spot it."

She didn't want to remind him that the road had appeared abandoned. And it wasn't as if the islanders were looking for places to play these days. Most were just trying to survive.

"How did that earthquake compare to the first one?" she asked.

"Hard to say," his soothing voice said in her ear. "My house made a lot of noise but the walls didn't come down."

Her vision was adjusting to the darkness of the cave but it was still impossible to make out the entrance.

"The first one could have loosened those rocks. Made it easier for them to fall this time." At least his words sounded good to her ears.

Trent shifted beside her and she sat up. "You should lie down. That wall on your back can't be comfortable."

"Sitting up will keep me awake."

Monica couldn't make out his expression in the dark. She rested her hand on his chest in hopes of comforting him. His voice was tight and his entire frame was rigid. "We might as well try and sleep. Even when Reynard realizes you're not coming home, it will take time for the clinic to get word to the doctors and for anyone to actually search for us. No one is going to spot your car in the dark."

Trent sighed and shifted his weight down from the wall. Monica had her leg propped up on her backpack and Trent used a rolled-up towel for a pillow. She used his shoulder as hers.

Once she was snug against his chest, and as comfortable as she could be for a night in a cave with a broken leg, she attempted to close her eyes.

She could tell that Trent was just as awake as she.

"You know," she whispered, "before the earthquake and the wall crashing down on me, I was having a really good time."

Her chest rumbled with his soft laugh. "I know how to show a girl a good time."

"I didn't think it would be possible to have any desirable memories from this crazy week."

"And now you're stuck in a cave all because I wanted you to myself."

She winced at the tone he was using against himself.

"Hey." She poked his chest with her finger. "I wanted you to myself, too. You had no way of knowing this was going to happen."

"I'll remind you that you said that in the morning."

She wiggled against him and jostled her leg with a hiss.

"You sure you don't want to take two of those Motrin now?"

She wasn't sure of anything. "I'll wait until I can't bear it anymore."

His hand stroked her hair and down her arm. The rhythmic movement lulled her eyes closed. She heard Trent mumble in her ear three words.

"I'm sorry, Monica."

"It's not your fault," she whispered back before she fell asleep.

The phone rang, jolting Jessie from her dreams. Beside her, Jack reached for the phone next to his side of the bed.

Her eyes swung to the digital clock across the room and noticed the time, 4:23 in the morning. Nothing good made the phone ring at this time of night . . . or day.

"This had better be good," was how Jack answered the call.

Jack paused and listened to the caller. "This is her husband."

Jessie leaned over and turned on the lamp. Jack was sitting up in the bed with his eyes wide open. He glanced at her, and his brow furrowed.

Jessie's heart sank. "What's wrong?"

"Ah, huh." He held up a hand, asking her to hold her question. "She didn't call? When was the last time anyone has seen her?"

Monica!

Panic gripped Jessie by the throat. She dug her nails into Jack's thigh. "Is it Monica?"

"Hold on," he told the person on the phone. "Monica didn't show up at the clinic last night. She and Trent haven't been seen since yesterday afternoon."

Jessie's jaw dropped. "What? That's not like her."

Jack returned his attention to the phone. "I didn't know there was a second quake," Jack said to the caller.

Another quake? Monica's missing? Jessie tossed back the covers and climbed out of bed. She found her purse next to her dressing table and removed her cell phone from the front pocket. She punched in Monica's number and listened to it ring. "C'mon, Mo. Pick up."

It went to voice mail, Monica's chipper voice telling the caller to leave a message. "Monica? Dammit, Mo where are you? Call me the second you get this. You hear me? Mo?" Her hand shook as she ended the call.

Jack approached her from behind and cradled her shoulders in his hands.

"What happened? Where is she?"

Jack shook his head. "That was one of the doctors. She went to Trent's house to sleep shortly after I left. Was due back at the clinic eight hours ago. When she didn't show up the nurse at the clinic left a message for the team leader at the hospital."

"Did they check Trent's house?"

"They're not there. A friend of his said they left midafternoon and haven't been seen since. With all the commotion after the aftershock, no one thought to search them out until nearly midnight."

"Monica wouldn't just leave. She's too responsible. Oh God, Jack. We need to find her."

"We'll find her. Shhh, it's OK."

Only it wasn't all right. Call it sisterly intuition, but she knew her sister and Monica would have to be half dead before she even called in sick for work. To not show up . . . not call?

Jack pulled out of her embrace. "You get dressed. I'll call the pilot and the family."

Jessie nodded, went into her closet, and grabbed the first thing she saw.

Monica moaned in her sleep but didn't wake. Trent's eyes had fluttered shut for only a few minutes at a time. He kept his ear tuned to the outside noises coming from above their heads. At first light, he planned on exploring the cave a little more. Maybe the quake opened up another passage, one with an exit. The cool air was coming from somewhere, and it wasn't from above their heads. In fact, the only warm air came from above the cave. The constant drip coming from the foliage above and into the pool was its own torture device. It was as if each second was ticking away on their clock of survival. Trent might have been able to deliver the little white lies Monica needed, but his own mind kept a constant ticker tape of doom.

As he saw it, his Jeep was parked off the main road. The lagoon and cave were secluded with few visitors. Reynard wasn't the one who showed him this little slice of paradise and Trent had no idea if his friend knew of its existence. Trent pictured the area from the air. The soft top of his Jeep wouldn't reflect in the sun, and the black color might not stand out enough to be seen. The beach outside the cave would look untouched. They hadn't even left a colorful towel to flag any would-be rescuers.

What the fuck was he thinking when he brought her here?

Sex. That's what he'd been thinking about. Horizontal alone time with his blonde angel.

He glanced down at her sleeping form. *Well, we're horizontal and alone.* He'd laugh if the situation weren't so dire.

Monica moaned in her sleep again, this time jolting awake. "Oh, God!"

"Shhh," he tried to soothe her fears.

Her body tensed as she woke. Trent couldn't see her face and was grateful not to have his own fears seen in her eyes.

"Not a dream," she uttered.

"Shhh, it should be light soon." The darkness was one more obstacle to overcome.

She was quiet for a few minutes, then her shoulders started to shake and a whimper escaped her lips.

Something inside him twisted and threatened to undo any resolve left.

"What is it?" What wasn't it was probably a better question.

"I-I have to pee," she choked out.

"Oh." To have her so torn up over something so simple made him realize her vulnerability. Up until now, he hadn't really seen that side of her.

He sat up, and helped Monica to a sitting position before turning on his cell phone to use the ambient light of the display screen to fill the cavern. When he shed the light on her, she turned away. "Hey." He placed a finger under her chin and met her gaze. "It's all right."

"It's embarrassing."

"This from a nurse who helps others every day?"

"I don't like being the patient."

He chuckled, trying to lighten the dark expression on her face. "Well role-play with me, won't you? How should we do this?"

She looked around the cave. "We have to assume we'll be here for a little while longer." She pointed to a dark corner. "I can hold on to the wall."

Trent scouted the area she considered, and dug into the sand with his shoe. He'd never been more happy to be a man than at that point. He returned to Monica's side and handed her his cell. "You light the way."

He lifted her as carefully as he could.

She still whimpered.

"Are you OK?"

She nodded, but even her nod lied.

Every step was carefully placed until he'd crossed the room and helped her stand on one leg. She kept the damaged one suspended.

"What can I do now?"

"I've got it." She braced a hand on the wall and handed him his phone.

Uncertain if he should stay and hold her up, or if she could actually accomplish the task without him, he hesitated in releasing her.

"You can let go. Unlike guys, peeing is a solo thing for girls."

"You sure?"

"I'm sure, Barefoot."

He released her slowly and waited for her to collapse.

She didn't.

He turned his back on her and she cleared her throat. "Uhm, can you ah, not look but point that light this way?"

A few paces away he lifted the phone in her direction and stood by.

"Talk to me. Tell me a joke . . . anything. I can't do this with you listening."

He smiled in the darkness and said the first thing that came to him. "Did you ever wonder how the professor on *Gilligan's Island* kept the radio working? It's not like they were hoarding batteries on the *Minnow*."

Laughter met him from her direction. "Someone told me there was an episode that explained the working radio, but I never saw it," Monica said.

"And what about the 'costumes' they always managed to come up with?"

"Or the never-ending makeup Ginger always wore . . . hey, Ginger. Is that who you named your dog after?"

"Yeah. I guess I answered the age-old question, Ginger or Mary Ann."

"Do you think Mary Ann hooked up with Gilligan or the Professor?"

"Popular opinion is Gilligan."

"That leaves the Professor and Ginger."

Trent shook his head. "I think the Professor was gay."

Monica laughed in the dark. "Oh, I don't know. He always seemed to have his eyes on the ladies. Besides, maybe Ginger and the Skipper hooked up."

"Eweh."

Monica giggled and the sound warmed him. "OK. I'm done."

Trent handed her the phone again and lifted her in his arms. "Good thing I don't weigh two hundred pounds, eh?"

"I bench press more than you weigh."

"Oh, now you're just bragging."

He lowered her to the blanket and didn't let go when she squeezed his shoulders. The ambient light of the phone gave him the proof he needed about her pain level. Her eyes were squeezed shut and she was biting her lip. "Where are those Motrin?"

"Backpack," she said between her tight lips.

He removed the phone from her grip and fished through her things until he found a ziplock bag with medicine inside.

"Which ones?"

"The orange ones."

He plucked them out of the bag and handed them to her with a bottle of water. She took them without complaint and handed him the water after barely a sip. "Thanks."

The phone indicated they still had an hour before any sun would filter through their skylight. After making himself comfortable beside her, he shut the phone down, determined to save the battery for as long as he could.

"I think Mr. and Mrs. Howell were the fortunate ones." He continued with their conversation. "The happily married couple stranded on an island together."

"All the money in the world and no way to spend it."

"All the clout and no one to care."

"Puts life in perspective. And here I thought it was just a sitcom. Thirty minutes of mindless entertainment. Guess I was wrong."

Trent ran his fingers down her arm, giving her a little massage.

"That's nice," she told him.

"Take your mind off your leg?"

"It helps." Translation: not really but don't stop. There that smile was again on his lips.

"Do you think they're looking for us yet?" Monica asked.

"I do."

Chapter Fifteen

Jack tried to talk her out of coming but there was no way she was staying in Texas when her sister was missing on an island in the middle of the Caribbean.

"There aren't any hotels to stay in," Jack had argued.

"I don't care. I'll sleep on the plane. I'm not staying here."

Katie and Dean flew to Houston with their young daughter, Savannah, and were staying with Danny at Gaylord's ranch. Jessie's father-in-law, Gaylord, was notified of Monica's disappearance but he was in Tokyo on business. His plan was to meet Jack in Jamaica to aid in the search.

Then there were Trent Fairchild's brothers. Between Katie and Jessie, they'd already learned where the Fairchild men lived and Katie had obtained a business phone number. Jack spoke with the local authorities and ascertained a phone number for Jason Fairchild, Trent's oldest brother.

The phone call Jack delivered to Jason was just as difficult as the one they'd received earlier that morning.

Jason and Glen Fairchild were en route to Jamaica and would be arriving within the same hour Jack and Jessie were due.

The pilot informed Jack and Jessie that they were on their approach, and to fasten their seat belts. Jack sat beside her, holding her hand firmly in his. "We'll find her," Jack kept saying.

"I know." She wouldn't lose hope. She couldn't even consider the alternative. Yet when the island appeared in the window, and the rough edges of the land displayed evidence of the tsunami that had destroyed much of it, a tiny bit of that hope chipped away. She swallowed the shock and simply stared out the window as the plane landed.

Before the pilot rolled the plane to a stop, and before the door was opened, Jack turned to her and captured her head between his hands. "Promise me something."

"What?"

"If there is any threat to you, to our child, that you'll stay here with Roy."

"What kind of threat?"

Jack pushed a lock of her hair from her eyes. "There are sanitation issues and illness is spreading because of . . . because of the dead."

Jessie wanted to argue. Instead, she said, "She's my sister, Jack."

"And we'll find her. But she wouldn't want you to risk yourself for her. Our baby needs you healthy."

Suddenly it felt like an inopportune time to be pregnant. "We're not leaving here without her."

"We won't."

Jessie nodded her agreement and the two of them exited the safety of the plane.

Jason Fairchild met them inside the pilot's room by the control tower. Jessie watched as Jack shook Jason's hand and introduced her.

"This is Monica's sister, my wife, Jessie."

Jason stood about an inch taller than Jack, his dark hair was nearly black and his gaze could only be described as guarded. He nodded in her direction and skipped a handshake. "I wish we were meeting under better circumstances."

Understatement of the year. "Have you talked with anyone here yet?" she asked Jason.

"We just arrived. Glen is checking the status of the helicopters so we can search from the air."

"Glen's your brother?" Jack asked.

"That's right. One of the security guards said that Reynard will meet us here to bring us up to date."

Jack ran a hand through his hair. "So we wait?"

Jessie didn't like the sound of that. "What about the physician who called us last night?"

Jack turned to his cell phone and used the number the doctor had given him the night before. "Dr. Eddy, it's Jack Morrison . . . we just arrived." He paused and both Jason and Jessie were staring at Jack as he spoke.

"OK. We'll find a ride. No, we'll come to you. Thank you. I don't have to tell you to call. Right. Bye."

Jack hung up and offered Jessie a wan smile. "He still doesn't know anything. He's at the clinic where Monica was supposed to report to yesterday."

"He's not looking for her?" *How can the people she knows here not be out searching?*

"The authorities have been notified."

That wasn't good enough. She was about to voice her protest when a man approached them.

Jason shook the man's hand with a familiar greeting. "Reynard. Please tell me you have something."

Reynard glanced around the room, his eyes devoid of hope. "Let's sit. I'll tell you what I know."

Jack pulled out a chair she had no desire to sit in and took one beside her.

Jason introduced Reynard as a friend of Trent's and someone who was helping organize the relief organization and transportation on the island.

"My wife and I, our home was destroyed after the first quake. Trent asked us to bring our family to his home. He said he was going to leave the island in a few days. Kiki and I arrived yesterday, before noon. Your sister," he said nodding to Jessie. "She was with Trent in his house. They said she would return to work last night. Trent informed me he would come home after."

Jessie sat forward. "What happened?"

"Nothing. We've not seen or heard from them. They left with a lunch and a few things."

Jason narrowed his eyes. "They went on a picnic?"

"Perhaps. My wife and I, we thought maybe we interrupted them . . ." His voice trailed off as he exchanged glances with the men.

Jack sighed and took Jessie's hand. "I told you she was flustered around him."

"OK, fine. I get it, they hooked up. Where would he take her to . . . hook up?" she asked Reynard.

"That's just it, Mrs. Morrison, there is nowhere. The hotels are not accepting guests. Trent may have taken her to a lovers' spot, but that could be anywhere."

"It can't be anywhere. It would have to be private. It would have to be close enough for her to return to the clinic by her shift." Jessie started wringing her hands together.

"Where has the search initiated from?" Jack asked.

Reynard looked between the men. "We've traveled the road to the clinic several times and then to the hospital."

"And?" *That can't be all they've done.*

"Everyone is searching for others on the island, Mrs. Morrison—"

Jason slapped a hand on the table. "Are you saying that there is no search party?"

Reynard's eyes grew wide. "Trent's friends are searching."

Jessie turned to her husband, her eyes pleading.

———•———

"You'll fall and break your neck." Damn foolish man and his idea to climb the wall. The cave wall without footholds or roots to hold on to or anything.

"I have to try."

"So what, we can both be unable to walk? What will that accomplish, Barefoot?" Without the ability to strike an indignant pose, Monica settled for a superior tone. Deep down she was scared to death that he'd attempt to reach the top of the cave only to fall and break his damn neck. "You need a good dose of my fear of heights and you'd understand the risk."

Trent was searching the walls of the cave, managed to get his toe into a crack or two only to have no other place to climb. All Monica could do was watch him pace the cavern like a caged lion and search for a way up.

The sun had come up to remind them the cave didn't hold a lost passageway that either of them could crawl through. It held a pool of water two feet deep and five feet wide that both of them had needed to drink. It tasted like dirt, probably because it was nothing more than runoff from whatever foliage sat above them. It drained somewhere beneath the sand, evident when there had been a downfall of rain shortly after the sun rose and the pool splashed about but didn't overfill.

"I can't just sit here," he said as he tried yet another wall.

"Oh, rub it in."

He sent her a glare worthy of a father to a teenage daughter trying to leave the house with a miniskirt and a biker boyfriend.

Instead of saying anything, he took a running jump to try to grasp an outcropping of rocks that was several feet above his reach. On the third jump, he managed to grab hold and hang above the ground. Monica didn't see any possible place for him to make his next move. Trent noticed something and reached for it only to lose his grip and fall to the ground with a thud.

Monica winced but he bounced back up to try again.

"I get it," she yelled at him. "You want to be the hero. But dead heroes aren't a lot of fun." Her insides crawled with every jump.

Why couldn't he see it was useless? Even if he managed to make it up ten, fifteen feet, there was nothing to grab ahold of at that point. Nothing.

If he fell . . .

Monica pushed herself up against the wall, using her back to inch into a standing position. The movement spread hot pain up her leg and made her head swim. For a brief moment, she thought she'd be sick to her stomach. She hoped to hell that was because of the pain and not because the water they were forced to drink was bad.

Trent hadn't noticed her stand and was still trying to climb a vertical wall without a rope.

She hopped on her good leg, using the wall for support. Monica needed to prove his foolishness to him. *Damn testosterone brain.* With one hand on the wall and the other gripping her scrub pants to hold her injured leg, she closed her eyes and tried to hop again.

"Crap!" she yelled when the movement made that white pain turn molten.

"What the hell?" Trent was off the wall and at her side with his hands around her in a second. "What the fuck are you doing?"

Tears, from pain or fear she didn't know which, swam in her eyes. "Getting used to being alone, asshole. You're going to get your-self killed and I'll be in here all alone," she choked out right as the first tear fell. She hated crying. So damn useless. Solved nothing and only offered a headache as a reward.

Still, once the tears started there wasn't any way to stop them. A sob escaped her throat and she punched the hard plane of Trent's chest. "Asshole," she said again just in case he didn't understand just how upset she was.

With able arms, he lifted her off her feet and placed her back on the blanket.

She swiped at the tears in her eyes as if they were unwanted ants at a picnic and refused to meet his gaze. "Ass," she mumbled again under her breath.

Trent plunked down beside her and released a frustrated breath. "I need to do something, Monica."

"You can do something. You can talk to me; take turns yelling so someone searching for us can hear us. You can tell me we're going to get out of here." They were coming on twenty-four hours and their food wasn't going to last. Thank God she'd carried a few protein bars and the Borderless Doctors version of MREs in her pack. But she'd only carried enough food to last a week while in Jamaica. She'd not eaten all of it thanks to the provisions provided by Trent while in his home, but no matter how one spun that bottle, her food was nearly gone. That left the lunch Trent packed the day before, the bananas scavenged off the tree, and that was it. Between the two of them, they had two days of food left.

After that, it was a slow death. Water would keep them alive for what, five days at most . . . under the best of circumstances. That was if the water . . . no, she couldn't think about that. They'd both drunk the water over three hours before and neither of them showed signs of it causing any turmoil inside their bodies.

"If I'm going to die in here—"

"You're not going to die."

Ignoring his words, she pushed on. "If I'm going to die in here I don't want to do it looking over your dead broken body. I've seen enough dead broken bodies." With her last words, she made sure her eyes met his.

"You're not going to die," he whispered.

Avoiding his pointed eyes . . . eyes of a man who didn't lie and had sounded so much more convincing when he'd uttered those words the day before, Monica's gaze fell on her leg.

Blood soaked her small bandage.

———

The night was worse. The dark . . . the quiet.

Trent gave up his need to climb the walls and helped Monica redress her leg before the sun set. The inside temperature of the cave was warmer than it had been the night before. Yet even as the thought crossed Monica's mind she knew the temperature of the cave was the same. It was *her* temperature that rose.

She had an open fracture and even though she'd jumped on cleaning it, dressing it . . . no use wondering what she could have done differently. Her leg was hot, her insides weren't right.

Luckily, Trent seemed well enough.

"I always wanted to learn how to play the piano," she said out of nowhere.

"Why didn't you?" Trent asked in the dark, her head cradled in his lap. He insisted on staying alert in case he heard something in the night.

"We didn't have money growing up. My mom still lives in the double-wide we grew up in. Jack offered to put her in something a little nicer, but she didn't want it."

His hand stroked her hair as they talked.

"Is there anything on your bucket list?"

He chuckled, thinking of something he wasn't saying.

"What?" she asked.

"I always wanted to go on one of those cattle ranch weekends with the guys. You know, live on the range for a few days."

"Like that movie . . . oh what was the name of it?" She pictured the lead actors but not the name of the film.

"There's one thing . . . only one thing," Trent said in his best cowboy voice.

"You only have to find out what that one thing is," she finished for him. "Who would you go with?"

"My brothers. They'd hate it." His chest moved with his laugh.

"Why?"

"They're the corporate type. Good guys, don't get me wrong, but they both like the office more than the outdoors."

"Stuffy?"

"No, no . . . just suited for the city. They didn't get why I moved here."

"Why did you move here?"

He took a deep breath, blew it out. "After my parents died I needed something new. I don't know, something different."

"Did you feel trapped when they were alive?"

"No. Not that. I just needed *something* else."

Monica ignored the warmth under her shirt and the sweat under her hair and closed her eyes as they spoke. "And now you're ready to go home?"

"Past time," he said.

Home sounded good. Really good.

Chapter Sixteen

They flew in search and rescue teams from Texas and California. The California team had members of the fire departments surrounding the hospital in which Monica worked. Several of the men knew her personally. Jessie was overwhelmed by their support and desire to drop everything in aid of finding her sister and Trent. Unfortunately, that support didn't find them instantly. It took hours for the teams to arrive and devise a plan.

While Jack and Jessie set up camp on Trent's property, which included actual tents for the company of men and women on the search, Glen and Jason flew in Blue Paradise Helicopters and did aerial searches.

There were over a dozen friends of Trent's, and a few new friends of Monica's that were on foot or in cars looking for the missing couple.

A new face pulled up in an old jalopy that rivaled the car she owned before she met Jack. The man parked beside the house and jumped out of the car. Jessie welcomed the new arrival, in fact she welcomed anyone willing to help.

"You must be Monica's sister," the man said.

"I am."

"I'm Walt. I work with Monica."

"One of the doctors?"

"Yeah. Dr. Eddy."

He ran a hand through his short brown hair. His hazel eyes looked as tired as Jessie felt. Jessie remembered a few conversations she'd had with Monica about Dr. Eddy, and for some reason never thought he'd be a young attractive man.

"Have we heard anything?" Dr. Eddy asked.

Jessie shook her head. Jack was on foot, somewhere, Gaylord at his side. Jessie stayed behind to help direct traffic and keep those who helped fed. Ginger barked at the newcomers until they greeted her with a pet.

"Not a word." Jessie looked beyond the doctor, half expecting him to arrive with more people. "Are there others coming?"

"Dr. Klein is still at the main hospital. The rest of the team has already left the island or are leaving in the morning."

They needed a village. "You're staying?"

Dr. Eddy kicked the dirt off his shoes. "I'm the one who introduced Monica to Borderless Nurses. I'm not leaving until we find her."

His conviction came through with a tight voice. Jessie couldn't help but wonder if maybe Dr. Eddy had deeper feelings for Monica.

"You know she was last seen with Trent Fairchild, right?"

Dr. Eddy shook his head, a small smile on his lips. "Yeah. Nice guy. They seemed to be getting along . . . well, getting along."

"And you're OK with that?"

"Me? Oh . . . you think Monica and I?" He shook his head, dismissing any thought in Jessie's mind about a romantic attraction. "Oh, no. Monica's like a sister to me. She doesn't put up with anyone's shit, she's the best damn nurse I've ever worked with, and if something's happened to her—"

She held up her hand, stopping him. "We'll find her, Dr. Eddy."

"Walt."

Jessie smiled.

She bent over a map of the island and pointed out where the current searches were taking place. "The helicopters are coming down with the sun. My husband and team one are concentrating their efforts here, team two is here." She pointed to places along the road.

"This is the clinic. Did anyone get beyond this point?"

"Not yet. Reynard thinks Trent would have stayed on the south side of the island because of the water damage. So far there's nothing along the shore to indicate they are there."

"The island is full of waterfalls, pools . . . Trent might have taken her someplace like that."

Jessie sighed. "Someplace romantic."

"Exactly."

"Yeah, we've thought of that. The locals are checking out the hot spots for romance. Most are met with clear roads and no signs of Trent's car."

"I'm guessing that he didn't take her to a house . . . a hotel."

"The hotels aren't taking in guests."

"And Monica is too dedicated to her job to toss her responsibilities to the wind for an island fling."

Jessie's heart flipped in her chest with worry. "Monica's the most responsible person I know. She's always been determined to make her own way. She'd never run away with any guy. It's just not the way she's built."

Walt studied the map. "Ice Queen," he whispered.

"What's that?"

He shook his head. "Nothing. So we agree that she didn't run off, and she's not in a hotel."

"Or if she was in a home, a cabin, something . . . and the next quake came along . . ." God, Jessie hated to think like that. But something was keeping her sister away. They processed Monica's personality and the map.

"It was a big jolt," Walt said. "I called the clinic after it hit. Portions of it came down. Luckily Monica had already moved the patients from that section when she noticed dust coming down a couple of days before."

Monica's bossiness followed her everywhere. "Her common sense wouldn't have put her in a crumbling house. Even for great sex."

"Where does that leave?"

"Open spaces? Secluded beach? I wish I knew this Trent guy better. Knew what he did around here."

"Monica wouldn't have volunteered for a helicopter ride."

"Right. Hates heights." Jessie was glad to know Walt knew that much about her sister.

"That leaves something close by." Walt tapped his hand on the map.

"You'd think."

Jessie swallowed the lump in her throat. "You'd think."

———

Something shook his leg, waking him. Trent opened his eyes to complete darkness.

Like a blind man waking for the first time in a dark world, it took him a moment to process where he was, why he couldn't see, and what had woken him.

The shaking started again. Accompanying it was a moan. Monica's moan.

He dropped a hand to her shoulder, expecting to wake her from a dream, only to remove his wet palm.

She shivered again, a violent trembling movement that should have woken her, but didn't.

Inside he started to panic. He ran a hand over her forehead, felt the heat radiating from her, the sweat.

"Monica? My angel?" His words were whispered at first and then became louder when she didn't wake. "Monica!"

She woke saying, "I'm cold."

Those two words let him know she was alive, coherent. "You're burning up."

He fumbled around in the dark for his phone. It took a few seconds to locate it and turn it on. The battery power showed half strength.

Her blonde locks were flush against her head, her face rosy with too much color.

Even in the dark, he noticed her eyes lose focus before finding him. "Motrin."

The backpack holding her belongings was under her leg. He lifted her injured limb away and once again fumbled around until he found what she needed.

Motrin would take care of it. *It's just a fever. Everyone gets them from time to time.*

Yet even as he thought the words deep inside he knew the larger danger. She'd been working with the sick, the injured for over a week. He'd seen her leg earlier in the day when she didn't think he watched. The angry skin had turned red and swollen beyond any wound he'd ever seen. She'd hid it from him quickly when he'd turned and looked.

He poured two pills into his hand and helped her sit up to take the medicine.

She swallowed the medicine with pinched lips. "Thank you."

Trent pushed her hair behind her ears. "You're hot."

She smiled, licked her lips. "You're not so bad yourself, Barefoot."

How could she joke? "C'mon, Monica. I'm out of my element. What can I do?"

"Is it cold in here?"

"No."

"Do I feel hot?"

He nodded. "Like hell on fire."

Her eyes dropped closed before she reached down and slowly removed her shirt. Her pink bra sat on pasty skin in the dark cave. She handed him her shirt. "Soak it in water." A tremor shook her as she spoke.

When he returned to her, soaked shirt in hand, she attempted to place it back over her chest. Her fingers fumbled in the task, her eyes sought his for help.

Trent slid the cool clothing over her hot skin, and tried not to wince each time she shivered. "I've got to stay cool."

"What's happened?" As if he didn't know.

"I don't think it-it's Ebola," she managed.

"That's not funny, Monica."

A smile met her lips, her glazed-over eyes found his. "Infection. Open fractures do that," she said.

"We cleaned it out."

She shrugged. "With dirty water at best." A shiver raked her frame, making her teeth rattle.

The light from his phone turned off and he grabbed it to make it light up the room again. Crazy how such a small thing lit a room.

"What can I do?" He'd never felt so helpless in his life.

"Keep me cool. Even if I beg, keep me cool."

Beg? Why would she beg? Then it dawned on him. Movies portrayed the sick as incoherent, unable to see reason. He'd never seen anyone lose it. Yet he sat there with a nurse who'd probably seen all that and more.

"I'm a sucker for a begging woman."

She licked her already dry lips, sipped more water, and lay back down. He had no choice but to return to his post as her personal pillow.

"I always thought Mary Ann was prettier than G-Ginger," Monica managed to say once the phone went dark.

Trent stared into the darkness and tried his level best to ignore the voice in his head that said they were both going to die in this goddamned cave.

"Homegrown. Midwestern girl."

"Hey," she managed to sound indignant through her fever. "I'm homegrown. California grown, but kinda small town."

He stroked her fevered brow as much for her as for him. "You don't seem the Ginger type. Did you want to be a movie star?"

"No. Too many people to depend on for that to happen. I need to take care of myself."

How much it must hurt to have to depend on anyone. Then it dawned on him . . . she hadn't needed to pee in hours.

Monica woke several hours later, her body full of heat and ready to explode. Unlike the last time she opened her eyes, this time the cave was filled with light. Almost blinding. "Trent?" she called out when she realized he wasn't at her side.

"Monica?" He scrambled from the far side of the cave. "You're awake."

"What time is it?"

"Nearly noon, I think."

A *tut tut* of her head pounded against her temple. The pain in her leg felt like a dull throb attached to her knee.

"Here." Trent brought her into a sitting position and helped tip the bottle of water to her lips.

The nasty taste trickled down her throat and threatened to come back up. She pushed his hand away when he tried to give her more. "I can't," she uttered.

"You have to drink more."

She met his worried gaze. "Later," she whispered. "Have you heard anything?"

Trent followed her eyes to the top of the cave. "A helicopter flew over hours ago."

"They didn't see your Jeep." Would they fly over again? Look harder?

"They might have." He rubbed at the three days of stubble on his chin and tried to smile. "We're getting out of here, Monica. I promise you, we'll get out of here."

She nodded, holding on to his lie. Giving up without a fight wasn't in her. Not yet anyway. "Well, when you put it like that," she teased. "Maybe our next date can be a little shorter."

The water dripping into the pool picked up its pace. They both focused on the hole in the cave. "It's raining."

"All these years I've been afraid of heights. When I get home, I'm going to sleep with the light on."

"And I'm going to paint my Jeep yellow."

"Good idea."

"You must be hungry." He jumped up, grabbed the bag with the food inside.

She agreed although she wasn't. *Not a good sign.* While he dug into their dwindling supplies Monica peeked under the bandage on her leg. There had been many times she'd seen infected limbs, but never could she actually feel the pain associated with them. She wiggled her toes, thankful that at least her circulation wasn't gone.

"Here." Trent handed her a protein bar.

Her fingers didn't cooperate with the wrapper. When Trent took the food from her, she tried to fist her hands and found it hard to do. The symptom struck her as odd, something that she should understand, but didn't.

"Did you eat?" she asked when she took a bite.

"Earlier."

The granular consistency of fake peanut butter and chocolate was hard to swallow. "I'll never eat these again," she said between bites.

Trent opened his mouth to comment when something from above caught their attention. Trent was on his feet standing next to the pool in a heartbeat. "Hello?" he yelled. "Hello?"

Monica strained to hear a reply, something.

Painful silence met the room.

Trent kept yelling. His voice growing more desperate each time he cried out.

Chapter Seventeen

Jessie clenched her phone in her hand, desperate to hear anything. Jack had left before dawn with the others. He called every hour, each time reporting the same thing. They'd not found the car Trent drove, or any sign at all.

The daunting task of updating her mother back in California, and Katie and Dean in Texas, weighed on her. Monica and Trent had been gone three nights and four days. Each passing hour chipped away at the hope of their survival.

Why couldn't Monica be the type of woman to tell her responsibilities to blow off and run away with a guy? Having a flaky sister was better than having no sister at all.

She squeezed her eyes shut, felt a teardrop down her cheek. Desperate, she called Monica's phone again. It rang, then voice mail picked up. "I love you, Mo. Please get this and call me. Please. I need you," she sobbed. "I love you."

Jessie dropped her hand in her lap and stared at the screen with Monica's picture. Her laughing eyes and beautiful smile.

Jessie had taken the picture when they were searching for bridesmaid's dresses for Katie's wedding. What the camera didn't show was the horrible dress Katie had made Monica try on. Katie's taste in clothing was impeccable, but as a joke, she told Monica how much she loved the ruffled taffeta in pea green. It was awful. Jessie had snapped a picture when Katie informed Monica that the joke was on her. Monica had been so relieved and then oddly proud of Katie's deception. She'd promised to make it up someday.

Jessie flipped through a few pictures on her phone. Most were recent and didn't contain any images of her sister. But the further she dug, the more she found. All of them were full of life, love.

Now all she had was Monica's voice on a cell phone.

Jessie called it again, listened to Monica's voice. The pain in her chest threatened to explode.

She sucked in her lower lip to keep from crying out at the unfairness of anything bad befalling her sister.

Wait.

"Kiki?" Jessie called to the near empty house. Only Reynard's wife was in the home. Their children had left with a grandparent the day before. Kiki remained behind.

Jessie jumped to her feet in search of the other woman. She found her in the kitchen, leaning against the counter with a crutch under her arm. "Kiki?"

Kiki turned around. "Did you hear something?" she asked, hopeful.

"No. But . . . what is Trent's phone number? His cell number?"

Kiki told her the number and Jessie punched in the numbers. The phone went directly to voice mail. No ring.

Jessie dialed Monica's again. Several rings, then voice mail.

"Her phone is on . . . still charged."

"What?" Kiki limped slowly toward Jessie.

"Monica's phone rings before the voice mail picks up. That means it's working. And if it's working maybe the cell company can narrow down where it is."

Kiki's eyes grew wide.

The skin on Jessie's arms prickled with promise. Hope.

Her next call was to Jack.

"Hey, darlin'." His voice was flat.

"Her cell phone is still working," she said without a hello.

"What?"

"Monica's cell still rings before her voice mail kicks in. It's still charged."

She met silence on the phone. "Jack?"

"Yeah, wait . . . are you sure it rings?"

"I've called a half dozen times. It rings five times then goes to voice mail."

"Oh, damn."

"I'm calling the service provider now."

For the first time in days, Jessie had hope.

Monica didn't finish the protein bar before she fell back to sleep.

Trent watched the rise and fall of her chest and prayed for the first time in years. They needed to get out of there . . . soon. He tried to keep her cool, changing her heat-soaked clothes with cooler ones soaked in the rainwater that dripped from above.

Every so often, he heard something above. He called out each time but didn't hear anything in response.

When he realized that Monica no longer woke up when he yelled, gut-wrenching fear sank into his blood. He shook her awake twice, and was met with glassy eyes and her saying she wanted to sleep.

At least he understood her. That had to count for something.

As dusk fell on their fourth night, he attempted to turn on his phone only to find the device completely dark.

Hunger took the place of hope, and he sat next to Monica, and placed her head in his lap.

She didn't wake.

Unable to stay behind at the house any longer, Jessie wore a raincoat and joined her husband. The cell phone company narrowed the phone to a few mile radius. The news came right as the sun set.

Ginger trotted alongside them as they walked along a forgotten road. Reynard had taken the Fairchilds on another road that led to a southern beach. The search and rescue team, Dr. Eddy among them, curled under their rain gear, using flashlights to guide them, and searched for any clue. The rain came in steady sheets now, making the search even more unbearable.

"You shouldn't be out here," Jack protested.

"You've already said that, cowboy. Let it go," she snapped at him.

She knew Jack was just trying to protect her.

"A little rain never hurt anyone," she said softly.

He grasped her hand in his as they used the flashlights to light their way.

The radio on one of the firemen's hips squawked. "Team one?"

"This is team one," the man said.

"We've found the car."

Jessie froze. Everyone stopped walking. *Monica?*

The man on the radio gave them directions to their location. Then the man said. "No sign of them yet. We've spread out."

Gaylord, who'd surprised her in his quest to find Monica, was quick to jog alongside the rest of them as they ran toward the second team.

Jessie ran to the Jeep when it came into sight. There were dogs sniffing around the car and walking in different directions.

Reynard was first to talk. "Her phone is plugged in."

Jessie glanced inside and then turned a three-sixty. "Where could they have gone?"

"They're searching the shore below. The lagoon is secluded here."

"Monica?" Jessie yelled at the top of her voice.

Ginger barked.

Somewhere in the dark forest, she heard search and rescue calling out Trent's and Monica's names.

Jason walked up to them, his breath short as if he'd run. "The beach is empty. Not even a shoe."

"They have to be here somewhere," Jack said.

Ginger barked again, excited over all the activity.

Jessie pet the wet fur of Trent's dog, and fell behind Jack and the others as they spread out and called to the dark.

———•———

Trent jerked awake. His heart beat too fast, his head ached with a throbbing pain so intense his back teeth felt as if a tiny colony of ants had taken up residency and were chewing away at the enamel one layer at a time.

Monica slept in his lap, her body shaking with the fever that violently racked her body.

He stroked Monica's hair, kissed her hot forehead. "Hang in there, angel."

As he let his eyes drift closed, again . . . he heard it.

His body stiffened, he tilted his head to the side. Rain dripped from above and had been all night.

This time when the noise came, he knew what it came from. "Here!" He yelled as he moved Monica's head from his lap with careful ease. Her head rolled to the side. The pitch black of the cave didn't allow Trent to see if Monica opened her eyes. "Here! We're in here!"

He heard a bark. On his hand and knees, he crawled in the direction of the falling water. When he splashed into the pool, he stood and filled the cave with a sharp whistle.

The barking continued, faster . . . closer.

His stiff hands fisted. "Monica? Monica . . . someone's here."

She didn't respond.

"Here! Help!" He whistled again, longer, louder. "Help!"

"Trent? Trent?"

He wanted to weep. They'd been found. "In here!"

"Trent?" The voice didn't sound familiar, but soon there were others.

"Monica?"

"She's in here."

Dirt from above rained on him, as did the glow of a flashlight. "Watch out. There's a hole."

"Everyone stop," he heard someone yell. "Back up."

"Monica? Monica are you in there?" The voice was female and frantic.

"She's here," Trent yelled back. "We're both inside a cave."

There were shouts of joy followed by the familiar bark of Ginger.

"Monica?"

Trent took a few steps away from the pool, careful he didn't trip over Monica as he hurried to her side.

"Monica?" The woman's voice started to edge toward panic.

"She's here."

"Why isn't she answering?"

He hesitated. "She's sick." *Really fucking sick.*

"Trent, it's Jason." Hearing his brother's voice was music to his ears. "Glen and I are here."

"I can't tell you how good it is to hear your voice."

Rocks from above fell again. Trent leaned over Monica's frame to keep any from falling on top of her.

"Everyone back! Mitch, tie me off. We have no idea how stable this ground is."

Trent envisioned the chaos above him. Couldn't help but wonder how long it was going to take to get them out of there. But holy hell they were going to make it out. Alive.

"Trent, my name is Radar. How far down are you?"

"We're at sea level. There was an opening to the cave on the shore. It collapsed with the last quake."

"OK. I'm dropping a flashlight down."

"There's a pool of water directly under the opening."

"Got it. One, two, three." The light hit the ground and lit the cavern. Trent grabbed the light, focused it first on Monica. She moaned, but didn't wake.

He shone his light toward the opening. "Is there a doctor with you?"

"Yes. Dr. Eddy is with us. We need to set up to bring you out. It's going to take some time."

Trent watched as another tremor shook Monica's body. "Listen, Radar." He thought of the woman above calling out for Monica. "I need to talk to that doctor. And ah, is that Monica's sister up there?"

"Yeah. The Morrisons are here. I pushed them back. There's no telling how stable the ground is up here."

"I need to talk to the doctor. Monica . . . she's not well," he said again.

"Hold on."

Trent soaked one of Monica's shirts and placed it over her head as he waited for the doctor to draw near. "Monica," he whispered. "We're going to be OK. They found us."

"Trent," she said his name without waking.

A few minutes later, Radar lowered a two-way radio in a basket and told him Dr. Eddy had the other end.

"Damn good to hear your voice," Walt said.

"You have no idea."

"Talk to me. How's Monica?"

"She's burning up. When the opening collapsed, her right leg was trapped under the rock."

"Is she still trapped?"

"No. We managed to free her, but her leg is jacked up."

"Bleeding?"

"Not anymore."

"Is her foot cold?"

Trent touched her foot. "No. It's warm." Hot actually.

"What about where she's cut? Do you see bone?"

Trent had slid her pants off earlier but kept the wound covered. "No. But it's bright red, swollen. It's obviously broken."

"Above the knee or below?"

"Below."

"OK. Can you wake her?"

He tried again.

She opened her eyes. "Sleep," she managed to say.

"She opens her eyes," Trent reported. "Don't think she's aware of what's going on."

Walt must have kept his hand on the radio because Trent heard every frantic demand on the other side. "Morrison," Walt yelled.

"Yeah," Trent heard Jack Morrison's voice.

"We're going to need to get Monica to a hospital as soon as she's out of there. Get a call to Dr. Klein, have him meet me at the airport."

The radio turned off, but not before Trent heard the panic in Walt's voice.

Since when did emergency physicians panic?

"Trent, you there?"

"I'm here."

"They're setting up ropes and a retrieving basket for Monica. What have you been eating, drinking?"

He fumbled with the radio, felt his fingers stiffen. "Monica had protein bars, some bagged food. We ran out of bottled water two days ago and have been drinking from the pool. Seems fresh enough."

"Not salty?"

"Tastes like dirt, not salt."

"No vomiting, GI issues, cramping?"

"No."

"What about you? Do you feel sick?"

Trent kept a hand on Monica as he spoke. "Headache, a little stiff, but otherwise fine." For a guy who's been stuck in a cave for nearly five days, he was perfect.

"Listen, Trent. When they bring up Monica, fill one of those bottles with the water you've been drinking, and send it with her."

Trent's gaze fell on the pool. "You think it's contaminated?"

"Won't know until I have a lab test it."

Someone above Trent shouted.

"I'm giving the radio back to Radar."

Radar told him to watch for the basket that would carry Monica out. They were going to test the ground with lighter equipment first, and then lower one of the medics down.

Trent felt helpless as the minutes ticked in painfully slow motion. When the basket finally breached the opening of the cave, he caught it and unlatched the hook. He fisted his hand a few times and dragged it to Monica's side. Next came a tackle box.

This time Trent couldn't blow off the stiffness in his fingers. *Maybe I'm not so great.* He rubbed the back of his neck and watched the rope elevate above him.

Finally, a man dangled above the hole. They lowered him slowly. A few rocks trickled down to splash in the pool. Trent stayed by Monica's side, talking to her although she didn't respond with anything other than a moan.

The medic slid out of his harness and moved to Monica's side. "I'm Miller," he introduced himself.

"Trent."

Miller took a quick look at Monica and said, "Damn, Queenie, what the hell happened to you?"

"Queenie?"

"Nickname. Some of us came from California to help search." As he spoke, he removed one of those blood pressure things and a stethoscope. Miller ducked into his work and spoke into his radio. "Walt?"

"Talk to me," Walt said on the other end.

"Blood pressure is 170 over 92, pulse 130, respirations 34." He rattled off her skin color, and several other things that Trent wasn't sure of their meaning. Miller attempted to wake Monica up, only to see her eyes open but then close.

Another man was lowered into the cave and pushed Trent away from Monica's side. The only thing he could do was stand by and watch as they worked on her. They started an IV and cut off the bandage on her leg. From the box, they removed gauze, tape . . . and proceeded to place a quick bandage over her wound. They wrapped something else around her leg, immobilizing it.

"Trent?"

Trent shoved around the medic to see Monica's eyes open and search for him.

"I'm here." He kissed her forehead. "I'm here."

She smiled and looked between the men. The guys working on her tried to talk to her, but she didn't say anything else before closing her eyes.

Between the three of them, they managed to get her in the basket and secured. Trent looked around the room, and then remembered the request for water. He filled a water bottle and secured it inside Monica's backpack, which he placed beside her.

He stroked her head again, and then she was being lifted into the air.

Trent held his breath until he knew she was safely aboveground.

"You're next."

It took another fifteen minutes for the rope to lower back down to ground level. And by the time Trent made it out, Monica had already been whisked away.

Chapter Eighteen

There came a point where life merged with death in a tug-of-war and the body in between could do nothing but grab a bowl of popcorn and watch. On one hand, death held a peaceful blanket of nothing left but an aching feeling that something was left out of place, something extremely important that needed to be done. On the other hand, there were the clawing nails of pain and anguish that instinctively you knew needed to be felt, to be triumphed over, in order to experience one more day.

That one day would be worth the struggle.

Images floated above Monica's thin layer of consciousness. Trent smiled above her, his face lit up by the glow of his cell phone. He kissed her, told her they were going to be OK. Then she was floating, and the ceiling of the cave floated toward her and panic set deep inside of her. *I'm not done*, she yelled at whoever listened.

Faces floated around her, of those who she worked with and beside, her sister, her brother-in-law . . . strangers.

Where's Trent?

The image of him inside the cave, alone, welled up inside her. "He's in there. Help him."

Then the water from the giant wave overtook everything and she couldn't catch her breath.

She fought to find the surface.

―――•――――

Jessie held her sister's hand throughout the flight. Not once did Monica wake long enough to utter one word that she was OK.

Walt flew with them to Florida where a team was waiting.

Jack kept telling her Monica would be all right. That she wouldn't allow anything as simple as a broken leg to get the best of her.

"Monica's tough," Jack told her.

From Monica's bedside, Walt chimed in, "We don't call her the Ice Queen for nothing."

"Ice Queen doesn't sound flattering."

"She's tough, Jessie," Walt told her. "She's going to be all right."

Yet there was a hint of doubt behind Walt's eyes.

The private jet didn't hold the necessary equipment to hold a gurney in place, so they improvised with what they had. The basket that had brought Monica to the surface was strapped into the couch of the plane. They secured an oxygen tank that helped deliver what Monica needed. Dr. Klein had met Walt at the airport with necessary medicine. Even to Jessie, Monica appeared as if she were sleeping and not struggling.

Yet when the constant beep of the monitor that displayed her sister's heart rate to the doctor slowed, Walt adjusted something . . . appeared frazzled. When Monica started to lose the contents of her stomach, the good doctor turned white.

Walt tried to hide his unease and mumbled under his breath, cursing the fact that he didn't have enough of what he needed to make everything perfect for his patient. His friend.

They landed in Miami. A medevac team met them and helicoptered Monica and Walt to the hospital.

When Jessie and Jack arrived at the hospital much later, they were ushered into a private waiting room for the longest hour of Jessie's life.

———

As much as Trent wanted to assure his brothers that he was alive, the desire to follow Monica and make sure she was being cared for was stronger.

"Where did they take her?"

Someone threw a blanket over his shoulders, which surprisingly he accepted. The cold night and rain should have been a comfort. They weren't.

Jason hooked an arm around his shoulders. "The airport. Someone said Miami, but I'm not sure."

Trent turned one-eighty and met with the bulk of a man he'd never seen. "Where did they take Monica?" he demanded.

"Miami General," the man said with a slight southern accent.

Trent twisted around. The world lost balance and someone was holding him up.

"Hold on, brother." It was Glen talking this time. "Let's have someone check you out."

"I'm fine," he insisted. He patted his pockets for the keys of his Jeep. He remembered them on the floor of the cave next to their food supplies. "Damn."

"Trent?"

Why were there two of Jason?

"What?"

Three . . . there were three of him.

The world tilted again and someone called his name.

Everything came into a fuzzy focus and then everything inside Trent's stomach emptied.

Maybe I'm not fine.

———

Trent recognized the inside of the family jet. It had been years since he'd been there, and wasn't exactly happy with being there now. Within one breath, he went from rescued survivor to patient. It was as if the mere mention of gastrointestinal issues made everything inside him twist on itself.

At some point, someone started an IV on him and he would swear that something soothing had been placed in his veins. The world dulled in flight. The noise of the engine lulled him to sleep. He hadn't slept much in the past several days, afraid he'd miss the sound of someone passing by. He slept now.

An ambulance met them at the airport and took him to an emergency room. He noticed the faces of everyone there, pictured Monica in her environment, shouting orders . . . running around. "Is Monica here?" he asked the treating doctor.

"The other survivor?" he asked.

Trent nodded. "Yeah. The nurse." It had taken Trent a few hours to follow behind her.

"She's here." The man didn't elaborate, which made Trent even more uncomfortable. "What about the doctor who brought her in? Walt? Is he here?"

"I'll see if I can find him."

When Walt didn't come to his bed fast enough, Trent pushed himself off the gurney to search out the man himself. Wearing a blue and white hospital gown with his ass hanging out the back end, he stepped outside the curtained room, and came up against his brothers.

"What are you doing?" Glen grabbed Trent's arms as he leaned up against the wall with an IV pole in his hand.

"Where's Monica? I told her she'd be OK. No one's talking to me." He was getting damn tired of people looking the other way and not answering questions.

"Mr. Fairchild." A woman appeared at his side. Her brown hair and pointed finger indicated a wheelchair someone had pulled up behind him. "Sit down before you fall and make everyone in this terribly busy ER work harder."

Trent sat . . . OK he fell into the chair. The woman he had to assume was a nurse stood over him, her hands poised on her hips. "You're looking for Miss Mann?"

"That's right."

"She's in the ICU. And if you want to see her you're going to have to let us stabilize you first. No one is going to let you go up there and fall all over her."

He could envision that this was how Monica scolded her patients. "How is she?" he asked.

"Stable."

Like that told him anything. "Is her family here?"

"In the waiting room. I'll tell them you're asking for them."

Trent exchanged glances with his brothers. "Thank you."

"Can I get you back in your bed now?" she asked.

Considering the fact that he didn't have enough energy to pull his ass out of the chair, the gurney didn't sound bad.

Back in bed, the nurse who'd put him in his place returned to hook him up to a monitor that sat above his gurney. His brothers sat in chairs at his bedside and watched him as if he were a fish in a flippin' tank.

"What's that for?" Glen asked the nurse.

"The doctor wants us to monitor his heart."

"It's still beating," Trent joked. Yet he wondered why after he'd been in the hospital for nearly an hour they were hooking him up to machines. Seemed like the longer the stay, the less need there would be for wires and tubes.

The nurse patted his shoulder when she finished and offered a half-assed smile. "Maybe the doctor just wants to keep you in your bed." She turned on her heel and walked out of the room.

Jason laughed and leaned back in his chair. "She's a sassy thing."

"Cute, too," Glen added.

That she may have been, but Trent couldn't think of any nurse save one. "Can one of you go and find Jack Morrison or even Dr. Eddy?"

"I'll go." Jason released a heavy sigh and headed out into the ER.

Several seconds passed in silence. When Trent's gaze met his brother's, he squirmed in place. "What?"

Glen's appearance always reminded Trent of their father. They shared the same cocky smile and hazel eyes. Glen turned those eyes on Trent now with a mixture of love and remorse. "We've missed you."

"Oh, Jesus, Glen. I was a few hours away by plane."

"You know what I mean. Reynard said you were planning on leaving the island before getting trapped in the cave."

"Yeah. I was."

Glen smiled, flashed his father's dimples. "Figure out where you're going to settle?"

No, he just knew that home wasn't on the island any longer. Jason and Dr. Eddy walked in the room. Walt shook his hand.

"How's Monica?"

"Stable."

Trent was starting to hate that word.

"Stable and the ICU sound like the ultimate in oxymoron."

Walt pulled up a rolling stool and sat beside Trent's bed. The doctor glanced over at Trent's brothers. "You mind giving us a minute?"

Glen stood and smiled. "I could use some coffee."

Trent flashed a smile at his family as they left the room.

Once alone, Walt's smile fell. "She's sick," he said. "But we've managed to bring her blood pressure down. We're jumping on the antibiotics."

"Has she woken up?"

Walt shook his head. "Not yet. But her fever is coming down, slowly. She needs to rest and we need to get her white count down before we can fix her leg."

"Is it bad?"

"Nothing that a few screws and a steel plate won't fix. They have a great group of orthopedic surgeons here."

That's good.

Walt glanced up at the monitor above Trent's head. "It's going to take a little time for the lab results, but I have the doctor here checking for lead and mercury poisoning on both of you."

Trent pushed his brows together. "That doesn't sound good."

"It's not. And usually toxicity takes time to occur unless you bite into a thermometer or eat paint. Both of you show signs of liver and kidney involvement."

Trent hadn't thought of his liver since he was in college testing his beer limit consumption. "Anything serious?"

"We'll want to keep you in the hospital to run some tests."

"You didn't answer my question." And he wasn't thinking of himself so much as the woman in the ICU.

"Serious enough to keep you here."

He guessed he didn't need to understand it any more than that. It sounded like there were unknowns at this point. "The water was bad, wasn't it?"

"That's my guess. The water you sent with Monica is at an outside lab and we won't get the preliminary results until the morning."

Walt stood and took Trent's hand in his. "I'm going to check on Monica again, and then find a cot and some food. I'll find where they put you in the hospital and keep you up to date."

"So I can't see her yet?"

"Let's get you fixed up, fed. I'll bet you're starving."

Trent tried to smile. "I could eat."

"I'll tell the nurses."

"OK. And thanks, Walt."

———

Muddy water threatened to pull her under again, but instead of allowing the thick desire for sleep to keep its death grip any longer, Monica forced her eyes to flutter open.

Bright, shiny light had her blinking several times, as the familiar smells and sounds of a hospital crept into her consciousness.

"Barefoot?" Her pasty lips tried to stick together as she spoke. "Mo?"

Monica turned her stiff neck to the right to find Jessie on the other side of a guardrail of the hospital bed she lay in. "Jessie?"

Jessie lifted Monica's hand to her lips, kissed the back of it. "Oh, God. You're awake."

Her sister had dark circles under her eyes, her hair was pulled back in a ponytail, and she huddled under a sweatshirt that looked like it belonged to Jack.

Monica squeezed her sister's hand, surprised at the effort it took to close her hand. "Where am I?" She remembered snippets. Trent's voice telling her they were going to be found. Him laughing at her attempt to sing the theme song to *Gilligan's Island*. Then there was an airplane and faces . . . some named, many nameless. Then a whole lot of nothing.

"Miami General."

"H-how long?"

"Only a day." Her sister's voice held a plea. "I was so worried."

"Ha! You and me both." Monica did a slow look around the room. The private room held every bell and whistle needed for a critical bed. A large glass door separated her from a center nurses' station with the rush of nurses, technicians, and doctors milling about. She rested her hand on the bed and noticed the IV connected to her wrist. She followed the tubing and noticed several plastic bags hanging from above her bed. She narrowed her eyes and read the labels. "Pressers?"

"What?" Jessie asked as she moved to the other side of the bed and turned on a light above the bed.

"Am I in the ICU?"

"Yeah. I'm going to tell the nurse you're awake. They wanted to know when you came around."

Monica released a breath and tried to stop being the nurse. "Jessie?" she stopped her sister before she left the room.

"Yeah, Mo?"

"I love you."

Tears welled instantly in Jessie's eyes. "Don't ever scare me like that again."

"I'll try."

Then Jessie left the room and returned a few seconds later with a nurse. With help from a complete stranger, Monica sat up in her bed and waited for the treating physician to make his way to her bedside. By the time the poor man left she'd drilled him on every medication he'd given her, asked for details about her lab work, made suggestions for tests. Yeah, the guy had steam coming out his ears by the time he left the room, but there was something else in the man's face. Admiration.

Jessie returned to the room and trailing behind her were Jack, and Renee, her mother.

"Hey, Mom."

Their relationship had always been strained, but it didn't mean her mother didn't love her. They simply didn't understand each other very well.

"Oh, baby."

Monica accepted her mother's kiss and offered a smile. "Sorry to drag you all the way across the country."

"Damn inconvenient," Jessie teased. "Be sure and think about that the next time you're trapped in a cave and try to die."

"No one is dying."

"Could have fooled us," Jack said. "Katie sends her love. She'll be here tomorrow."

Monica shook her head. "That's not necessary."

"Would you stay away?" Jessie asked.

Why did Jessie have to be so perceptive? Monica tried to roll her eyes and feign indifference. Instead, her eyes closed and she had a hard time opening them back up.

"I think maybe we should let you get some sleep," her mother said.

She was wiped out after only being awake for an hour. It still felt wrong to push her family out the door after she'd scared them half to death. "They want to take me to surgery tomorrow," she told them.

"Walt said something about that," Jessie said.

"Walt's here?" Monica opened her eyes again.

"He flew with us. You don't remember?"

Monica shook her head. "I don't remember much," she uttered with a yawn. She remembered Trent kissing her forehead. "Trent. Where's Trent?"

"Who's Trent?" her mother asked.

"The man with her in the cave. He's downstairs," Jack told her. "They're keeping him for a couple of days."

"Is he OK?"

"Yeah."

Good. That's good.

Damn she was tired.

The next time she opened her eyes the room was empty and dark.

Chapter Nineteen

Trent pulled on a second undignified gown so his butt wasn't out there for everyone to see, and rolled the pole holding his IV as he trekked up the hall from his room. Jack had visited him earlier in the day to tell him that Monica had woken and that if Trent was going to sneak up to see her he might want to do it tonight as she was scheduled for surgery in the morning and would be out of it for hours after.

The entry to the ICU was locked and Trent needed to sweet-talk, and name-drop, in order to gain access to Monica's room.

When he rounded the corner into her room, she was sitting high in her bed and eating.

She noticed him in the doorway and the most beautiful smile spread over her lips. "Barefoot!"

He picked up a slippered foot and wiggled it. "You can take the man off the island, but not the island out of the man."

He pushed a chair next to her bed and sat. "You look good."

"I feel better. It's amazing what the right antibiotics can do for you. What about you?"

Trent waved away the IV pole at his side. "This is overkill if you ask me. Damn yellow bag makes it look like they're injecting urine into me."

She giggled. "It's vitamin packed," she told him as she gestured to a like bag hanging over her head. "They're giving them away today."

"I heard you're having surgery tomorrow."

Monica wiggled her foot. "They need to put me back together."

"How's the pain?"

She blinked a couple of times and he noticed the slight glaze in her eyes. "Good drugs."

"There's something to be said for that."

After nibbling on a cracker, she said, "They finally let me eat. I know I won't want to tomorrow."

"This is your first meal?"

"Yeah, well, I didn't want much earlier."

He liked this. The easy conversation and comfortable buzz he felt just by being with her.

She sighed and placed her hands in her lap. "We made it out."

"We did. They tracked your cell phone."

"Really? No one told me. I don't remember anything other than you telling me we were going to be OK and then waking here."

Trent recapped what she'd missed. "When they were lifting you up I kept thinking it was a damn good thing you were out of it. I know how much you *love* heights."

"Glad I don't remember."

"There were a few guys from your neck of the woods that jumped in on the search."

"Pomona Fire?"

"Apparently."

"Wow. I'm surprised I've not seen them."

"They didn't follow us here. You'll see them when you get home." It dawned on him at that point that she'd be headed in one direction when she was well enough to travel, and he'd go in a different one.

Before the wall crashed down and they'd brushed with death, she'd made it clear that they were a fling, a temporary diversion from life.

Yet brushing with death changed that. Didn't it?

He sat back in the chair and glanced at the newscast that was playing on the flat screen. When he returned his gaze to hers, she smiled. "When are they releasing you?"

"Walt said I could go tomorrow if the blood work continued to clear up."

"It's scary, isn't it? I thought the water was fine."

"Tasted like city tap water to me," he said.

"I'll suggest that rescue workers leave with water purifying tablets in the future. We were lucky."

"Very."

The nurse took that moment to come in the room to retrieve the food tray. "Not much longer," she said to him.

Monica tsked. "He's fine."

The nurse stared down her nose at Monica and lifted her hand to the monitor. "Your blood pressure is going up as is your heart rate since he arrived." Then to emphasize her point, Nurse Hard-Ass took a tympanic thermometer, placed it in Monica's ear, and turned the device around so Monica could see the number. "And you're spiking a fever again." Nurse Hard-Ass had a point. She swiveled toward Trent and placed her palm up and spread her fingers. "Five minutes. And no arguments from you, *Nurse Mann.*"

The woman left the room in a huff, mumbling something about nurses and doctors being crappy patients.

"Boy, I thought my nurse was rough."

A sad smile spread over Monica's lips. "She's right. I'd kick your ass out too if I was her."

Trent took the hint and stood to leave. For an awkward moment, he wasn't sure how to say good-bye. He placed a hand over hers, smiled.

"You'll come by tomorrow?" she asked.

"I will." Since Trent wasn't good at white lies, he knew he'd found a reason to see her again. Maybe that was how this would work. One day at a time.

One day at a time.

———

Walt entered Trent's room early the next morning; the admitting physician led the way. "Good news, Mr. Fairchild," Dr. Simons said. "Kidney function, liver function . . . all your labs are back within normal limits."

"That mean I can leave today?"

Walt smiled. "Means you're one lucky bastard. And yeah, you're going to be discharged."

Trent stood from the chair he'd been sitting in and with as much dignity as one could have wearing a drop cloth, shook both the doctors' hands. "I already know I'm lucky," he managed to say with a smile.

Dr. Simons went on to tell him how he wanted Trent to see his personal physician in two weeks for follow-up blood work. Also Dr. Simons wanted him to have his doctor request the files from the hospital so they could jump on any long-term effects of the large exposure to lead and mercury, both of which saturated the water Trent and Monica were forced to drink to survive inside the cave.

Trent would never again look at a pool of water and think it anything but poison. Tasteless and odorless poison.

"I'll write the order for discharge. It will still take a couple of hours to get you out of here."

Trent thought of Monica. "S'OK. I'm not in a hurry. Need to get ahold of my brothers."

Dr. Simons left the room, leaving Walt behind.

"I'll be headed back to California after Monica's out of surgery."
Walt took a chair across from Trent.

"How's she doing this morning?"

"She didn't have an ideal night, but she's tough. They're going
forward with surgery. The surgeon thinks there's something left inside her leg that's keeping her from progressing."

"Surgery is going to fix it?"

Walt nodded. "We think so."

"You're a good friend," Trent told him.

"Monica's good people."

When Walt took to his feet, Trent followed him. "I can't thank
you enough."

"I'm glad I was there to help. Maybe we can have a beer sometime, watch a game or something."

Trent smiled. "I'd like that."

"Take care of yourself."

Trent called Jason who was staying at a local Morrison Hotel,
courtesy of Jack and Jessie. Glen had to fly back home but was making room for him at his place until Trent decided what he wanted to
do and where he wanted to do it.

He didn't push his discharge, instead he waited around until
they practically kicked him out so that he could linger past the time
when Monica would be returned to her room after surgery. He
needed to see her. He'd make an excuse to see her again.

The nurse from the night before recognized him and allowed
him into the ICU. "She's sleeping," Nurse Hard-Ass told him. "I
don't want you guys waking her up."

Trent assumed "you guys" referred to Monica's family, yet when
he walked around the now familiar glass door into Monica's room,
seated at her bedside and holding her hand in a familiar way was
a man.

He hesitated and cleared his throat softly so as to not wake Monica. She slept peacefully, or at least it appeared that way. Her leg sat elevated on some contraption, the bulky dressing on it evidence of the trauma her limb had gone through.

The unknown man lifted his bloodshot eyes to Trent. His face grew cold. "Yes?" he asked as if Trent had no business in the room.

"How is she?"

"Resting."

Trent couldn't help but notice how the man held Monica's hand.

"Who are you?" Trent found himself asking.

"I'm Monica's boyfriend."

Everything inside Trent froze.

"Well, nearly her fiancé."

Trent's stare moved to the woman on the bed. The warmth inside of him turned ice cold. Now it made sense. No need to think he was anything more than a fling. Wasn't that how she put it? Of course she'd have someone back home.

Didn't everyone Trent found himself falling for?

Ignoring the fast rate of his pulse, he swallowed hard and turned off any emotion, any one-day-at-a-time thought.

He wasn't going to fall into this again.

He'd been down this road and it drove him to a fucking island and cost him his parents. This was *not* happening again.

"Who are you?" Monica's fiancé asked.

Trent shook his head. "No one."

Without any more words, he left the ICU and the hospital, and put her out of his mind.

———

The next day blurred together. It didn't help that her fever had spiked in the night, delaying her surgery by several hours. Monica met the orthopedic surgeon, signed consents, and met the surgical team right as they were putting her under.

There's something about being at the total mercy of others to humble the strongest of characters. In all her nursing years—admittedly, she didn't have many of them—Monica had never been the patient. Not on any level that depended on someone else to breathe for her.

Her eyes opened briefly in recovery, the pain in her leg so immense she simply uttered a moan. The need of something to keep her from screaming was her only thought. And then the world dimmed again.

Her next moment of lucidity was in the early morning hours of the next day. A lone figure sat beside her bed. His frame filled the chair, his eyes sought hers with concern.

She blinked several times, confused.

"John?"

Chapter Twenty

"W-what are you doing here?" Speaking clogged her dry throat. Staring into the face of her ex was simply too much the minute she woke from surgery. Where was Jessie?

"I couldn't stay away. Good God, Monica, I thought I'd lost you."

John held her hand in his, kissed her fingers. Pain sat behind his eyes.

"You didn't need to come." He shouldn't have come. Hadn't she made herself clear before she left?

He wasn't listening. The gentle stroke of his fingers along her hand began to feel like an emery board grinding a fine layer of her skin away. "I had to come. I love you, Monica."

She closed her eyes, not ready to hear his confession, nor ready to tell him she wanted nothing to do with his love. Her feelings weren't on the same level as his. He knew this.

"Where's Jessie?" She needed her sister to intervene.

"She and Jack went to the cafeteria."

"John . . ."

"You don't have to say anything. When I was told you were missing, that they thought something awful happened to you, I realized that I can't walk away from you."

"You didn't walk away. I did."

John's grip on her hand increased, his eyes stayed with her as if he didn't hear a thing she said.

"We can talk about this later," he told her. Not that her mind would change about their relationship.

"Yes. Please." Monica reached for the call light, desperate for any intervention.

Nurse Hard-Ass walked in, a rare smile on her face. One glance and she asked John to leave the room.

"I'll wait outside."

Once he was out of hearing range, Monica whispered to the nurse. "Please have him stay in the waiting room."

The nurse narrowed her eyes. "He said he was your fiancé."

Monica squeezed her eyes closed and shook her head. "No. He's not. Where's my sister? I need Jessie."

"OK, OK, I'll get her. Calm down."

"Please."

The nurse stepped out of the room and spoke with John just beyond the door. "I'm going to have to ask you stay in the lobby for now."

"I'm a nurse," John argued.

"And a friend. You know the rules. She just woke up and isn't ready for visitors."

Just go, John.

The sound of footsteps moving away from the room helped calm her rapid heartbeat.

"Thank you," Monica said when the nurse came back in the room.

Twenty minutes later Jessie walked into the room, a smile on her face. "Look who's awake."

Monica attempted a smile. "Is John still out there?"

Jessie slid into the chair. "In the lobby. How come I don't know about him? He said you guys were serious."

"Since when am I serious about anyone?" she asked. "He wanted serious, I cut him off."

"Oh." Jessie's face fell.

"I need my sister to get him out of here. I can't deal with him right now. I told him we were over before I went to Jamaica."

"He probably got scared like the rest of us when we heard you were missing."

"Yeah, but it didn't change how I feel about him. Please, Jessie. I need my big sister to make the man go away."

Jessie giggled and stood. "Consider it done."

Monica shivered. "Be nice. OK. I know he wanted more. Tell him I'll talk to him when I get home."

"I'm the good cop, remember. Just relax."

Jessie started toward the door.

"Jessie?"

"I'm not getting very far here, sis."

"I know. Have you seen Trent?"

"No."

"Oh, OK. Well, he can come in. You know . . . if he shows up."

Jessie offered a smile and a wink. "Got it. Anyone else I should know about?"

Monica wished she had something to throw at her sister, instead she settled on a wicked look.

Trent didn't show up. And once they transferred her out of the ICU the next day and into a private room Monica called reception and asked if Trent Fairchild was still a patient and could her call be transferred to his room. Monica was met with the response, "Mr. Fairchild was released yesterday afternoon."

Monica stared at the phone in her hand for several minutes, all the while thinking, *He said he'd come by.*

Jessie and Jack flew with Monica to their home in Texas. It didn't matter that Monica lived in California, there was no way around letting her big sister take care of her until she could walk.

It wasn't like there was a rush to return to her home anyway. Deb, her friend from work, had called on several occasions, checking up on her and giving Monica the rundown of the ER drama.

Walt had returned in a fiery fit about Monica's job being placed on hold. Once she was able, she'd have to go in front of the review board to see if the hospital had grounds to terminate her. For once, maybe being a part of the union would be helpful. She'd fight the issue now if she was able to work.

John had returned home after sending a massive bouquet of flowers with a card. He added accolades of their time together and how he wanted to take up where they'd left off. He agreed he'd rushed their relationship and wanted another shot at being her perfect guy.

The letter should have made her heart do something other than freeze. The fact that when she did return she'd have to once again put him off made her tired. It was hard enough to tell the guy they were over the first time. Now after he'd flown all the way across the country only to be put on the next plane home after one brief audience, it was going to be even harder doing it again. If she were in high school, she might send Jessie to do it for her.

Sometimes being an adult sucked.

"Maybe I should play for the other team," she said one day while perched in Jessie's den watching DVDs of *Supernatural* and *Buffy the Vampire Slayer*. Katie stayed behind in Texas and was "babysitting" Monica while Jessie and Jack were out shopping for some family surprise they planned on presenting that night.

Katie had tucked Savannah into bed for a nap and it was just the two of them watching mindless television. Well, Sam and Dean weren't mindless, but the play of muscles as they kicked another demon's ass was mind-numbing.

"The way you're drooling over this show proves you could never *play for the other team.*"

They'd been talking about guys and Monica's inability to connect with any of them.

"Well I've got to do something. I'm obviously the problem."

"Why do you say that?" Katie had set up shop at Monica's feet and proceeded to paint her toenails. A pedicure was out of the question, but with her toes peeking out from beneath the temporary cast Katie thought it was her duty to gussy her up.

Monica ate up the sister time. Though not a sister by blood, Katie was a sister of the heart. Jessie really lucked out when hooking up with Jack. His entire family was something out of Mayberry only loaded to the umpteenth degree.

"I don't want them for very long. I swear I should have been a guy."

Katie laughed, holding the polish aside to avoid a smudge. "Because you enjoy sex without strings?"

"Because I enjoy sex and want them to leave when we're done."

Katie regarded her with a tilted chin. "You don't do the cuddle thing? Spooning?"

There'd been only one guy she'd come close to spooning. And that was in a cave while doing her best I'm-going-to-die-soon interpretation. "Not really."

Katie bent her head toward her task, blew on Monica's toes. "What about the guy in Jamaica?"

Monica's head popped up. "Trent?"

"Well at least you know his name. Some guys don't bother to remember the girl's name."

"He doesn't count."

Katie moved on to her other foot. "Oh, why not?"

"Near-death experiences have a way of skewing the facts."

"What facts are those?"

"That we were never going to be anything but temporary. A nice diversion from the crap on that island." OK, a *mind-blowing* diversion. A *rock your world* diversion. A *nocturnal emissions* diversion.

"There's that look again, darlin'. And you're not even watching the hottie on the TV."

"What look?"

"The 'Is it getting warm in here?' look. So, you and this Trent guy . . . you spooned?"

"Not spooned so much as he was my personal pillow. The cave was pitch black at night. And so damn quiet." She shivered with the memory. "I could hear the constant drip from the hole above into the pool of poisoned water and kept thinking I knew what Chinese water torture felt like. The only thing that broke it up was if it started to rain."

Memories flooded her senses. The smell of the cave, of Trent. He'd certainly become more earthy as the days had passed but Monica had never been put off by it. They used the one towel to wash off as best they could, but a lack of shower for that many days resulted in discomfort. She still hadn't been able to take a completely proper shower. A bath with her leg hanging out to avoid soaking her cast was the best she could manage. She wondered if Trent lingered in the hot spray for an hour once given the opportunity.

"I'll bet you were scared," Katie said, pulling Monica out of her thoughts.

"Shitless. But he made it better. We talked about stupid stuff. Old movies, whatever we could to get our mind off the fact that we might . . . well, that we might not make it out."

Katie sighed. "And you spooned."

"Cuddled. Kind of."

They paused for a moment, both thinking and not talking.

Then Katie said, "Sounds like you connected with him."

Monica shrugged. "Must not have. He didn't even say good-bye when he left."

"But you wanted him to?"

No. Actually . . . Monica didn't want to say good-bye at all.

———

"We're pregnant." Jack stood at the head of the table with Jessie at his side and made the announcement just about everyone was expecting.

Monica glanced over at Katie and said, "You owe me five bucks."

Katie rolled her eyes and Jessie laughed. "You guys knew?"

"Guessed," Monica told her.

Gaylord walked around the table and bear-hugged his daughter-in-law before taking Jack's hand in his. "Well, I didn't know." His face beamed and his cheeks warmed to a rosy color. He glanced back at Jessie and hugged her again, lifting her off her feet.

With the exception of Monica, everyone took their turn hugging Jessie and Jack and offering advice to Danny. "I'd jump up for a hug, but my jumping days will have to wait."

Jessie walked over and leaned down for a sister hug. "I'm happy for you," Monica said.

Jessie lowered her voice. "So different than the first time."

Monica understood. When Jessie found out she was knocked up in high school, they both thought her life was over. Their mom had been good about it. As much as a mom could be, but never once did Jessie think being a parent on her own at such a young age was going to be a picnic. Still, she brought Danny into the world, alone because the dirtbag who didn't glove up split soon after she announced she was expecting, and put her life on hold to raise him. This time she'd have a husband, a family to support her . . . everything a new mom could want.

Monica reached up and hugged Jack. "Congrats, stud man."

He beamed.

Danny took that moment to pull on Jack's sleeve. Without hesitating, Jack scooped Danny up into his arms. "Can my baby brother sleep in my room?"

Jack ruffled Danny's mop of hair. "Maybe. What if you have a baby sister?"

Danny regarded that possibility and dismissed it. "I don't think Mommy can have girls."

Jack shook his head and laughed. "She might have a girl."

"As long as she doesn't have too many dolls, she can sleep in my room."

The adults at the table laughed.

They settled into their seats again, and champagne was served to everyone but Jessie, who opted for milk in a crystal flute.

Sometime before the meal was over, Danny asked a question that had Jack earning his daddy stripes.

"Daddy?"

"Yeah, sport?"

His young brow pitched together as he picked his words carefully.

"How did Mommy get the baby in her belly?"

A hush went over the table.

Katie and Monica exchanged glances and awaited Jack's reply.

"I-I ah, I put the baby there."

Dean chuckled under his breath and drank his beer.

"Yeah, but how?"

Jack ran a hand over his chin and glanced around the table. Not even Gaylord was offering any help.

Then Jack sat a little taller and said, "A special hug."

Danny pushed out his lips and looked at his mom. "Oh." And then he went back to the food on his plate.

Chapter Twenty-One

Jessie sat with Katie on the split rail fence surrounding the corral that held Danny and his horse. Jack had insisted Danny learn to ride shortly after they moved to Texas. He received no complaint from Danny, who loved all animals big and small. The kid was going to either be a veterinarian or a rancher.

"Maybe it's the hormones, but the thought of everyone leaving is making me weepy."

"It's gotta be the hormones cuz we're all a pain in the ass." Katie nudged Jessie's shoulder, knowing full well that none of them were difficult.

"And I'm worried about her."

The doctors had put Monica's leg in a walking cast after four weeks. Not that she was ready to go back to work, but she felt the need to get back to California to fight for her job.

Jessie didn't need to elaborate who she spoke of. She and Katie had a few quiet conversations about Monica's disposition since she had returned from Jamaica.

"Oh, don't do that," Katie scolded.

"Do what?"

"Make me worry any more than I'm already doing. She's a mess, isn't she? I mean, you'd know better than I would."

"She's not joking, smiling . . . finding any reason to get out of the house."

"Maybe getting back to California and fighting back will help."

"I think whatever is bugging her has something to do with what happened in Jamaica and less about her job."

Katie placed a hand over Jessie's shoulders. "She did nearly die."

Jessie winced. "I can't even think about it. You think it's some kind of post trauma crap?"

"Maybe. What else could it be?"

Jessie thought about the question for a minute. "Has she said anything to you about the guy she was in the cave with? Trent?"

"Only that he bolted as soon as he was discharged and didn't say good-bye."

Jessie waved at Danny who managed to stay on the back of his horse despite the trot and uneven gait of the animal. "Don't you find that odd? I mean, even if they didn't hit it off, wouldn't someone you'd damn near met your maker with deserve some kind of *see ya later*? *Have a nice life*. Something?"

Katie seemed to consider the question for a while.

"And it's not like Monica to not call a guy on their bullshit. I'm taken aback by the fact she hasn't tried to call him out."

"Call him out on what? Not being into her? Can't blame anyone for not feeling the same way. Look at that John guy. He keeps sending flowers and she's not led him on at all. Maybe she's worried about *that* conversation when she gets home. Or maybe she's worried she won't get her job back. I've tried to tell her that we'd help her out if she needed money."

"Monica won't accept it."

"I know," Katie said. "I've tried. I had to go behind her back when I lived with her last year to pay the landlord directly."

Jessie pulled her cowboy hat farther down her face to keep the Texan sun from burning her nose. "Monica hates depending on anyone. And if that anyone has a penis, forget it. That's the by-product of growing up without a dad and having your mother keep a revolving door of wannabe replacements nearby."

"Funny, I always thought it would be better if my dad dated after my mother left him. Now I'm thinking I was wrong."

"We had all, you had nothing. There's got to be something in the middle. Divorce happens. That doesn't mean the end of your life."

Katie nudged her again. "Not that you'll ever have to worry about that."

"Said the pot to the kettle." Jessie sighed. "God I love your brother."

Katie giggled. "Married life is the best. Now if we can just help Monica find the right guy."

Jessie rubbed a hand on her still flat belly and smiled. "Yeah."

The beer in Trent's fist had become a constant companion. At least when his mind traveled to the island . . . to her.

Which was daily.

The door to Glen's home slammed, telling Trent his brother was home.

"Jesus Christ, Trent." Glen's profanity barely made Trent lift his eyes to his brother. "What the fuck are you doing in the dark?"

"It's not dark." Well, actually, the curtains were drawn and there wasn't a light on in the masculine den. The only company came from the radio that knocked out heavy rock. But there was still a glow from the outside to drive away the dark.

Glen crossed to the stereo, jabbed a finger down on the knob, and turned off the sound.

Ginger, who had been curled up by the couch, snapped her head up and barked.

His brother tossed his jacket over a chair and glared at him. "Enough! I'm not going to watch you do this to yourself."

"Do what?" Trent dropped his feet from the table and reached to set his empty beer aside.

"Do nothing. Drink all the fucking time. Sit in the dark. Is this what you did in Jamaica?"

No. Well, in the beginning there had been a lot of drinking. Eventually he found his rhythm again. Maybe that's why he escaped to the island, to mourn in peace. His brothers wouldn't have allowed him to find the bottom of a bottle for long.

"I could have died in Jamaica."

"But you didn't!" Glen yelled. "Do you think that little blonde number is soaking up her liver like you are? She sure as shit had it worse than you."

That may have been, but Monica had someone to share the night with.

"Fuck you."

"No, fuck you." Glen turned around and slammed his fist against the light switch. "And turn on a fucking light."

Glen stormed out of the room. Trent had half a mind to follow his brother and lay a fist into him. His other urge was to grab another beer. He squelched both desires and found his way to the room he called his since he returned. In his bathroom, he turned on a light and looked in the mirror.

"Oh, damn." When was the last time he shaved? His eyes were bloodshot, and a quick sniff told him he needed a shower.

He turned on the tap, watched the water as it ran down the sink. He wondered if Monica was as happy about healthy tap water as he was.

How was she doing? Was she back in California or still in Florida? Maybe she stayed with her sister in Texas for a while? Or maybe she moved in with her fiancé?

Trent grabbed his razor and removed several days of stubble. When he turned off the water he could hear his brother through the wall talking on the phone.

"I'm about to pull the family intervention shit, Jase. It's fucking crazy."

So Jason and Glen were talking about him.

"If I didn't care, I'd kick his ass . . . hell maybe I will kick his ass. Something needs to wake him up."

Trent moved out of earshot and leaned against the wall. Since when did he become the family bum? The first week home, he told himself he deserved a little R and R. Some downtime from life. He'd shared several beers with his brothers. They talked of old times, about their parents. For the first time since their death, Trent felt he could remember the good times and not choke on regret and blame. He didn't tell his brothers about Monica outside the obvious. They didn't bat an eye when he left Florida. Both told him to take all the time he needed to acclimate.

So he took the time.

Winter was losing its grip on the east and the spring sun was starting to stay up later. Trent moved to the window and realized the glare of sun was still out there.

Ginger sat on her haunches looking at him with that dopey dog expression. The one that said, *Well . . . are we going out or what?*

Trent ran a hand through his hair, hair that needed a good cut, and pulled on his shoes.

He grabbed Ginger's leash, which resulted in a rapid series of barks.

Trent stepped out of his brother's home and let the late afternoon chill wake him. The lingering scent of cold rain felt heavy in the air. Ginger pulled and tugged, excited to be out and peeing on every bush.

He walked the block, then the next. A few kids were playing outside their homes and somewhere the sound of a lawn mower hummed. It was the time for cut grass and flowers.

The thought of flying over fields of wildflowers reminded him of how much he'd been missing since he attempted to remove the memory of Monica with beer.

By the time he made it back to his brother's, the sun had set in the far west. His thought lingered on whether Monica was watching it over the ocean tonight.

The smell of a grill made his insides churn. When he let Ginger loose in the backyard, he smelled the sizzling scent of steaks on the barbecue.

Glen turned a couple of steaks and closed the lid before focusing his attention on him. Without words, Trent grabbed a Coke from the outside fridge and tossed his brother a beer. Glen's eyes opened wider.

"I can't work in the office," Trent said, placing his ass in a lounge chair. "You know how much I hate that shit."

Glen leaned against the side of the house and opened his beer. "It's been a while since you've been around. A lot of our pilots don't even know you."

"Yeah? So?"

"We have a couple of locations where more hours have been logged into flight time than were expected. We could use some investigating."

"Find out if someone's using the birds for their personal use?"

Glen smiled. "It's not in the office."

Yeah, and it wouldn't be boring and leave him with hours to think.

"Where are the problems?"

"Biggest one is in Seattle."

Seattle. Cold, wet . . . and miles from anyone. "You'll watch my dog?"

The walking cast might have aided in walking, but in driving . . . not so much.

Monica's first stop once she finally shook Katie loose was at the fire station where the majority of guys who'd come to her aid worked. It was about four in the afternoon, and the station was quiet. Quiet was not a word she'd say out loud for fear of jinxing the vibe of the day.

She stepped into the familiar garage that housed the big red trucks and knocked on the wall. "Hello?" she called out for someone to notice her.

Out from the weight room walked Stan. A veteran of the department for nearly twenty years, his hair was peppered with gray but he was still stacked with muscles he should have lost in his forties.

"Queenie? Holy cow. Guys?" he yelled in the back. "We have a visitor."

Stan walked over and pulled her into a hug. She hugged him back and meant it.

"So damn good to see you." Stan stood back and took her in.

Her bootleg pants didn't hide her cast, but they did hug her ass. She wore a simple button-up shirt and whimsy scarf. The guys were used to seeing her in nothing but scrubs. She knew she looked different to them in plain clothes.

"Monica?" The next hug came from Radar. Not his real name but a nickname these jokers gave him because of the glasses he often wore. That's what they told her anyway. Rumor had it he actually had a stuffed animal his kid gave him by his cot.

After Radar was Clive, no nickname there. Then came Spock, his name because of the word games he was so fond of playing in their downtime. Even their captain had his hug turn. Charlie might have been about four years away from retirement but he wasn't anything but hot. In fact, all the guys surrounding her could easily be placed on one of those hot fireman calendars. Even dirty, these guys would sell thousands of copies.

She remembered the first time she'd done a ride along. They did their best to make her feel like she belonged. They kicked back when the radio was silent and hauled ass to the next emergency when needed. It was a learning experience to help her call appropriate shots over the radio from the ER.

She trusted these guys.

Even she knew that trust was rare.

"Come in, come in." Charlie opened the door to their man-cave and gave her one of the prime seats so she could put her foot up.

"How you doing?" Radar asked.

"Remarkably well. I was told that some of you volunteered for the search."

"Yeah, well . . . you might not wear blue, but you're part of our family here."

Oh, damn . . . there were actual tears welling behind her eyes. "Uhm, I'm not even sure who was there. I don't remember anything."

Radar and Spock raised their hands. "Mitch on B shift was with us, and Miller from 73."

"Wow. That's just . . . wow." She blinked several times trying like hell not to let tears fall. "I know the rest of you had to shuffle shifts." She turned to Charlie. "And your boss had to let you go." She grabbed Charlie's hand because he was close. "Thanks isn't the right word."

They were smiling at her and taking her appreciation with a shrug. "It's how we work, right? You'd have come for us."

Yeah, she would.

Another knock grabbed their attention. "Delivery."

The smell of barbecue sauce followed the delivery guy as he stepped inside the fire station.

"Who ordered? I thought we were going out?" Stan asked.

Monica waved the deliveryman over once he placed the bags on the table. "On me," she said as she signed for their dinner. She'd scheduled dinner for the guys for the next few days to make sure everyone managed at least one meal on her.

"Oh, hell no."

"That's not gonna happen."

More than one of them pulled a wallet from his back pocket.

"C'mon guys. I have to do something." She shooed the delivery-man off before someone could grab the ticket and circumvent her gesture.

They didn't like a woman paying for their food, but that didn't stop them from digging in.

She ate with them and they talked about some of the things they'd seen while in Jamaica. A couple of them talked about joining a team of emergency aid for future disasters.

"I've seen my share of crazy shit, but that was huge," Spock said between bites.

"Did you see the clinic?"

Radar nodded. "After we got you on the plane, nice digs your sister has by the way, we took some of the locals back home."

"I didn't know you were related to the Morrisons."

"I'm not. Well, my sister married Jack. But—"

Clive waved a rib at her. "That's related in my book. Morrison offered a huge incentive for us to look for you."

Monica stopped eating mid chew. "He did?"

Charlie rolled his eyes. "Like we needed it or something."

Knowing these guys didn't come because of money made her smile linger.

"Word from the ER is that you lost your job."

They all watched her now, with eyes over their food and serious concern on their brows.

"Pat's been out to sack me forever. Not sure why."

"She's jealous," Radar said as if it were common knowledge.

"Jealous of what?"

"You're single, gorgeous, all the guys fawn over you, and you could take her job in a heartbeat if you wanted it," Clive said.

That had Monica squirming in her chair.

"Way to make her uncomfortable, Clive."

"What?" Clive had this cleft in his chin that dug in with his smile.

"Aren't you married?" Monica scorned.

"Happily. But I'm sure as hell not blind," he said with a wink.

That made her laugh. "Remind me to kick your ass when I get this thing off." She lifted her leg as she spoke.

"She can't really fire you for helping in Jamaica, can she?"

Monica blew out a breath. "I don't know. I have a meeting with human resources tomorrow to find out what exactly is happening."

"Well, we have your back if you need anything from us."

The guys nodded right as the blaring alarm forced them from their hot dinner and had them running for the door. She knew the drill, wasn't offended in the least.

"Would have been too much to ask for ten more minutes," Stan said. He patted Monica on the shoulder as he made it out the door.

"Thanks, Queenie."

"Thanks, Monica."

"Come by again soon."

One by one they left her alone in the station with boxes of barbecue and a crazy lump in her throat.

They were a damn good group of guys.

Chapter Twenty-Two

Monica walked . . . well limped, out of the human resources building with a pink slip and an attitude. She was half tempted to walk into the ER and ask Pat what the hell her problem was. Now that Monica was back in the States, a formal investigation would take place. Of course that took time to happen and it wouldn't transpire until all parties involved could be reached.

All parties involved. *Who the hell could they be talking about?* On the surface the case had very little ground. Monica had covered her shifts. Except one of her colleagues had gotten sick and the shifts then defaulted back to Monica. It became her responsibility to have them covered. She wasn't exactly around to fix the schedule, being knee-deep in shit on the island. The scheduling problem had taken place the first hours on Jamaica and there wasn't a damn thing Monica could do to fix it.

It wasn't proven yet, but it appeared that Pat had kept at least one nurse from coming in to help solidify the case against Monica. The whole thing was stupid.

Monica sat in with Mrs. Levine, the HR representative, who began with the facts, and then started to embellish them.

"It doesn't help your case that you were on the island enjoying the sights."

"Enjoying the sights," Monica practically yelled. "What are you talking about? I worked my ass off the whole time I was there."

Mrs. Levine, with a polished expression of disbelief, peered at Monica over her cheaters. "According to one nurse at the clinic, you left on more than one occasion with a local for a . . . an affair."

Monica felt steam come out her ears. "An affair? What the hell?"

"We still need to obtain her statement, but she said it was well known that you slept in this man's home instead of the accommodations provided by Borderless Nurses."

"There weren't any damn accommodations. I was transferred to a clinic far away from anything. Dr. Eddy and Dr. Klein were both there. They'll vouch for me."

Mrs. Levine removed her dime-store glasses from her nose and crossed her arms over her chest. "Are you saying you didn't spend time with a man on the island? A man who wasn't a colleague or a patient?"

Monica stood at that point and crumbled her pink slip in her grasp. "I feel like I need a fucking lawyer."

"Cussing at me will not change the facts. And that wasn't an answer, Miss Mann. It's one thing to leave your post with the intentions of helping others abroad. But to do so and use the good of our system for a free vacation with a lover . . ."

Monica wasn't prone to violence, but she'd never wanted to punch someone so bad in her entire life.

She hobbled out of the building and practically ran into a familiar and unwelcome guest. "Dammit. What are you doing here?"

John tucked his hands in his pockets and peered behind her. "That bad?"

"They're stupid. Have no idea what I've had to go through."

"Wanna talk about it?"

Yes, but she didn't think that someone to talk to about it was him. Her conversation with him held a whole different set of words.

In her haste to get out of the building she stepped down the stairs with the wrong foot and damn near ended up on her butt.

John managed to keep her upright, his hand lingered on her arm longer than she wanted.

"Thanks," she said as she stepped away.

"C'mon. I'll buy you a drink."

She rubbed a hand over her face. "John . . ."

"Just a drink. I know we have a lot to talk about. That can wait. Let's just pretend we've only worked together and we're shooting the crap after a bad shift. OK?" Some of the charm he'd held that encouraged her to go out with him the first time presented itself with his smile. She didn't want to be his enemy, or the bitch in his life that he would judge all others against.

"Just a drink?"

His smile started to crack. "One cocktail. Or soda . . . your choice."

Soda wouldn't do for this day. "One drink."

He smiled. "Want me to drive?"

Yeah, but she didn't want to be without a car, or have an excuse to have more than one drink. "I'll meet you at Joe's."

Joe's was around the block from the hospital. The jukebox held some of the latest pop favorites and several from the eighties and beyond. The music wasn't rap and filled with hate, which made it a decent spot for the staff to meet up after work. The last thing they needed after twelve hours was headache-inducing bass.

The cocktail waitress took their order and disappeared after leaving a bowl of salty pretzels on the table. Smart move. Monica started nibbling on them the minute she walked away.

"Pat's been bad-mouthing you ever since you left," John told her once their drinks arrived. Monica opted for a beer. It would take a while to get through and wouldn't leave her hungry when she was done.

"I'm sure she had an audience with you." Monica wanted to slap the words back into her mouth instantly.

John shrugged. "I wasn't happy with you when you left, but I didn't join her tirade. We had a really busy shift the day Shel called in sick."

"I can't help the fact that my replacement was ill. What was I supposed to do an ocean away?"

John tipped his drink back. "More than one person called Pat on her shit. Didn't stop her from going to the DN."

The director of nursing was Pat's best friend. They'd known each other since nursing school, back in the Stone Age. "Great."

"I wasn't at work the day we heard you were missing. Deb called me at home."

For once, Monica felt bad for John.

He took another swig of his drink, popped a few pretzels in his mouth.

"I survived."

"Not before we all thought the worst. God, Monica, when I think of how our last conversation went—"

"Not our last conversation," she reminded him. "I'm here now."

He gave her a half smile. "Well. Pat seemed to have some remorse. Word got out that some of the fire guys took off to look for you, Pat didn't even come to work. Then when she found out you were rescued . . . I don't know, it's like there was never any hitch in her plan. She went right back to bitch mode. Said if you were there only for work then what were you doing in a cave to begin with."

For a minute, Monica thought of defending herself, her actions. Then she realized who she was talking to. She might not owe John an explanation, but she didn't want to flaunt her behavior either. Especially since her lapse of judgment nearly got her killed and the guy involved didn't stick around for a proper good-bye.

Maybe it was karma for the Ice Queen, a taste of her own medicine.

"It was hell on that island. I hardly ate, barely slept. When all this is hashed out it's Pat that's going to look like the witch she is." Monica finished her beer.

John placed his hand over hers.

Monica slipped away. "John?"

"No. We said nothing more than work shit."

She smiled and sat back for a moment.

"But I'm damn happy you didn't die, Monica."

She laughed at that. "Me, too."

For a few more minutes, they talked about the hospital, about some of the gossip she'd missed while away. When she left, Monica felt a little less like an Ice Queen.

———•———

Monica shot out of bed in a cold sweat screaming Trent's name. The panic didn't start to fade until she turned on her bedside lamp and filled her room with light. As the terror of being back in the cave that was still fresh in her mind from the part dream, part memory faded, the pain in her leg brought her back to reality in a flash.

Under the stiff, unrelenting cast, her leg cramped. A charley horse of monstrous proportions gripped her and didn't let go. Tears instantly appeared. She jumped out of bed and tried to walk off the cramp but with the inability to flex her foot, the pain didn't stop. In her bathroom, she fumbled with the bottle of muscle relaxers and swallowed one without the aid of water.

Everyone complained about the itchy and smelly part of having a cast restricting one's movement. She'd take the itchy and smelly over the crampy every day of the week. Lighting her way into her kitchen, Monica found a banana and ate it. She knew the potassium would help ward off more cramps, but probably wouldn't make this one go away any faster.

She leaned against the counter and forced the banana down. She considered the peel, the color . . . and thought of the bananas Trent had cut from the tree right before they descended to the beach and hidden cave.

"How can I miss someone I barely know?"

She did. She missed talking to him, seeing him . . . smelling him. Even in the dark he'd whisper in her ear and chase away the shadows.

Monica swiped away the tear on her cheek and realized the pain in her leg had eased.

The pain in her chest, however, grew.

Once the peel was in the trash, she moved into the living room. It might have been three in the morning, but that didn't mean she had to sleep. Besides, ever since she returned, sleeping at night had become more difficult. Maybe when her job was reinstated she'd ask for the graveyard shift. Then at least she could sleep during the day, when her room was never really black. She could roll over, peek through half-opened eyelids, and know she was safe.

She turned on her computer and opened her e-mail. A few on-line bills came through reminding her that her savings was dwindling. She'd accumulated some sick time, but the last of those checks had come the previous week.

Now that the medical bills were accumulating, her bank account had a hard squeeze around its neck.

She turned on Pandora radio and listened to her private station while perusing the inbox. She clicked on an e-mail from the Board of Registered Nurses. She assumed it was some kind of spam, some notice of pending changes within the organization.

Instead, she was faced with a direct e-mail to her.

Dear Monica Mann RN,

It has come to the attention of the Board of Registered Nurses that pending litigation and grievances have been filed against Monica Mann RN. Temporary suspension of Miss Mann's license is in effect immediately.

Monica's vision blurred. She kept reading, and at the same time found herself hyperventilating. The letter went beyond an internal issue between her and the hospital for unsubstantiated reasons for her termination. This letter accused her of acting outside her license and endangering the lives of patients. It took Monica three times reading the letter to recognize the name Shandee Curtina. Curtina meant nothing to her, but Shandee?

Nausea rose in her throat. How could this be happening?

All her life Monica only wanted to be independent. Helping people and finding fulfillment from it was a by-product of the profession she chose.

Fighting for her job at the hospital was one thing . . . this was entirely different. If she wasn't a nurse, what was she? Who was she?

She needed help. She reached for the phone and realized the time. Up until that moment Monica had been willing to step back a little and let the wheels of the hospital investigation take place. Let the union hold court. Not anymore.

This was *not* happening.

Three hours later, Monica was on the phone with Jessie relaying all the shitty details. "I'd never ask if I thought I could do this on my own," she told her sister. "I'll pay you back."

"Don't be stupid, Mo. What they're doing to you is wrong on a colossal level. How the hell will Borderless Nurses or Doctors ever recruit anyone to help if they get away with this?"

The anger in Jessie's voice matched that boiling in Monica's blood. "I know Jack and Gaylord have a team of lawyers."

"Say no more."

"I think I'm going to need character witnesses from the island. Shandee wasn't happy with me at first, but I can't believe she'd throw me under the bus." Her name was on the actual complaint, so obviously Monica wasn't a good judge of character.

"We'll let the lawyers figure out who needs to be brought in. I'm so sorry you are going through this, sis. What else can I do?"

Hold her while she cried. "Just see if we can assemble a posse and make Pat and her minions shit their pants."

"Oh, hon . . . we'll do that. And I'll call Katie, too."

"OK."

"How are you otherwise? Are you sleeping?"

Monica hesitated. "Ah, yeah. I'm . . . yeah."

"Why don't I believe you?"

"My leg hurts at night." That certainly wasn't a lie.

"When do you get the cast off?"

"Next week. Then I'll start physical therapy." She knew walking with the cast was easy compared to what she had to look forward to in the coming months.

"That's something at least. I'll bet you'll feel better then."

Yeah, her physical wounds were healing. That was something.

———

Trent huddled under his windbreaker, cursing the cold wind. His blood had certainly thinned in the last couple of years. That was proven as he stood on the private airstrip just south of SeaTac International shivering his ass off. He'd been introduced to the management of the Pacific Northwest team as TJ Childs. He wasn't sure how far he could convince any of them that he was a pilot new to the company and considering a transfer to Seattle.

Trent circled around the Citation, inspecting the seven-passenger private jet. The hours logged into this aircraft exceeded what the flight log suggested. The FAA wasn't happy about the discrepancy and it was going to end up an external investigation if Trent and his brothers didn't find the culprit.

"She's a beauty, isn't she?" Frank was a hotshot thirty-six-year-old who'd flown for Fairchild Charters for a few years. He reminded Trent vaguely of the high school football star who always wanted to be the center of attention. After only a couple of days, Trent's gut told him that Frank was their man. He had yet to prove he used the aircraft for anything other than work, so Trent kept his thoughts to himself as he acted the curious observer.

"She's sweet. Take her out often?"

"Often enough," Frank said. "We have a couple of execs that request her on a routine basis."

The door to the hangar that housed the plane was open, whipping in the wind from outside. How did the locals handle the constant drizzle? He'd been there for only a few days and was already done with it.

Trent asked questions, though he knew the answers. "How long is her range?"

Frank told him the miles the bird would fly and the cargo weight restrictions. He knew his planes.

"It would be nice to have your own. Go anywhere . . . anytime." Trent planted the seed and waited for Frank to bite.

Frank lowered his sunglasses over his eyes and looked up at the engine. Who wore sunglasses on rainy days? "We'd have to be doing more than flying them in order to own them. Besides, we have the privilege without the headache."

"Oh, how's that?"

"The cost of housing, maintaining . . . fuel. You know what that all adds up to?"

Yeah, he did.

"But you're flying other people where *they* want to go."

Frank shrugged. "Works out sometimes." With that, he turned and walked away.

Trent removed his cell phone as Frank walked away, with the intention of dropping Frank's name on Glen. He noticed two missed calls, both from numbers with which he wasn't familiar.

The callers didn't leave messages so he went on to text his brother and then turned the ringer on.

Twenty minutes later, his phone rang. "Yeah?" he answered.

"Trent?"

"Jase, how ya doing?" He ducked away from any ears, stood outside the hangar doors, and watched the rain pelt the runway.

"I got your text and have Sally checking what we know on him."

"Sounds good. It's a hunch. I don't have anything solid."

Jason laughed. "Listen to you sounding all spy-guy."

"Call me Bond."

"How does it look up there?"

"Rainy. But the operation runs well. Management is efficient and the planes are in great shape." He walked out in the rain and elaborated on the business.

"It sounds like you have it figured out," Jason said. "Oh, another reason for the call."

"Yeah?"

"I got a call from Jack Morrison. He's looking for you."

Monica!

Trent turned away from the wind. "Did he say why?"

"Something about his sister-in-law needing your help. Isn't she the one you were in the cave with?"

"Monica . . . yeah. Is she OK?" Something inside tightened and felt as if it were going to snap.

"How would I know? I told him I'd pass on the message. He did say he wouldn't have called if it wasn't important."

Trent thought about the missed calls on his cell.

"Do you know his number?" Jason asked.

"I got it. Thanks."

His throat tightened when he dialed Jack Morrison's cell. As the phone rang, Trent walked farther away from the building.

Jack answered on the second ring. "Morrison."

"Jack? It's Trent Fairchild. I hear you're looking for me."

"Yeah, I am. Can you hold on a second?"

"No problem."

A few seconds passed before he came back on. "Sorry 'bout that."

"It's OK. What's up?"

"It's Monica."

"Is she OK?"

"If you're asking if she's healthy, yeah. Much better than when you last saw her."

Part of Trent relaxed. "That wouldn't have taken much."

Jack didn't laugh. "She was fired."

Trent wasn't sure what that had to do with him. "Yeah, there was trouble before she left. I'm sorry to hear about it." He was more than sorry, but shouldn't the person holding her hand through this be her fiancé? "I'm not sure what I can do to help."

"It's more than her job. There's a huge blowup, and investigation . . . they stripped her license."

"What? How can they do that? And investigate what?" And why did he care?

"I have lawyers all over it, Trent, but what they need is your statement."

"About what?"

"They're accusing her of taking the assignment in Jamaica to obtain a free trip to see her lover."

If the wind hadn't chilled him to the bone, Jack's words did. "Me?"

"That's what they're saying. They're also accusing her of working outside her license. Rushed her job to meet with you."

"I met Monica on the island. If she rushed to do anything it was to keep people from dying."

"I know that. But my lawyers need to hear you say it. They want a deposition before she goes before the board."

Trent rubbed the bridge of his nose. "That is seriously fucked up."

"I know. Monica's not going to be happy that I called you. But I promised my wife I'd do whatever was needed to help Monica. It's hard enough that Monica won't take any money. She's drowning in debt and refuses to let us help. I'll pay for your flight down, hotel . . . whatever. Or I can have my lawyers come to you."

"That's not necessary, Jack. When is the deposition?"

Jack hesitated on the phone. "Yeah . . . uh, it's tomorrow in LA. Sorry for the short notice."

It didn't matter. There was no way he'd be able to rest until he knew he dispelled any rumors about Monica's reasons for going to Jamaica. Yeah, she'd probably be pissed to have her fiancé know the details about their brief affair, but it was better than losing her career.

Trent ended the call to Jack and called his brother back. "Hey, Jason."

"Everything OK?"

"No, actually. I need to go to LA." He glanced into the hangar at his ride. "And I'm going to blow my cover to get there."

"Seriously? Must be bad . . . or good. You gonna be a daddy or something?"

Trent actually stumbled when he walked into the hangar. He hadn't even considered the possibility.

"Trent?"

"Ah. No." *Shit . . . maybe.* "It's important."

"Do what you gotta do. We have your back." Jason hung up.

Trent opened the hatch to the Citation and jumped inside. He took in the cockpit, checked the hours, did a quick once-over, and then exited the plane. He noticed one of the airport mechanics and waved him down. After a quick instruction, he made his way into the pilots' lounge and dispatch. The girl behind the desk smiled as he approached.

"I need the Citation fueled and a flight plan filed for a one-way to LA. I'll be leaving in an hour." He wanted to get out of Seattle before the storm that was following this drizzle set in.

She narrowed her eyes. "I didn't get a call."

Frank heard him and walked over. "Watcha doing, TJ?"

Ignoring him, Trent walked into the manager's office. Frank followed and took his ridiculous glasses off his face.

The manager, Cornelius something or other, shared a confused look as Trent went to the logbooks to check the maintenance schedule. "I'm taking the Citation. Probably be gone a couple of days."

"Excuse me?"

For the first time he realized he looked like a lunatic. Trent grabbed the book he needed and turned toward the boss. He extended his hand. "Trent Fairchild. Call Jason if you need a replacement." He flashed a smile at Frank and took a brisk walk to his car. He could be at the hotel he was staying in, pack a bag, and be in the air within an hour.

Chapter Twenty-Three

Monica sat beside not one, not two, but three lawyers who wore suits so expensive that she'd have to work for a month to pay for all of them, and this was only half of the team. Mr. Goldstein was the senior lawyer in this trio. Back in Texas Mr. Goldstein had two other associates whom Monica lovingly referred to as Mr. Silver and Mr. Platinum. Not their names, but it was how they presented themselves.

Goldstein sat beside her with his sharp suit and cologne that was a little too potent for her taste, but she had to admit he smelled nice. It was as if the olfactory nerve was on trial and he planned on beating anyone within a foot into submission.

"This is only a deposition," Goldstein told her. "You're not on trial, though you might feel you are."

"Do I have to answer everything they ask?"

"Yes. If they ask anything objectionable, I'll stop them. Answer everything as truthfully as possible and don't elaborate. If you don't remember, say you don't remember and leave it at that."

Goldstein had already spent several hours with her talking about the case. He determined early on that she had nothing to hide. That didn't stop the hospital attorneys from attempting to make a case against her. Not that Monica had any intention of working there again. But a discharge based on the crap they were spewing—

and a loss of her license—would certainly prohibit her from working anywhere else.

Katie took her shopping before the deposition. Monica wore a pencil skirt, matching jacket and the perfect flats because her leg had only been out of the cast for a week and she couldn't wear heels without falling on her face. Monica felt like she belonged next to these high-powered lawyers. More so, she was bent on proving she wasn't some needy woman desperate for a vacation who would use a charity to score a free airplane ride.

She may not have been one to flaunt her sister's new family, but she didn't have any problem helping her accusers connect the dots so they could see how asinine their claims were.

A petite woman made her way into the conference room first. She reached over and shook the hands of Monica's attorneys. She introduced herself as the court reporter and set up a laptop.

Monica sat up straight in her chair and rubbed her leg absently. Goldstein spoke with his colleagues in hushed tones as they waited for the hospital representation to arrive.

A lone man stepped into the large room, his abdomen preceding him by a good six inches. The sweater-vest he wore with a lack of a jacket, mixed with the thinning hairline, was a testament to the man's disregard of the case. Monica couldn't help but notice his general lack of polish. Suddenly she realized that her team knew exactly what they were doing, dressed the way they were. Her team stood and shook hands with the opposing attorney. He smiled at her, but didn't bother putting his hand out.

Good. I don't want this guy to think I like him or who he represents.

Mr. Hudson set his papers on the opposing side of the table, but didn't sit.

"Looks as if the nurse union has stepped up their attorneys," he said with a laugh that could only be described as guarded.

Goldstein sat back and said nothing while his colleague corrected him. "Oh, no, Mr. Hudson. There isn't any union representation here."

Hudson shot a look at Monica. The cocky smile on his face fell. "Is that right?"

"That's correct, counselor. Miss Mann has waived her right to a union attorney."

Hudson started to smile again. As if he knew something none of them did.

Goldstein's right-hand man, literally, removed a card from the inside pocket of his suit and handed it to the other attorney. All the while Goldstein had said nothing.

Hudson glanced at the card and Monica would swear she could hear his heart palpitate from where she sat. She really hoped this guy was healthier than his fast food lunch gut made him appear. It would suck to have to render aid to the enemy.

"If you'll excuse me?" Hudson said as he left the room.

"Where's he going?" Monica asked as she watched him retreat.

Goldstein reclined in the surprisingly comfortable conference chairs.

"Recruiting reinforcements." A smile played on her attorney's face.

Suddenly Monica had a new appreciation for lawyers.

Ten minutes later, Mr. Hudson returned with two more attorneys, one woman in her midthirties with sharp eyes and a pinched face, and a man somewhere in his fifties dressed to the nines. Would you look at that, Monica mused. Mr. Hudson found his jacket.

Everything began with cordial tones. State your name for the record, show us your ID, and your nursing license so we have that as well . . . everything Goldstein told her to expect. Forty-five minutes into the deposition and the only questions raised were about where Monica went to school and where she was raised. She didn't see the importance of her childhood home address but Goldstein didn't stop her from answering the questions.

Finally, after what felt like hours, they asked about her involvement with Borderless Nurses.

"How long have you been on their list of recruits?"

"A year and a half," she answered.

"And have you ever gone on an assignment with them before the recent relief effort in Jamaica?"

"No."

"They've never sent you anywhere?" Hudson asked.

"No . . . well there was a training I went to in Florida."

"Mandated?"

"Yes. The first few days were mandated, I opted to stay for the more detailed course since I was there."

"So a week in Florida?"

She smiled and felt like she was being led. "Yes."

"Did you meet anyone on this trip to Florida?"

"Sure. There were a lot of physicians and nurses from all over the country all there for the same training."

"Anyone else?"

Monica glanced at Goldstein. He sat forward and for the first time during this deposition said something. "What are you getting at, counselor?"

"Did you meet anyone romantically, Miss Mann?"

Her face grew cold.

"I don't see what this has to do with Jamaica," one of Monica's other attorneys said.

"It's OK," she interrupted him. "I didn't see anyone in Florida. The hotel was on the beach and the organization did spring for a farewell dinner the night before I came home. Didn't even stop in Disney World or anything."

"So you enjoyed your time in Florida?"

Monica placed a syrupy smile on her face. "I was doing what I love to do with many other people who feel the same way. It didn't suck."

Goldstein placed a hand on her shoulder to encourage her to remain composed. She took a deep calming breath through her nose and slowly exhaled. Didn't work.

"When was the last time you took a vacation, Miss Mann?"

"A friend of mine married last summer."

"Where did you go?"

"Texas." Katie and Dean were married in the same church Jessie and Jack tied the knot.

The opposing lawyers spoke to each other under their breaths before the woman started asking questions.

"How much money do you make as a nurse a year?"

Monica glanced at her lawyer, who nodded.

"I claimed a little under sixty thousand last year." And she was damn proud of her accomplishments.

"So your take home was what, forty-five?"

"I guess. I didn't add it up."

"Student loans?" Hudson asked.

"Yeah."

They spent the next twenty minutes whittling away at what Monica made. By the time they were finished with the questions, she felt like a pauper.

"So according to your own accounts, you don't have the finances to fly to Jamaica for a vacation?"

"Objection!" Goldstein sat forward, his stare penetrated the wall behind the lawyers on the other end of the table. "Save that for a trial, counselor."

"It's OK, Miss Mann. No need to answer that question. I think we have a clear picture of what we need."

Monica shook her head.

For the next two hours, they talked about what she did on the island in reference to her job. Easy questions and in Monica's head, nothing damning.

When they took a fifteen-minute break, Monica turned to Goldstein. "Why don't they ask how I can afford you?"

"My guess is they already figured that out."

"Wouldn't my sister and Jack dispel the questions of my using Borderless Nurses for a free ride?"

"That depends. Have you ever taken money from your sister in the past? Asked to use their air accommodations for your own personal use?"

"Of course not. It was hard enough asking that they help me out with this."

Goldstein raised a brow. "All of which would be brought out in court. They don't have the actual answers to those questions, and they don't want to look like the idiots here. They'll ask for your bank statements, credit card statements, phone records."

"I have to show them all this?"

"You do if you want to keep your license. Your job."

She shuddered. "I feel violated."

Goldstein placed a reassuring hand on her shoulder. "Try not to show it. If they think you're weak, they'll pounce."

"Why? It's them trying to screw me. I should be suing them for unlawful termination, slander."

"Pain and suffering," Goldstein's second hand said behind her back.

"Exactly."

Goldstein gestured to his colleague, who placed his briefcase on the table and removed a stack of papers.

"I've taken the liberty of having these drawn up." He handed the packet to Monica. She glanced at them, confused.

"What is it?"

"The papers to file suit."

Her eyes slowly looked up. "Seriously?"

"Right now they think of themselves as the hunters. As long as they think they have a case they'll continue. When they're done they will either mess up your life just to walk away, or they will *violate* you and walk away. Or *violate* you, pay you for your trouble, and walk away. Your call."

Hell yeah. These assholes shouldn't get away with this.

Monica held out her hand. "Does someone have a pen?"

"We'll file them at lunch," Goldstein told her.

If Monica thought she was violated before the personal questions began, she was wrong.

They didn't bother with any easing into the personal when they reconvened.

"Did you have an affair on the island?"

She swallowed. "Yes."

"How could you have had time for an affair if you were busy every minute of every day?"

"I had to sleep, eat?"

"Having an affair is more than sleeping and eating."

"That's not a question," Goldstein stated.

"How many days were you in Jamaica?"

"Six before we were trapped in the cave. Five after."

"And of those, how many did you see your lover?"

Monica clutched her hands at her side to stop from throwing a punch. Since when had she become so ready to hit someone? "He wasn't my lover the whole time."

"Answer the question."

It wasn't possible for her to answer the question without it damning her. "He flew the helicopter to the main hospital the first day there. Early the next he was my ride to the clinic. The clinic that didn't have any place for me to sleep except beside my patients."

"So you decided to sleep somewhere else?"

"Trent offered a bed, to sleep. I was exhausted."

The lawyers smiled at each other.

Monica wondered if she could sue them all twice.

"So the third day you spent with your lover?"

"He wasn't my lover then."

Hudson ran a hand through his thinning hair and sneered.

"Since there is no one to agree or disagree with that point—"

Goldstein broke in. "We'll call the man by his name for the record. Skip the dramatics, counselors. It's common knowledge that Miss Mann and Mr. Fairchild were rescued together. Miss Mann has told you of her brief affair. Get to the point."

"Did you see *Mr. Fairchild* daily while in Jamaica?"

"Yes," she muttered.

Hudson leaned back, smug. "I think that's all for now."

The woman on their team offered a smile to Goldstein. "We'll break for twenty and bring in the next witness."

Goldstein nodded.

Everyone stood, except Monica, who felt her knees shaking so badly she didn't think they would hold her weight.

Once the other lawyers left the room, Goldstein helped Monica to her feet. "You did well, Monica."

"Really? They made me sound like a whore."

Goldstein offered a sympathetic look. "I'm sorry for that."

Not half as sorry as she was. She reached in her purse and sent a quick text to Katie to let her know she was finished. "I'm exhausted."

"Go home, rest."

"What's next?"

"We have one more depo today. We're meeting with Dr. Eddy tomorrow, and flying to Kansas to meet with Dr. Klein in two days to obtain his statement."

Stiff from sitting, her leg didn't cooperate as she took a few steps toward the door. Goldstein lent his arm to help. He opened the huge wooden doors to the law office to let her out. "I have it from here," she told him.

"You sure?"

She ignored the pain and took a step out the door without his aid. "I'm good. Thank you."

He stepped into the hallway with her as she turned around.

She gasped and held her hand out when her gaze collided with Trent's.

Goldstein took hold of her arm again, and kept her from falling. Trent stood outside the door of the lawyers' office looking nothing like the man she'd met on the island. He wore a three-piece suit that rivaled her attorney's. His hair had been cut short, much more than it had been when she met him. He was just as tan, just as magnificent as she remembered. His eyes sparkled with appreciation before something clouded over them. "Barefoot?" she whispered.

Chapter Twenty-Four

Trent thought he was prepared to see her again.

He wasn't.

"Monica," he said her name, tasted her on his lips.

The man at her side stepped forward and reached out a hand. "You must be Mr. Fairchild."

Monica moved aside and watched him.

"Larry Goldstein. We spoke on the phone."

Ah, the lawyer. Trent shook the man's hand.

"Wait, you two spoke?" Monica asked.

Mr. Goldstein nodded. "Early this morning."

They all had to step aside as someone from inside the office exited. Monica stumbled and Trent shot a hand out to hold her up.

Her lawyer held her as well. "Are you sure you're OK to walk downstairs?"

Trent's hand and arm sizzled with the contact.

"I'm fine," Monica said. "The more I move, the better it gets."

Trent's gaze moved down her leg. A thin pink line where they'd put her back together, peeked from under her skirt. A skirt that hugged her too-thin curves. She'd lost weight. He had too, but managed to put it back on after leaving the cave.

Mr. Goldstein offered a smile and nodded toward the office. "We'll be inside when you're ready," he told Trent, who hadn't let Monica's arm go.

"Call if you have questions, Monica. We'll be in touch."

He should retreat with the lawyer, but it didn't seem as if Monica was rushing off and Trent couldn't let her leave without seeing her smile again.

Why torture yourself, Trent? he asked himself as if he were on the outside looking in. *She belongs to someone else.*

Without realizing what he did, he glanced at her left hand and noticed it bare.

"I'm sorry they're dragging you into this," she said as she took a step back.

He let his hand drop or risk looking as if he was holding her.

"I'm hardly a hostile witness," he said.

"Still, I'm sure you have better things to do."

"Not really." Why had he admitted that?

"Oh? You seemed to be in a hurry to leave Florida." She sucked in her lip, as if wishing she hadn't uttered her words. "I thought you'd say good-bye."

Was that pain in her eyes?

"I tried."

She pinched her brow together.

"I went to the ICU. Your fiancé was there." He'd gone over their conversations so many times. Remembered her saying that she didn't mess around with two guys at the same time. Yet when faced with a man claiming her as his, Trent stepped aside.

Her face went white. "M-my what?"

He swallowed. "Never mind."

"Never mind? What are you talking about? I don't have a fiancé." Her voice was elevated now and her pale skin turned pink with what Trent assumed was anger.

"The guy in the ICU told me he was—"

"John? John told you we were engaged?"

"Yes."

"And you believed him?" She was enraged now and controlling her words as they left her mouth slowly.

Maybe not now. Damn, could he have been wrong?

The ding from the elevator kept him from answering the question. Out of it walked a tall, slender blonde with dark sunglasses over her eyes. "There you are," the blonde said. "I thought I was meeting you outside."

Monica blinked and dismissed him. "Sorry, Katie. I was detained." Monica stepped toward the woman she called Katie with an obvious limp.

Trent reached for her again.

Monica snapped out of his grip as soon as he touched her. Her glare kept him from reaching for her again. "I have it, Trent!"

His insides twisted. Could he have spent the last two months accusing her of being just like Connie only to find out he was wrong?

Katie removed her glasses and stepped to Monica's side. "Trent Fairchild?"

Monica nodded. "C'mon Katie. I've had a shitty day and can't wait to get home."

Katie glared in Trent's direction as she helped Monica walk away.

"Monica?" Trent walked between the two of them and the elevator. "We should talk."

"Why? So you can pretend to listen and then think the worst of me later? I don't have anything to say to you."

The door behind them opened. "Mr. Fairchild? We're ready for you."

He glanced away when he heard his name. Dammit, he'd screwed up. So completely screwed up.

"Monica, please."

Monica gripped Katie's arm. "Let's get out of here."

Trent had no choice but to let her go. As they stepped into the elevator, Monica studied the floor and Katie dug a hole into him with her glare, and buried him six feet under.

———— · ————

Jessie held the phone to her ear and tried to make out what Katie was saying.

"I don't know what I interrupted. Monica looked as if she were about to commit a serious crime when I stepped out of the elevator."

"And you said Trent was there?" Jessie asked.

"Yeah, looking like someone had just taken his puppy. I don't care what anyone thinks, there were some serious vibes going between them."

Jessie smiled. "Good vibes?"

"Deadly ones. At least from Monica. Trent looked like he wanted to throw up."

"And Monica hasn't told you what happened?"

"Said she didn't want to talk about it."

Sounded like her sister. When something really bugged her, she clammed up. "She's mad?"

"At first. Then I heard her in the bathroom sniffling, and she doesn't have a cold."

"Crying? She was crying?" Now Jessie was worried. "Monica doesn't cry over anything."

"I know."

"You didn't leave her alone did you?"

"I'm on my way back with wine . . . and ice cream. I told Dean I was staying over so she won't be home alone tonight."

Jessie sighed. "I'll fly in tomorrow."

"Good. I'm pulling into the parking lot now."

Katie hung up and Jessie called their pilot.

———

Trent's head was still spinning as he sat next to Monica's lawyers. Across from the sharks trying to paint her as something other than the angel he knew.

Dammit, what had he done? How could he have thought of her as anything but an angel?

Mr. Goldstein had told him this wouldn't take long. But that it was imperative he do this face-to-face.

What Trent really wanted to do was find Monica and make sure she was all right. Explain.

Explain what? What an asshole I am?

"Mr. Fairchild can you tell us, for the record, where you're currently living."

Trent told them his brother's address since he had yet to set up his own residence since leaving Jamaica.

"You do own a home in Jamaica?"

"That's right. I left the island after the quake."

The woman, Leslie something or other, smiled and asked, "And you fly helicopters for tourists?"

"That's right."

"When did you meet Monica Mann?"

"Two days after the first quake. We were flying the medical staffs back and forth to the hospital."

"You'd never met her before?" the fat lawyer asked.

"No."

They paused. "Are you sure?"

Trent felt a smile on his lips. "She's a beautiful woman, I would have remembered seeing her before."

"Assuming what you say is correct, when did you start sleeping with her?"

"Objection!" Mr. Goldstein sounded just as pissed as Trent felt. "If you're going to call my witness a liar then we will end this now and you can find out what he has to say in court."

Leslie held up her hands in retreat. "When did you and Miss Mann become intimate?"

"I don't see how that is anyone's business." He'd left high school and bragging about girls a long time ago.

"Just answer, Trent. Monica has already told them," Mr. Goldstein said.

"The day the cave collapsed, trapping us inside."

"But you spent nearly every day with Miss Mann."

"So?"

"You said yourself she's a beautiful woman."

"Is there a question?"

The oldest attorney opened his mouth. "Isn't it true that you frequently flew in and out of Florida while living in Jamaica?"

"The tour company has a base there. It wasn't uncommon for me to fly into Miami or Fort Lauderdale."

"Were you there a year and a half ago?"

Trent shrugged. "I don't remember."

"That's convenient."

Mr. Goldstein shook his head.

Trent stared at Monica's attorney. "What are they getting at?"

Mr. Goldstein turned to the court reporter. "We'll take this part off the record."

The tiny woman rested her hands in her lap and waited.

"Monica was in Florida a year and a half ago for training. They believe you two met then."

"That's ridiculous. Even if we had," he turned toward the trio of shitheads, "what of it?"

"They think Monica took the assignment to Jamaica to obtain a free ticket to meet you."

Trent couldn't help it. He laughed. He laughed until his insides started to cramp. Mr. Goldstein chuckled alongside him.

Trent waved a hand at the court reporter once he got himself under control. "Can you get this?"

"Now that you're finished," Leslie said. "What—"

"Ask me what I do for a living," Trent demanded.

"You already told us you flew helicopters for a tour company."

Trent's smile fell. He slammed his hand on the table. Everyone jumped. "Ask."

"OK, Mr. Fairchild, what do you do for a living?"

He leveled his eyes with the older silent lawyer, the one who seemed to ask a minimum of questions but who appeared to be in charge of these two. "Nothing. I don't have to work."

"You said you flew—"

"The company I fly for is one my brothers and I own, Fairchild Vacation and Charter Tours. We have twenty-five locations world-wide in seven different countries. In addition to helicopters, which just happen to be my favorite to fly, we have executive jets that hold anything from four passengers to sixty." The other lawyers were listening now and Mr. Goldstein sat with a smug look of contentment. "If I wanted to hook up with Miss Mann she wouldn't have needed a free ticket. I'd have sent the Lear, that is worth more than any of you sharks will make collectively in your lives, to pick her up."

The vein in the fat man's face started to bulge.

Trent could have heard an ant crossing the room in the silence.

The older attorney recovered first. "Nice performance, Mr. Fairchild. But we're here not only to determine what nefarious reasons Miss Mann had in going to Jamaica, but to determine if she in fact abandoned her post both here and on the island. The fact is, she did take a lover, left her patients to do so—"

"Objection!"

"—and worked outside her license."

Mr. Goldstein stood and slammed his hand down this time. "Objection."

The lawyers faced each other.

"We're done," the opposing lawyer managed.

The court reporter was the first one to move as she gathered her things. Trent reeled in his anger and understood how drained Monica must have been after hours of this. Trent had only been there for one.

Each one of them stood and started to leave the room. Before the other team made it to the door, Mr. Goldstein stopped them.

"Mr. Richardson?"

So that was the old guy's name.

"Yes, counselor?"

Mr. Goldstein handed a stack of papers to the other attorney. "You'll get these through the proper channels of course, but I couldn't help but hand-deliver them myself."

Mr. Richardson opened the file. A flicker of doubt flashed so quickly Trent would have missed it had he blinked. Then the others walked away.

Once alone, Trent asked, "What was that?"

"Monica's suing."

That made him smile. "Good."

Mr. Goldstein gathered his papers, stacked them in his brief-case. The two other lawyers on his team shook Trent's hand and left the office.

"I'm hoping that after today they drop the case and settle the suit quietly."

"There's no possible way they'd win."

"They won't win. But the longer it draws out, the harder it will be for Monica. She's a lot more vulnerable than she looks."

Trent remembered her in the cave, the fear in her voice when he tried to scale the unscalable wall. "She's tough."

"Maybe the woman you knew on the island was. The one I know is fragile. If this draws out, she's going to need every penny we can squeeze out of these people. Talk about no good deed going unpunished."

"You're not kidding." If Monica ever decided to help others again, she'd do it with gloves and body armor.

Chapter Twenty-Five

"You see, Trent, I've gotten mighty attached to my balls over the years, and if I plan on keeping them, I can't go telling you where my wife's sister is. She's downright protective of her baby sister."

Trent gripped his cell phone while sitting in the parking lot of the law offices of Old, Fat, and Uptight. He hadn't even twisted the key in the ignition before he called Jack Morrison to learn Monica's address.

"I dropped everything and rushed down here—"

"Which I'm sure you understand now was important," Jack interrupted.

"I need to talk to her, Jack."

"Hold on."

Trent heard Jack over the line talking to Jessie.

"Jessie, darlin', Trent's on the phone asking for Monica's address."

Trent envisioned Jack holding the phone up making it clear that Jessie knew Trent was waiting on the phone.

"If you know what's good for you, you'd hang up that phone and help me pack."

"Did you hear that?" Jack asked when he got back on the phone. "You know what they say, happy wife, happy life."

"I'm not leaving LA until I have a chance to talk to her."

"Suit yourself. You staying at our hotel?"

"Yeah."

"I'll make sure the girls know where to find you."

"The girls?"

"Yeah, Jessie's on her way there, and Katie, my sister, lives there."

"Great!" Trent hissed between his teeth.

Jack chuckled. "Good luck."

And he hung up, leaving Trent to stare at his phone.

"Wine is the answer to heartbreak. That and ice cream," said Katie as she shoved a spoonful of mint chip between her lips and followed it with a swig of Chardonnay.

"I'm not heartbroken!"

Katie topped off Monica's glass. "Bless your heart, why don't you have another glass and tell me how unheartbroken you are."

Monica sipped from her second glass and felt some of the tension in her shoulders dissipate. "He thought I was engaged. Me? Engaged! Stupid man."

"Trent?"

Monica took another drink. "How could he think I was messing around with him and have someone back home? Who does that?"

Katie lifted a knowing brow. "Well, actually . . . a lot of—"

"But this is *me* we're talking about! I don't fly that way." Monica thought about the lawyers, their accusations. "They treated me like I was a slut."

Katie nearly spit out her wine. "Trent?"

"No, not Trent. The lawyers. Kept calling him my lover. Said I'd purposely agreed to go to Jamaica for a free plane ride to the island. Acted as if I needed a fucking booty call."

Katie laughed.

Monica glared at her. "It's not funny."

"It will be when they find out who Trent Fairchild is."

Monica dipped her spoon in the double Dutch chocolate and asked, "What do you mean *who* he is?"

"A Fairchild."

Maybe it was the wine, but she wasn't following Katie's line of thought. "I don't get it."

"Fairchild Charters . . . Fairchild Vacations." Katie dropped her spoon. "You don't know who he is?"

"Well, of course I know who he is. He owns the helicopter tours on the island. But he's not going to be booking tours there anytime soon." She sipped more wine.

"Oh, bless your heart, you have no idea who he really is."

"I do, and stop with that *bless your heart* crap. I may not be from the South but even I know that's your way of calling me an idiot."

"If the shoe fits."

Monica tossed a pillow at her friend. "I liked it better when you were trying hard not to have an accent and southern roots."

"I can't help it. Dean's family is so down home. When we all get to drinking and shooting the shit, the South in me just comes out. I'll blame the wine." Katie's cheeks were rosy with wine and the twang in her voice became more apparent.

"Well, my southern belle, why don't you tell me why I'm an idiot."

Katie set her glass on the table, but only to add more liquid to the glass. "I think we need popcorn."

"Katie!"

She stood and followed Katie into the kitchen as she pulled out the microwave variety of uncooked kernels, removed the plastic wrap, and tossed it in to cook. "Where's your tablet?"

"Charging on my desk."

"Well go get it and look up Fairchild Charters."

Monica grabbed her Kindle Fire and accessed the Internet. She typed in Fairchild Charters and the website popped up. At first glance, she thought she typed in the wrong IP address. Then she looked closer. The page was sleek and featured a rotating banner of jets available to charter. Monica dropped in the chair at the kitchen counter and clicked through a few pages. When she found the About Us page there was one group shot, and then three individual pictures of the co-owners. Jason Fairchild, Owner & CEO Fairchild Charters & Fairchild Vacation Tours, Glen Fairchild, Owner & CFO Fairchild Charters, and Trent Fairchild, Owner & CFO of Fairchild Vacation Tours.

She blinked. The picture of Trent and his brothers had been taken on a sunny tarmac in front of the largest private jet Monica had ever seen. The Fairchild men were all the same height, with bright smiles and sunglasses hiding what Monica knew were laughing eyes. What a hunk of trouble they must have been in school. She thought of the story Trent told her about hijacking his father's chopper.

The individual pictures had the guys wearing those hats that pilots were fond of. Jason, the oldest brother according to the bio, lived close to their headquarters and ran the company. Glen, the middle son from what Monica could tell, looked like a player of the highest order. His smirk in the photo reminded her of Trent. He ran the financials and coordinated the jet charter end of the company. Monica found her mouth hanging open when she noticed the number of locations their planes flew out of. Then there was Trent. He had his jacket tossed over his shoulder as he posed for the picture in front of a huge helicopter. His smile played on her hot buttons and reminded her of his smooth voice and unforgettable kiss.

"He's rich," she all but whispered to her tablet as she clicked around to learn more about him.

"Ah, yeah! Daddy's worked with the Fairchilds for years."

Monica glanced at Katie. "You know them?"

"Never met 'em." Katie retrieved Monica's glass and set it in front of her. "My dad knew their dad."

"Before he died?"

"Yeah."

Another link took her to island tours. There she found a more recent picture of Trent wearing the clothes she associated with him. Shorts, a company pullover short-sleeved shirt, and flip-flops. "How come he didn't tell me he was all this?"

Katie leaned against the counter and set the bowl of popcorn between them. "Guys brag about stuff like that to get laid."

Monica stared at the picture of Trent. "He didn't need to brag to get laid."

The room grew quiet and when she glanced at Katie, her friend studied her with sad eyes. "Was it great?"

"Trent?"

"Yeah, Trent." The *bless your heart* was implied.

She allowed the silly grin to spread. "I didn't know sex could be like that. Where you feel it from head to toe and so many ricochets in the middle you know it can't be real. Then you open your eyes and he's still there, smiling . . . feeling it too."

"Sounds perfect."

If it was so perfect then why did he run off? "Then the walls collapse, you almost die, and he runs off at the first hurdle. Must not have been so *perfect* for him." She tipped her glass again.

"Asshole!" Katie yelled.

"Fucktard!"

Katie giggled. "Fucktard is such a funny word."

Monica drove the melancholy away with alternating sugary and salty bites. Katie cursed Trent with one breath, then poked a little more and sighed into the warm parts of their story, until Monica was certain Katie could write a book on the romance that wasn't.

They polished off nearly three bottles of wine by the time Monica made it to bed. She had no problem falling asleep with her fuzzy brain.

Seeing Trent again led to dreams so real Monica could smell them in her sleep. When she revisited the moment the rocks fell on her, she looked over and saw Trent lying lifeless under the rubble. She woke screaming his name. Her heart raced from too much wine and too many memories. She flipped over, desperate to chase away the dark.

Katie ran into her room and Monica lost it.

The tears she'd been pushing back all night fell.

———

Jessie no sooner met Monica's doorstep than Katie whisked her away after leaving a note on Monica's fridge saying she went for a walk.

"She's asleep?"

"Finally fell off a couple of hours ago. Oh, Jessie, it's worse than I thought."

They'd only gone a few blocks and Jessie wanted to turn around. "Then we need to be with her."

"You need to hear this first."

Katie almost never left home without polish, and here Jessie looked into the eyes of her millionaire sister-in-law with hair that had barely been tied back in a ponytail and not a stitch of makeup and knew it had to be bad. "Don't stop now."

"She loves him. I mean really loves him."

"C'mon, she knew him for two weeks. Monica falls in bed with guys, but not love."

Katie stuck out her hand. "Five bucks?"

Jessie shook her head and shook Katie's hand. "Sucker's bet. Tell me what you know."

"Yesterday was awful. Those punk lawyers should be horse-whipped for what they put her through." Katie recapped the deposition for Jessie, leaving her angry.

"She wasn't expecting Trent."

"Did he say why he ran off?"

"Remember a guy named John?"

Jessie hesitated as they turned a corner in her old neighborhood. "Yeah. Oh, wait, Trent saw John and got the wrong idea?"

"Worse. John told Trent they were engaged."

Jessie stopped that time. "Shut up!"

Katie nodded slowly. "So Trent, feeling like a third wheel, runs off."

Jessie started marching again. "Monica doesn't need a man who's going to run off at the first sign of trouble."

"It's not like that."

"What's it like then?"

"I couldn't sleep last night. I looked up old stories about the Fairchilds. Trent's parents were killed in a plane crash a few years ago along with a woman."

"OK?"

"I haven't confirmed it, but this married woman was listed as a friend of the Fairchilds' only her *husband* didn't know them." Katie looked as if she was sitting on a pile of answers but Jessie was a little lost.

"Help me connect the dots, Katie."

"I need Jack to talk to Trent's brothers. I think there is more to the story about who else was on the plane when it went down. Right after the accident Trent moved to Jamaica."

"You think Trent loved the woman?"

Katie shrugged.

"And she was married to someone else?"

"Happily, according to the papers. But the whole thing stinks. Like there's a story there not being told."

Jessie turned the block and headed back to Monica's. "OK, so let's say Trent loved this woman. If he knew she was married then why was he troubled to think Monica was hooked up with someone else? A guy who helps a wife cheat . . ." she shivered. Again, all lines drawn said this Trent guy wasn't the one for Monica.

Katie held Jessie back. "What if Trent didn't know she was married?"

Jessie froze. "You think that's possible?"

"Does every cheating wife tell her lover she's married?"

Jessie blinked a few times.

"I've known men who said they were single just to get laid when they had a wife back home."

"That's awful," Jessie said.

"If men lie, women lie. And if you were Trent and you thought Monica was ready to marry someone else and playing around in Jamaica, wouldn't you run far, far away if you felt bad shit happening again?"

"We don't know if that's true." But there was doubt hovering over Jessie's mind.

"We need to find out, hence my thought that Jack needs to talk to Trent's brothers."

He sure did.

They were nearly back at the apartment when Katie stopped Jessie again. "One more thing."

There's more? Her poor sister.

"Monica's having nightmares. Woke up last night screaming for Trent and didn't settle until I turned on the light. Then wouldn't go back to sleep without the light on."

Jessie bit back tears. "Oh, Mo."

Chapter Twenty-Six

Trent hesitated when he answered the knock on his door to find Jack Morrison standing on the other side.

"Morrison?" The knowing smile in Jack's eyes told Trent the man was there for a reason.

"Fairchild!" Jack glanced behind him and nodded outside the room. "Can I buy you a drink?"

It was noon. "Sure." Trent retrieved his wallet and key, left his room, and followed Jack.

"How's your stay?"

"Everything I expected, Mr. Morrison."

Jack chuckled, tipped his Stetson farther back on his head. In the elevator, he waved a passkey over a sensor Trent didn't see and instead of the elevator taking them to the bar on the ground floor, it ascended.

Saying nothing, Trent rocked on his heels and waited for his host to lead the way.

They reached the penthouse level and stepped past a private foyer and into the suite. The room had every amenity Trent expected, plush carpet, hardwood floors, and stone countertops in the open suite, which hosted a kitchen to one side. By Trent's guess, the suite housed a minimum of two bedrooms, maybe three. Impressive.

"What's your poison?" Jack asked as he made his way to the wet bar.

"It's early. How about a beer?"

"Dark or light?"

"Dark."

Jack passed him a beer and twisted a cap off one for himself, took a swig.

"What brings you to LA?" Trent cut the ice with his question.

"Monica."

Trent drank from the dark longneck bottle, hardly tasting the hops and barley the company making it wished he'd taste. "Funny. That's the same name that's keeping me here."

Jack tilted his beer back again, crossed to the plush couch, and sat. Trent followed.

"Yesterday was brutal," Jack stated as if he was there. "Larry gave me a blow-by-blow."

"If you need help paying for those lawyers—"

Jack waved off his offer with a flick of his hand. "After yesterday I might have to insist that Larry take the check. Seems everyone has a soft spot for a nurse."

"He's a lawyer, he'll take it." Though Trent thought perhaps Jack could be right.

"My sister spent the night with Monica."

Trent hung on Jack's word.

When Trent didn't say anything, Jack continued. "Then this morning my wife calls me, tells me to call your brothers."

That got Trent's attention.

"I couldn't exactly tell my wife that men didn't work that way. And she better not find out from you that I didn't bother with a call to your relations."

Trent held up a hand. "Man code is safe with me."

Regardless of how women might operate, men simply did it differently. Women might go behind, around, over, and under others, but men went straight to the source.

Jack hesitated, acted as if he wasn't going to continue.

"What did your wife . . . it's Jessie, right?"

"Yeah."

"What did Jessie ask you to find out from my brothers?"

Jack drank his beer a little quick for just after noon. He obviously wasn't sure if he should say anything to Trent.

"Monica's having nightmares."

Trent gripped his bottle and lowered it to his lap. "What kind of nightmares?"

"The kind that make you scream, wake up, and chase away all the bad with a bright light."

The half smile that had been on his face the entire time he'd been in Jack's presence slid, as did Trent's gaze. He drew in a shuddering breath.

"I don't think Jessie wanted you to tell my brothers that."

Jack set his empty bottle to the side, crossed one ankle over his knee. "The girls are smart. Wicked smart."

Trent knew Monica was sharp already.

"Somewhere between scoops of ice cream and glasses of wine, my sister decided you ran from Florida because you were spooked."

It was Trent's turn to drink his beer.

Jack continued, staying within the man code of not making the other guy talk about his *feelings*. "Katie asked Jessie, who asked me, to find out the details about your parents' unfortunate passing."

Trent's head started to pound and the desire for his beer to turn into something stronger nearly made him head to the bar.

"More importantly, the woman who died along with Beverly and Marcus."

Hearing his parents' names made him cringe. He swallowed half his beer in one drink.

After a few minutes of reflective silence, Trent said, "Your family must blow every surprise you ever try and pass by them."

Jack laughed at that. "Katie's the worst. Hires a stealth PI when she needs information."

Trent flipped his gaze to Jack.

"Though she hasn't gotten that far . . . yet," Jack said.

Trent finished his beer. If the women in Monica's life had somehow figured out his past, it was only a matter of time before they told Monica.

"Monica's dad left when she was a kid," Jack told him.

"She told me that."

"It impacted both Jessie and Monica. It's hard for them to trust and depend on anyone. Especially men. After Jamaica, I'm not sure Monica will trust anyone again."

Trent wasn't sure what to say to that. He hadn't meant to blow Monica's trust. They were barely getting to know each other and everything went to a dark, hungry hell.

"I like you, Trent. You seem like a good guy. But Monica . . . hell, she's family. I love that girl and she needs someone who isn't going to run off without an explanation. If you get my meaning."

Loud and clear, cowboy.

"So, are you going to give me an address?"

Jack shook his head.

"No. That would be too easy." This little "get to know the real you" session only went so far.

"Remember our earlier conversation?" Jack indicated his balls. "I've grown used to them. No. You can't get Monica's address from me."

Dammit.

Jack readjusted his hat and said absentmindedly, "She did work at Pomona General. Hung out at Joe's Bar around the corner after her shift once in a while. Had to work those nasty twelve-hour shifts. Hard to find a night without someone on staff hanging out after say . . . seven thirty at night. I'm sure nurses were real good about designating a driver."

A half smile met Trent's lips as he stood. He had hours to kill before seven thirty. "Have you had lunch?"

"I could eat." Jack stood, tucked his hat farther on his head, and walked beside Trent as they left the suite.

———

Joe's was one loose brick short of a dive. Yet, as Trent glanced around the room, the dive portion was restricted to the outdated décor, wood paneling, and crappy lighting. To be a true dive, Joe's needed the scent of stale beer and a resident drunk hanging off the bar. On second look, it just needed the stale beer. The guy at the bar looked as if he'd been there since noon.

Finding the ER staff wasn't difficult. Something about the uniform gave away hospital employees like nothing else. Instead of waltzing over to the table of scrubs and stethoscopes, Trent found a stool at the bar, flagged the bartender for a beer, and watched.

He twisted around to thank the bartender and found a hand on his shoulder.

"Trent?" Walt stood beside him, holding out his hand. "I thought that was you walking in."

Standing, Trent shook Walt's hand complete with a hearty pat on the back. "Monica said you guys hung out here once in a while." *Little white lie number one.* Wasn't it Monica who tutored him on telling white lies?

"Is she here?" Walt looked around the room.

"No, her sister is here from out of town. Thought I'd give them some alone time."

"You're staying with her?"

"Yeah." That lie bordered on gray. Walt bought it.

"I thought you two might hook up." He looked like he wanted to say more. "And I owe you a drink."

"I'm not one to pass up free beer." Trent pulled his beer to his lips and downed it.

Walt waved the bartender over. "Hey Roy, can you hit him again . . . on me? I'll have my usual."

Roy nodded.

"Let me introduce you to some of the staff, then let's find a quiet table. I'd like to know your take on what the hell is happening with Monica."

There were six ER employees at their table.

"Hey guys. This is Trent. He flew the helicopter in Jamaica."

Walt started naming names, all of which Trent quickly forgot. A pretty brunette smiled. "You're the guy that was in the cave with Monica."

"Yeah," he confirmed.

"We have some catching up to do," Walt told his friends.

The staff murmured and watched him as he and Walt ducked to a quiet corner of the bar.

"Seem like a good group of people," Trent said as they took their seats.

"They are."

The bartender brought their drinks and disappeared.

Trent took a drink and then stared into the glass. "Damn, maybe I shouldn't drink this."

"Why?" Walt tested his cocktail.

"I've already had a couple and I'm driving."

Walt waved him off. "I'm not far from Monica's. I'll give you a ride."

Trent smiled, sucked the foam off his beer, and looked around for the large red button . . . the one that said *that was easy* when you pressed it.

"Half the staff is ready to quit," Walt told him. "The union is awaiting the depositions to complete and if they like what they see, they're going to rally a protest."

"A strike?"

"No. But signs, banners . . . bad PR for the hospital." Walt nibbled on the peanuts as he talked.

The thought of that kind of support put a smile on Trent's face. "How many people do you think will participate?"

"Nearly all the ER staff, those who aren't working that is, techs from radiology, lab, the trauma surgeons, and then there are the guys from fire."

"Wow. Does Monica know about this?"

"I don't think so. Like I said, the union is holding off until the preliminary legal crap is over. I'm not sure of their logic. Seems to me that the sooner we put this shit behind us the better. I'd really like to know why the hospital is pursuing this."

"Monica's boss doesn't like her."

"Pat's not loved right now."

"Was she ever?" Trent asked, remembering the name from Monica's conversations in the cave.

"Managing independent-thinking nurses isn't easy. Especially when you have management on one side pulling on you to cut costs, nurses on the other hand telling you they're understaffed, and unions mandating what you can and can't do. The average length of employment for an ER nurse manager is less than five years."

"How long has Pat been there?"

"Nearly six."

"Past due."

Walt shrugged. "So how's Monica doing?"

Trent could only replay their last encounter, but if he let Walt think he was lying about staying with her, Trent wouldn't get his ride. So he bullshitted with educated guesses based on what he'd learned from Jack at lunch.

"The deposition knocked her back. But her lawyers are brutal. Jack put his top guys on her case. When they're done, the hospital and anyone slandering her are going to run away with their tail between their legs." His voice rose as he spoke.

"It's so wrong. And the shit about working outside her license? What a bunch of crap. We try to protect our nurses with every contingency. Give standing orders for patient care. Not every scenario is thought of. Hell, there wasn't enough of anything to carry out all our orders. Not quite enough medicine, not quite enough hands, not quite enough room to put the patients . . . the bodies." Walt shuddered, took another drink. "Not quite enough of anything."

Walt sat through another beer and nursed his one drink while they talked about Jamaica before turning their conversation to sports to avoid the memories.

The ride to Monica's apartment complex wasn't long. Once there, Trent thanked his driver and offered to drive the next time they went out. Walt drove off with a wave and Trent walked over to the mailboxes. Only last names were listed on the boxes. He was damn happy her last name wasn't Gonzalez or he'd have been knocking on doors half the night.

He found her name and apartment number with a grin. Between here and Seattle, Trent had turned into quite the investigator.

If the airplane thing doesn't work out, I have new skills to exploit.

It was just before nine at night and the apartment complex was relatively quiet. He heard music playing from one of the upstairs units and more than one TV cluttering up the quiet. But there weren't any obvious parties going on or loud fights spilling into the street.

He found Monica's apartment and sucked in a deep breath before knocking on the door.

He heard the volume on the TV from inside go down. *Good, she's home.*

When he didn't hear her walking toward the door, Trent knocked again and stood back so she could see his face through the peephole.

"Go away, Trent," she said through the closed door.

Damn. It didn't occur to him that he'd find her only to be sent away.

Chapter Twenty-Seven

Monica leaned her head against the door and closed her eyes.

"I shouldn't have run off," he said through the door. "Let me explain."

"You don't owe me any explanations." And she'd just bullied her sister and Katie into leaving an hour before. Emotionally, she was exhausted. It didn't help that last night's wine reminded her of why she didn't drink that much. "Just go." She turned away from the door, ready to follow through with what she needed, which wasn't to hash out anything with Trent tonight.

"Her name was Connie."

Monica stopped.

"I'd flown her over to see me, to meet my parents since I thought I loved her enough to marry her. She was furious. Didn't want to meet my family. And then she told me there was someone else."

Monica brought her hand to her mouth. His words soaked in.

"I had no idea. I asked my parents to fly her back home. They never made it, Monica. The plane went down—"

Monica grabbed the door and opened it wide, stopping his painful flow of words.

Trent stood with his hands poised on either side of her door, his head down.

She tugged him inside her apartment, glanced around the outside to see if anyone had witnessed Trent's explanation, and then closed the door.

He stood in place staring at her. The usual smile on his face was absent. "When John told me you were engaged, I ran."

It took very few words to bring to light his swift departure and give Monica a reason to open the door of communication.

She tilted her head to the side and sighed. "Can I get you something to drink?"

He smiled now. "Coffee would be nice."

She stepped around him and into the kitchen. Preparing the coffee gave her the equilibrium she needed to clear her head. Trent seemed to be waiting for her to say something, so she asked, "How did you and Connie meet?"

He sat on a stool and stared off at the wall. For a second, Monica wasn't sure he was going to answer her question. "I was flying a lot. Personally overseeing some of the pilots we were using within the company. Connie was a flight attendant."

"Did she work for you?"

"No," he said with a quick shake of his head. "Domestic flights. Her main hub was in Chicago, but we only saw each other there once in the six months we dated. I'd join her all over the country, but not Chicago."

"Because she was married?"

He winced. "Yeah. The night before the crash, I picked her up in Virginia and brought her home to meet the parents. It was a surprise. I thought women liked that stuff." He offered a joyless laugh. "She wasn't happy. It was then she told me there was someone in Chicago. I didn't know the someone was a husband until after the crash."

"How could you have known?"

"I realized later the signs were there." He sounded disgusted with himself.

"But you loved her. Love is blind I'm told."

"I thought I did." Trent looked directly at Monica now, his eyes softened. "But I was wrong. If I had loved her then I would have mourned her. Sure, at first I was so damn mad and dead inside over my parents. Everyone told me it wasn't my fault, but I was the one who asked my dad to fly her home. I couldn't do it." The words flew from his mouth.

"You blamed yourself. That's normal." The psych nurse in her was coming out.

"I missed my parents." He paused, took a breath. "I never missed her. If I loved her, I would have missed her after the anger faded."

"She screwed you over. It's hard to care about someone like that." Monica was mad for him.

He shook his head, as if shaking off what Monica was saying. "After, whenever I dated, or found myself attracted to a woman, I always made sure they knew I was temporary. I think the island helped me with that lifestyle. Vacationing women either do so with their husbands or their girlfriends. Very few married women take off with their friends until they're hitting the cougar age."

Monica laughed at that. "I can see the cougars going after you."

He smiled at that, and Monica felt the hair on her arms go up. Ignoring his effect, she turned toward the coffee pot and poured him a cup.

She set it on the counter in front of him. When he took the cup, his fingers grazed hers and those upended hairs grew to tingles across her shoulders, up her neck, and down her spine.

She moved her hand away, but Trent kept hold of her with a soft grip.

Their eyes met and Monica's lower lip trembled.

"I missed you," he whispered. "Even when I thought you were someone else's, I *missed* you."

The lump in her throat was hard to swallow. "You can't tell me you love me. We hardly know each other."

"I don't know what to call the feelings inside of me. But for the first time I want a chance to explore something more permanent than an island fling."

Oh, damn . . . she did not need Trent to see her cry. On the one hand, she wanted to embrace him and give him a chance, and the other said they were doomed from the start so why put herself through more heartache. "People who go through what we did often have a connection because they survived something traumatic together. What you're feeling might be fleeting."

He was stroking the inside of her wrist. "It might."

She stiffened.

"And it might not," he added. "I had decided to leave the island before you and I were trapped in that cave, remember?"

"Yeah."

"I'm fairly certain I would have needed to fly to LA soon after you returned."

There were serious butterflies taking flight in her belly. "You probably would have called . . . to see if the sparks were still there."

"Oh, they're still there."

He tugged her around the counter and ran a hand up her arm. "What about for you? Are they still there for you?"

"Fishing for a compliment, Barefoot?"

His hand tucked around her waist and pulled her between his spread legs. "Fishing for permission."

She lifted her head and offered her lips, giving him all the permission he needed.

He was soft, sweet, and sensual as he kissed her. Those sparks flew with such bright light she had to close her eyes to contain them. His arms felt so secure as they drew her farther into him. His closed-mouth kisses had her opening to him with tiny licks of her tongue seeking his. Trent moaned, changed his angle, and deepened their connection.

He stood there, holding her, kissing her, forever. When he came up for air, he murmured, "I missed you."

She missed him, too, and the Ice Queen was legendary for flicking off lovers, never missing them. The need to warn him, to protect him had her pulling away. "Trent?"

He didn't let her go far. His kiss lingered on her lips and chased tingles down her jaw.

"Wait," she said, stopping him from moving too fast. "I'm a risk," she said. "I suck at relationships."

His lopsided grin made her melt. "Trying to scare me off?"

"Yeah. No. I think I should warn you. Monica Mann should come with a warning label. Caution, Ice Queen on board. I cut guys out when they get too close." Everyone knew that about her.

Trent ran his hand down her back, and hesitated on her hip before moving back up. "Am I getting too close?"

"You already broke through the imaginary line," she said.

He brought both arms up to hold her face with his hands. "Uncharted territory?"

She nodded, the sheer terror of knowing she didn't want him to leave unsettled her.

"I can deal with that. I *want* to deal with that," he said.

"I'm scared." Her words were barely above a whisper.

"Oh, Monica. Standing outside the door and wondering if you were ever going to open it . . . that was scary. This." He kissed her briefly. "This isn't scary at all."

"What if this, the physical, is all we are?"

He laughed at that and let her go. "We can abstain. Test your theory."

Monica was positive a look of absolute horror passed over her face. "No sex?"

"Sure."

"You're serious."

He seemed to be liking the idea as the seconds ticked by. "Yeah. Why not?"

Had she ever had a romantic relationship without sex? Not since high school, and those dates didn't really count.

"I like kissing you," she confessed.

"Kissing isn't sex," he said and placed a hand on her arm.

"So kissing and holding, but no sex."

He swallowed, his Adam's apple bobbing up and down. "Yeah."

"For how long?"

"Until you know this is more than just physical. Until you stop referring to yourself as the Ice Queen."

Talk about uncharted territory. This was safer, somehow, and if their experiment didn't work Monica would know that she hadn't ruined him for other women.

She reached down and held his hand. "So, what do two people, who want to jump each other's bones, but can't, do on a Tuesday night?"

"I don't know. What were you doing before I came over?"

"I had the TV on, but I was on the Internet."

"Playing games?"

"No. I was searching for schools."

The smile on his face fell. "You're going to get your license back."

She squeezed his arm. "I'm sure you're right. I'm looking into going back to school, getting my masters in nurse practitioners. That way no one will ever be able to accuse me of working outside of my license again."

He motioned toward the couch. "Show me."

They walked to the couch and when she sat down beside Trent he pulled her into his side and looked over her shoulder as she showed him the different schools that offered NP classes. "At first I thought someplace close by. But I'm not going back to Pomona General. I can't, not after all this."

"So where are you thinking?"

"There are a couple places in San Francisco. I'm not sure if I'll like living in the city and it's so expensive." She clicked the next page and Trent pointed at an East Coast location. "That's close to our headquarters."

Monica found herself grinning at him. "There's always San Diego. Warm beaches. Sunshine."

Trent clicked the page back to the East Coast selection. "Don't be afraid of a little snow. Warm fires and hot cocoa. It's an option."

They spent the next couple of hours talking about schools, locations, all the while not having sex.

"I should get some sleep," Monica finally said when it was close to midnight.

"That's my cue, huh?"

Yet she didn't want him to leave.

"I need to call a cab."

"A cab?"

Trent itched the side of his face and glanced at the floor. "Yeah, I left my car at Joe's."

"The bar?"

"Yeah. Kind of a dive."

"Very much a dive. What were you doing there?"

He still didn't look at her. "I may have 'accidentally' run into Walt."

"Accidentally?"

"And I may have told him that you and I hooked up and I was staying with you."

She wanted to be mad at him, but his confession was said with such a cute face all she could do was grin. "Is that right?"

"And I may have had *one too many* and asked him to drive me here."

"Wow. I'm impressed. Seems you got over the *don't tell white lies* rule you had." It was nice to know he worked so hard to find her.

"I guess I did." He stood and stretched his arms over his head with a yawn.

The thought of him leaving emptied something inside her. "It's late. Why don't you just stay?"

He cocked his head to the side. "You sure?"

"Yeah. It's not like we haven't slept beside each other without . . . you know."

"That would have proven difficult under the circumstances."

She closed her laptop and set it aside. "If you want to go back to the hotel . . ."

"I didn't say that."

She wanted to clap but settled for a smile. "You can't sleep naked. That would be like dangling a carrot before the horse."

He lifted a brow. "A carrot?"

"OK a sausage before a bowl of spaghetti."

He busted out laughing. "Not sure that's better."

"I'll take the bathroom first."

When they were both finished freshening up for a night of sleeping and not sex, Trent crawled into bed beside her and pulled her into him. Monica looked over her shoulder and kissed him. "Good night."

"Good night, Monica."

Chapter Twenty-Eight

The first time she woke in the middle of the night, Trent stroked her hair, and helped her fall back asleep. She curled next to him like a cat and murmured his name as she dozed. The second time Trent didn't think she would remember. He felt her stirring beside him and realized he'd rolled over while he slept. Once he pulled her close, she settled.

He sat awake after that for some time. He'd had his share of nightmares since Jamaica, but never more than one in a night, and only a couple per week in the beginning. In the past month he could count on one hand the times his sleep had been interrupted with memories. Although he hoped her restless night was a rarity, he heard Jack's words in his head and knew it probably wasn't.

Trent kissed the top of her head and dropped off again.

The sound of water flowing in the pipes of the apartment woke him. Inside the bathroom he heard Monica humming and Trent felt a smile on his lips. What would it take to slip into the shower with her?

His body responded to the thought and he rolled over with a groan. Had he actually agreed to a no-sex relationship with the most beautiful woman he'd ever known?

God, he must have been desperate last night to agree to that stipulation. Then it dawned on him, he'd suggested it. Maybe he had drunk too much yesterday.

Trent slipped out of Monica's bed, pulled on his pants, and padded with bare feet into her kitchen. He found her supply of coffee and prepared a pot.

The apartment was well laid out. The furniture looked to be new, the flat-screen TV would do a game day proud. There were silk flowers instead of live ones and a few childish art pictures hanging on her refrigerator along with a magnetic picture frame housing the artist. He was sipping his coffee and studying the picture of what Trent thought was a boy holding the leash of either a really big dog, or a very skinny horse. "To Auntie Monica," was written on the bottom followed by, "From Danny."

The fresh floral scent of Monica's skin preceded her into the room. She walked into the kitchen and Trent forgot to breathe. Her skin was pink and scrubbed clean, her face was void of any makeup, and her hair was still wet, dripping. A small bead of water fell down to her shoulder, past the slim spaghetti strap of the small top she wore, and disappeared between her breasts.

He set his cup of coffee down before he dropped it. She wore yoga pants that fit like a second skin. Her toes peeked out from below, with pink sparkly polish finishing her off. As his eyes roamed back to her face he found her hungry gaze on him. She held a towel to her hair but had stopped attempting to dry it as she took a moment to look him over.

One step and he had her up against the wall and his lips on hers. *It's just a morning kiss.* A good-morning-where-have-you-been-all-my-life kiss. She tasted like mint and smelled like spring. His body raged with the need to put more than his tongue in her, but he pushed those thoughts aside and just kissed her.

Just kissing with his hands on her breasts and over the curve of her ass. Her hand fisted in his hair and pulled him tighter and when her hips pushed into his he came up for air.

"This abstinence thing is really hard," she said.

"It's just a morning kiss." He returned his lips to hers to prove it, and he would completely ignore the hard parts of him seeking the warm soft parts of her. Just kissing.

She was the one to pull away the second time. "Morning tonsil hockey is more than a morning kiss, Barefoot."

"Want me to stop?"

She shook her head and he dipped down for further exploration of her clean teeth and tasty lips.

Minutes later, pulling away was one of the hardest things he'd ever done in his adult life.

Her laughing eyes sparkled when they looked at him. "Two adults really should have more control," he scolded the both of them.

"You'd think."

He reached down and picked up the towel she'd dropped on the floor and handed it back. "I think I'll take a shower." Because if he stayed there, he'd have Monica horizontal and naked . . . or vertical and naked.

He groaned and adjusted his pants to accommodate his need.

Monica chuckled as he walked away.

Monica dropped Trent off at Joe's to pick up his rental car. The yellow Jeep made her laugh. "Not leaving anything to chance," Trent had said.

With a list of errands to run and a physical therapy session to occupy her day, Monica knew she'd have plenty to keep her mind busy for the few hours she'd have by herself.

Trent had kissed her again as she dropped him off.

"I'll pick you up at six," he told her between kisses.

"You will?"

"For dinner. Wear something nice."

She huffed out a breath, pretending disgust. "What, you don't like my workout clothes?"

He ran a hand down her back and cupped her butt in his palm. The sparks his touch created were better than any Fourth of July.

"These clothes make my mouth water."

She kissed him, tasted the water he spoke of.

"Are you asking me out on a date, Barefoot?" she managed once she came up for air.

"Do I need to ask?"

She thought about that. Releasing some of the control in her relationships had always been hard. With Trent, it felt right. Even if it was just asking if she wanted to go out. She knew she wanted to spend time with him. He knew it, too. "You don't need to ask."

"Good." He managed one more quick kiss and opened the door of her car.

Physical therapy wasn't as daunting as it had been two days before. The therapist thought they'd have her walking fast on a treadmill before her follow-up appointment with the orthopedist. She was one step closer to her morning runs, and one step closer to being released from disability and able to return to work. It was one thing to not be able to work and not have a job, it was quite another to be physically able to work, and be told you couldn't.

Monica shoved those thoughts aside while she prepared for lunch with Katie and Jessie. They hadn't brought the kids over when they'd all but ambushed her for an intense "girl talk" session. But that was yesterday afternoon, before Trent had found her . . . before he spent the night and didn't sleep with her. Well, didn't make love to her. She was thinking about their *no-sex* deal as she walked into the restaurant where she was meeting her family for lunch.

The Morrison Family Inn was the brainchild of Jack. It wasn't the luxury hotel that the Morrison chain promoted itself as, but that didn't mean it wasn't posh in many ways. The family-friendly and family-affordable accommodations were evident in every foot of the establishment. All the rooms were at least one-bedroom suites. There were rooms pre-equipped with cribs and Murphy beds, hide-a-beds in the sofas, everything a family could need. The grounds were a child's paradise. Even the restaurant Monica was walking into had families on the mind when it was laid out. The round tables left room for toddlers to move around without bumping into others. The lower ceilings helped muffle the noise of the room and instead of every television in the room hosting the local sports team, half of them were dedicated to kids' television. Although the restaurant was part of the hotel, it had become an instant hit with the suburban community of Ontario.

For Monica, it was always a pleasure to eat with her family. Danny always had a smile when he was with them. Which might have less to do with the fact that mac and cheese was on the menu, and more to do with the fact that Jack had named the restaurant "Danny's."

Monica noticed Jessie waving at her from one of the booths across the restaurant and made her way to their table. Danny jumped up from his seat and ran to her with a hug. She missed her nephew and knew that one day those hugs and kisses would become gross and out of the question, so she made the most of them now and kissed his cheeks until he pushed her away, laughing. "Hey, cowboy." She tilted the cowboy hat he wore down on his head a little farther. Ever since Gaylord had bought the hat for her nephew, he hadn't taken it off. "How is your restaurant running?"

"It's not really mine, Auntie Monica. It's just named after me."

She didn't want to correct him. He'd own that restaurant and more when he grew up.

"Hey," she said as she approached the table.

"Someone looks happier today," Katie said.

"That's because I get to see the kids." She leaned down and dribbled kisses over Savannah's cheeks. "Look who grew a foot."

Savannah was nearing her second birthday and stringing enough words together to actually be understood.

Monica settled next to Jessie and made a fuss out of looking at the pictures Savannah and Danny were creating. Savannah was great training for Danny. Monica had commissioned a custom T-shirt with *Brother in Training* written over the front. He'd loved it.

When the table grew quiet, Monica looked up to find Katie and Jessie staring at her.

"What?"

"What's up with you? Yesterday I wasn't sure you had teeth for the lack of smiles. Today you're . . . you're . . ." Jessie squinted her eyes as if searching for the answers would be easier by wrinkling the skin on her face.

"I'm what?"

"Happy," Katie managed.

"Auntie happy," Savannah giggled at Katie's side.

"Almost glowing," Jessie said.

"There are only two reasons a woman glows and I don't think you're pregnant," Jessie told her.

"I'm not preggers."

Jessie glanced at her son and asked, "Any special hugs you wanna talk about?"

Monica thought of all the hugging, which was special, but not *that* special. "There was some hugging."

Katie's eyes grew wide. "Trent?"

She sighed. "He came to the apartment last night after you guys left."

Both the other women squirmed and glanced at their kids. Monica knew they had a thousand questions and they'd all be asked in code. As to keep the delicate ears and even more transparent tongues of the kids from listening and wagging.

"He did?"

"How did he find out where you lived?" Jessie asked.

Monica glanced between the two women. "*Someone* told him that I used to hang out at Joe's after work."

Katie shrugged. "Don't look at me. I haven't seen him since I picked you up at the lawyers'."

"No phone calls?" Monica asked.

"No."

She glanced at Jessie. "Not a word with him since Florida."

"Well someone has talked to Trent. There are plenty of after-work options for a drink."

Danny bumped Monica's leg as he bent down to retrieve a crayon from the floor. "Trent's nice," he said.

The three of them focused on Danny.

"You met Trent?" Jessie asked her son.

"Yesterday. He and Daddy were at the hotel when Grandma dropped me off."

Jessie closed her eyes and shook her head. "Busted."

Monica had to laugh. Poor Jack didn't stand a chance. "Go easy on him," Monica suggested. "He didn't give Trent my address, just a hangout. He hung out, ran into Walt, and finagled a ride to my place." It was just this side of romantic how hard Trent had worked to get her address. The thought had her smiling again.

"So what happened?"

"I'll give you details later, but let's just say there was a really good reason he spooked and ran off. Once he realized I wasn't engaged when we met, and hadn't lied to him, he wanted a chance."

"A chance?"

"To see me, to date."

"And *hug*?" Katie asked.

Monica shook her head. "No, actually. We're not going to *hug*."

Jessie looked at her like she was crazy. "Not *hug*?"

"I always *hug* first and get to know the guy later. Which usually ends up with the it's-not-you-it's-me talk." It had always been her and not them.

"Wow!"

The waitress gave their conversation pause as they ordered.

"So if there's no hugging going on, why are you glowing?" Jessie had always been so observant.

"Can't a girl be happy about a guy and glow?"

"I guess."

Their drinks arrived, and Monica sweetened her iced tea while she talked. "It helps that I slept last night. I didn't realize how much Trent taking off in Florida bugged me." She sipped her tea. "When I dropped him off at Joe's this morning, he told me he'd pick me up at six tonight for a date." She laughed. "I never let guys *tell* me we're going out." The memory of his take charge tone had her thoughts drifting from her current company. When Monica glanced back up, the girls were staring at her again. "What?"

"He spent the night?"

"Uh-huh."

"On the couch?" Jessie asked.

Monica rolled her eyes. "Aren't there nights you and Jack sleep without hugging?"

"We're married," and as if the bump in Jessie's belly wasn't obvious enough she patted it and said, "and pregnant."

Monica laughed. "You don't have to be married or pregnant to sleep without hugging."

The code talk was making Monica dizzy, and the confused expressions on Katie's and Jessie's faces were priceless. "The glowing might be from all the kissing without hugging."

"And he agreed to this?" Katie asked.

"He suggested it."

"Seriously?"

Monica laughed. "Crazy, huh?"

"Certifiable."

"Maybe. But it's kind of nice. I'm not sure how long it will last, but it's fun."

Katie disregarded Monica with a flick of her wrist. "You're nuts."

Katie looked at Jessie and held out her hand. "You owe me five bucks."

When Monica asked why, neither woman said a word.

Their food came and the conversation shifted to Katie and Dean and their decision to move back to Texas. The thought would have saddened Monica if there wasn't a real possibility of her moving away soon as well.

They ate lunch and then took the kids to the swimming pool and continued talking for hours. In what felt like no time, Monica had to break up girl time to get ready for her date.

As she left the hotel, Monica glanced in the rearview mirror and caught her reflection.

She glowed.

Chapter Twenty-Nine

"They're hedging," Mr. Goldstein told Monica on the phone a few weeks after her first date with Trent. "But they haven't dropped anything yet."

Monica sat on the small patio off her apartment with her phone cradled to her ear. "I wonder why they think they're going to win this. Seems the more information you obtain, the less of a case they have. Didn't you tell me that the statement from Shandee was fabricated and that she didn't want anything to do with coming here to testify?" That information had come midweek, at which time Monica and Trent thought the case would be dropped.

Apparently that wasn't the case.

"She recanted her statement. It wasn't made under oath, so there was no holding her to it."

"I don't get it."

"It's the union. The hospital doesn't want the union there." The union had only been voted in a couple of years before Monica began working there. So far, the contracts they'd negotiated hadn't made life for the nurses that much easier. There was some chatter about a vote to eliminate their presence.

"Why? Seems the nurses are the ones who have to pay the union dues and we aren't getting a lot for it." Her annual raises weren't much to write home about.

"When was the last time you sat in on a union meeting?"

She hadn't sat in on any. "Never."

"You might be happy to know that the next contract, which will begin negotiation this winter, is going to favor the staff much more than the previous one. Even with the depressed economy the union feels that with all the health care reform dollars going into the budgets, they can find a way to get that into your hands. They want to see that your health care benefits remain the same. A lot of companies are having to downsize, but big hospitals can't. Instead they're eliminating raises, cutting benefits. The union wants to be proactive."

"So if the hospital can make it look like the union isn't able to keep an innocent nurse employed now, then the members might think, what good are they?"

"Yeah, that's what we think. It's not written anywhere, but that's our theory. You were convenient. Add a boss that doesn't like you, and you're the target. The hospital made one fatal error. They underestimated you and your ability to seek counsel."

Could it have been as simple as the hospital looking at her resumé's previous addresses to assume she didn't have a family with money? "That sucks."

"When you didn't show up with a union lawyer, they were undoubtedly confused and had to find out how you could afford us."

"I can't afford you," Monica said with a laugh.

Goldstein chuckled at that. "What you can do is see if you can have your union push up the protest. I already spoke with Jack, and he said he'd chat with his sister about making sure the media was there snapping pictures and making the hospital squirm."

"You think it will make a difference?"

"I can't believe they haven't dropped the case yet. Let's give them a reason to drop it before the fall."

Before fall classes. She might not have picked a school to apply to, but she had made the decision to go back once the case was behind her.

"I'll make a couple of calls."

"I'll look forward to hearing from you." With that, he hung up.

The next hour she started her calls with Walt. She asked if he could rally some of the staff in the next twenty-four hours for a protest, to which he told her he'd do everything on his end. The union was just as eager to move on a protest so Monica put all the wheels in motion making calls to Katie, to Monica's friends at the fire station, even some friends from nursing school.

When it was all set she called Trent, who had left that morning to join his brothers for a business meeting in Connecticut. It was the second time he'd left her side in the few weeks they'd been a kissing and dating couple. He'd returned the jet he'd flown down from Seattle and needed to stay in the Pacific Northwest long enough to confirm that Frank was the employee who was flying their planes for his own pleasure. After Frank was dismissed, Trent decided it was time to put into place a benefit program in which longtime employees could request certain flight privileges to avoid any issues in the future.

As Trent told her, ever since his parents' deaths, his brothers had taken up the slack in the company and it was time for him to get back in and ease some of the burden. That meant flying back home for a while.

Monica would have worried about him leaving if he hadn't told her he was coming back. His life wasn't in Southern California, however, and she knew that eventually if they wanted to keep seeing each other one of them would have to make a residential change. The thought would have scared the shit out of her a month ago.

Now she found herself searching for masters in nursing programs close to Trent's company. She wondered if she could trust them as a couple enough to make such a leap.

The couple of nights he planned on being away would help give her the space she needed to think. She already knew that sleeping without him would be difficult and figured she could *think* then.

Their cuddling, kissing, and not making love hadn't made her want to be around him less. She knew when she saw him their conversations and time together were going to be about something beyond the physical. The overwhelming desire to talk to him about the protest was a testament to the changes happening within her. It wasn't often she bothered talking about her problems with the guys she dated. Nothing on a deep level in any account. With Trent, Monica talked about everything. Her dreams, nightmares, future goals, and bucket list achievements.

Share time wasn't limited to her. Trent told her some of the things he wanted to see happen within the company. Now that he was finished with island living, he wanted to be a larger part of the company. His brothers had carried him for some time. Taking part in the daily decisions was a task he wanted to become a part of again. He was once again putting his life on hold, but this time it was to give their relationship a chance.

At some point, Monica knew she had to take a leap of faith and follow her heart. The leap was from a huge height, however, and the fear of falling made her hesitate.

Her call to Trent went to voice mail, which he returned later that night.

"Hey, California," he said on the phone, his voice sleepy.

"Did you just get home?"

"I forgot how annoying commercial flights are."

"Slumming with the rest of us?" Monica joked.

"It's a pain when I know there's a better way. Besides, I don't like someone else driving."

"Control freak."

"Look who's talking."

She brought him up to date on the protest, told him it would take place in two days right before rush hour. "Katie suggested we blow up a picture I took in Jamaica of me at the clinic, and another one from the ER. Make sure the people in the area know which nurse they're rallying for. I'll be at the printer tomorrow and then Katie and I are going to get together with a few of my friends to make the signs."

"I can change my plans and come back early." He'd planned on staying home for a few days.

"I'd love for you to be here, but it's OK. How are your brothers?"

"They're good. They want to meet you."

She smiled at that thought. The last woman he'd tried to introduce to his family ended up breaking his heart. "I'd like that."

"When the hospital drops the case, can I convince you to come here for a visit?"

She curled her feet under her. "You can convince me to visit even if the hospital doesn't drop the case."

He hesitated and Monica could hear the smile in his voice. "All right then."

"All right then," she repeated. They talked for a while longer, both of them reluctant to hang up. When she heard Trent yawn for the second time she told him she missed him, and that she'd call him the next day.

As she hung up she realized that missing him was simply her way of saying she loved him.

And that made her smile.

The day of the protest started early. Monica and Katie put the finishing touches on the posters and arranged for a last-minute permit to be approved so the protest wouldn't get them all arrested. Strategically, the protest was scheduled one hour before the end of the business day. If the lawyers of the hospital, and the administration itself, decided to drop the case, they could minimize the damage of the protest by calling a stop to all the attorneys. Goldstein had told her not to expect a call from him until after five. Even if the hospital decided to drop the case as the first picket sign went up, he'd conveniently get the call to Monica after five. "Make 'em bleed," he'd told her.

She was quite happy to have Goldstein on her side.

Monica staged with off-duty employees, nurses, doctors, union reps, and more members of the fire and even police department, in a park across from the hospital. As four o'clock rolled around, they took the short walk down the street like a flash mob.

Katie held Monica's hand as they approached the sidewalk in front of the hospital. Media vans were already there and Monica noticed the cameras swing their way as they approached. They no sooner touched the public sidewalk than the union reps began marching with Monica's friends and colleagues and shouting through their bullhorns about wanting justice. About unfair practices. It grew loud in a heartbeat.

Katie pulled Monica over to a reporter and facilitated the interviews. Even if the hospital made the call, the damage would have been done. None of which bothered Monica in the least. They wanted to make an example out of her, and instead she'd make an example out of them. *Pick on someone your own size* was the theme of the day. The posters were heartbreaking and the media was all over the story.

Monica told the reporters what she could, all practiced words Goldstein had told her to say. All true, but nothing that would keep her from countersuing the hospital.

The crowd grew with faces Monica didn't even recognize. Between interviews, she thanked people for coming and often found tears on her face as they offered their support. Katie's husband, Dean, had shown up with Savannah in a stroller. On the stroller was a picture of Monica holding Savannah as an infant. The picture had been taken right before Monica had gone to work so she was wearing her scrubs. A thought bubble above Savannah's head said, LEAVE MY AUNTIE ALONE, BULLY!

Cars drove by honking in support, there were discussions of hospital politics, and there were many nurses who mentioned that it could very well have been them that had fallen prey to the hospital's actions.

It was all so very overwhelming. Monica thought of calling Trent, to share the moment with him, and was pulling her phone from her back pocket when a man approached her from behind.

"Nurse Mann?"

Monica turned around and smiled. The stout clean-cut man was terribly familiar, but recognition didn't come instantly. "Hello."

"I wanted to say thank you." As he spoke shock rolled over every inch of her.

"Oh, my God. Gary? Gary Owens?" How was that possible? He looked sober, healthy. Even a little attractive maybe. What he didn't look like was the man she'd read the riot act the last day she'd worked in the ER.

A coy smile passed over his mouth and he nodded confirming his identity. "Almost four months sober." He held up his wrist, which had some kind of charm bracelet denoting his sobriety. "I wouldn't have tried if you hadn't pushed me."

There was no stopping the tears in Monica's eyes. In her peripheral vision she noticed a camera on the two of them.

"You look great." And he did.

"I feel good. When I saw this on TV, I had to come."

"Wow, Gary. I'm not sure what to say."

He shook his head, had tears of his own he was brushing away. "You don't have to say anything. Sometimes it only takes one person to make you realize what's important. You did that, and I'll always be grateful."

"I'm so happy for you."

He shuffled for a bit, then asked, "Can I hug you?"

Monica opened her arms and hugged a man she once thought she never wanted to see again. "Best of luck to you," she said before he walked away and picked up a picket sign.

Another voice interrupted her thoughts. "Was that Gary Owens?" John asked.

"Yes. Can you believe it?"

"Some people do change," he said.

She turned toward her ex and grinned.

"I heard you were with the guy from Jamaica."

They hadn't really talked about the two of them since she returned. He'd called a few times, tried to get her to go out with him, but she never said yes.

"I am."

He shoved his hands in his pockets. "I don't stand a chance, do I?"

Now there were tears in her eyes for other reasons. "I never meant to hurt you."

"And I wish I was the guy who made you happy."

"I really do mean it when I say I'd like to still be friends, John."

He opened his arms and Monica had no problem going to them. When he pulled away, he kissed her cheek. "Take care."

She twisted around to watch him walk away and her eyes collided with Trent's.

His face was stone-cold.

Her heart did a hard kick in her chest and she waited for him to move. The excitement of seeing him was mixed with the fear that he'd misinterpret what he'd just seen between her and John. But if they were ever going to move forward, he needed to trust her, and she needed to trust that he wasn't running off without explanations.

She fisted her hands at her sides and waited for the cold stare to melt, and just when she thought he'd turn and run, he opened his arms.

Those movies where the woman ran into the arms of her guy had always seemed contrived until that moment. Trent lifted her into his arms and whirled her around. "I missed you," he said, his voice tight.

He set her on her feet and kissed her, and not a little peck but a full-on tongue-to-tongue bedroom kiss that wasn't suitable for television. She was a little breathless and pink cheeked when he let her go and found some of the staff staring and catcalling.

"Looks like Queenie is thawing," she heard someone yell.

Monica waved off their comments. "I didn't know you were coming."

"Looks like I need to stick around or risk someone pushing in." He was smiling as he said his words.

"They can push, but they'll never get in."

He kissed her again, briefly.

The phone in her back pocket buzzed and she reached for it. It was after five, and the call was from her lawyer.

Her hand shook as she took the call and plugged her opposite ear to hear. "Please tell me you have good news," was how she answered the phone.

Goldstein laughed. "They dropped the case, Monica. Congratulations."

She reached out for Trent and squeezed his arm. "You're serious."

He laughed. "I'll call you next week about the countersuit. They're already talking settlement."

Trent stared at her now, searching for answers with his gaze.

The grin on her face stretched from California to Boston. "Thanks, Larry."

"Have a great week, Monica."

She screamed when she hung up and threw herself into Trent's arms.

Katie walked over, Dean and Savannah at her side. "Well?"

Monica found her feet again, but Trent kept his arm around her. "They dropped."

Hugs and congratulations spread until someone put a bullhorn in Monica's hand.

"Can I get your attention. Everyone?" She waited for the crowd to turn her way.

Trent picked her up and put her on a chair so she could look above the heads of the people gathered.

"I just got off the phone with my attorney. The hospital dropped the case."

When the clapping died down, Monica thanked everyone for their support and effort in helping her.

Katie took the horn from her when she was done. "We have a banquet prepared over at The Morrison for all of you to help celebrate. So let's get the party started."

———

The banquet was complete with a full buffet dinner with champagne fountains and a DJ.

"How could you have known they'd drop the case?" Monica asked Katie as she stood beside Trent, Dean, and Walt as they toasted a successful day.

"I didn't. But I love a party and figured we'd thank everyone for coming."

"I knew they'd drop the case," Dean said.

"Me, too." Trent hugged her into his side.

"Well, I'm glad they did. Now I can move on."

"What are you going to do now?" Walt asked.

She'd already told him she wouldn't be returning to the hospital to work. "I think I'm going back to school. Get my masters."

"Nurse practitioners?"

The more she thought about it, the better she liked the idea. "Yeah."

Walt's smile fell. "I guess you won't be back to Borderless Nurses."

"I've not ruled it out, Walt."

Monica noticed Gary Owens walking by some of the staff and shaking their hands. He had a Coke in his steady hand. "Don't take me off the roster yet."

She and Trent stayed until the last guest left before heading back to her apartment.

As they walked inside, she came to the realization that her time there was coming to an end. "I'm going to miss this place," she muttered as she walked into the living room and kicked off her shoes.

Trent sat next to her, and pulled her into his lap. "Are you leaving?" He asked his question with a smile on his lips.

"Seems silly to have a two-bedroom apartment when it's just me here."

His smile fell, but Monica didn't relieve his thoughts quite yet. "You didn't run away."

There wasn't a need to explain what she referred to. Trent nuzzled her neck. "I wanted to deck him."

"But you didn't, and you didn't bolt, either."

"I want to say it didn't enter my mind, but the feeling to leave was brief. My desire to stick around and fight for you was stronger."

Monica pushed a lock of hair that had fallen forward away from his eyes. "You don't have to fight for what's already yours."

He leaned in to kiss her and she pulled away. "Wait. I need to say something."

His eyes searched hers and he leaned back to listen.

"I figured out what my one thing is. You know, that one thing in my life that I need to make every day worth living." Her heart fluttered in her chest as she realized without a doubt what that one thing was.

"Oh, what's that?"

As if he couldn't figure it out. "I more than miss you when you're gone. It's like I'm empty inside. It's you that I need."

His coy smile slid and he didn't let her pull away as he kissed her, soft and intimate with lots of sparkly promise.

"Wait, I'm not done."

He leaned his forehead against hers and waited.

She took a deep breath and leapt from the tallest obstacle on which she'd ever been perched. "I'm going to tell you something. I don't expect a response." She hesitated. "I love you."

Trent closed his eyes. "Say that again," he whispered.

"I love you, Trent."

He found her gaze and stared deep inside. "Thank God."

The edge of despair in his voice placed a smile on her face.

"I didn't want to fall alone. I love you, Monica." He held her face in his hand and said, "God, do I love you!"

Yeah, she might have told him he didn't have to repeat the words, but damn it was good to hear them. Any ice left of the queen was shattered with his words.

Her lips met his in a hungry kiss, greedy and full of desire. His arms circled her waist, pushed under her shirt.

She sucked his tongue into her mouth and feasted on his lips. Lips she loved, with the man who broke through her walls and emotional boundaries. It no longer mattered where their relation-ship would lead so long as they were together on the journey.

Monica squirmed on his lap, not content to feel his rising need pressed against her thigh. There were much better places for that part of his anatomy than her thigh and damn if she wasn't ready to experience it . . . him again. Using the sofa for leverage, she lifted her knee over his legs and startled him. Even between their clothes, their combined heat burned. She arched into him with a low moan of pleasure.

Skilled hands ran along the edge of her bra, undid the clasp, and filled his palms with the weight of her breasts.

He broke the kiss and held her to him with both hands as he lifted both of them from the couch. Clasping on with her legs, she used her lips to suck on the lobe of his ear. "Jeez, Monica, you make it hard to walk."

She giggled. "Oh, you're hard. Very yummy and hard."

In her room, he fell with her onto her bed, pinned her, and thrust his hips into hers.

"We have way too many clothes on, Barefoot." She tugged at his shirt, freed it from his shoulders, and tossed it away.

Trent helped her out of her shirt and leaned in to taste her needy breasts. Their endless foreplay had ended right here for weeks. Not this time.

She reached for his pants, undid the clasp, and thrust her hand inside.

He pulled away from her long enough to groan. Using his sur-prise she shifted her leg over him until she rode on top. "I think it's my turn to be on top," she said.

He laughed. "Whatever the lady wants," he promised. "Just get naked."

She slid off the bed and pulled his pants with her until he was there in full naked mouthwatering glory. When she kicked the rest of her clothes off, she reached for her bedside stand, found protection, and returned. She sheathed him slowly, running her hand up his length and back down. When his eyes glossed over and closed she did it again.

Trent reached for her hips and guided her close. With her spread over him, he rounded a hand in front and cupped her. Monica rode his hand for a moment until the rhythm carried her close to the breaking point.

When Trent lifted her up and onto him, he plunged and carried her weight. The angle brought depth and fired off explosions and heat. Monica wanted to think she had control over him, but he managed to take her over and over, guiding her hips and finding the perfect angle for her world to spiral and break free in a rush of pleasure.

He flipped her under him, so unexpected, and so damn hot, and pushed her into the soft bed.

"More," he said in her ear as if a promise. "I want more from you."

"I don't know if I—" But he moved a little higher and—hell yeah—heat built again until she was moaning his name and her eyes went blind.

He pushed himself farther once, twice, until pleasure rippled over him with his release.

The world stopped spinning on its axis yet the two of them kept moving, hearts beating, heads spinning, until she heard Trent draw in a breath. "If . . . if you tell anyone I agreed to not do that with you, I'll tell them you're the liar. Fair warning."

Her laughter filled the room. "Wanna do it again?"

The rumble of his chest against hers was quickly followed by him climbing off her and vaulting off the bed.

Stunned, she leaned up on her elbows and gaped. "Where are you going?"

"Coffee," he said. "We're going to need coffee to stay up *all* night. Make up for lost time."

The man she loved glanced at the door, jumped back on the bed like a kid, and kissed her. "I love you," he whispered. Then he made good on his threat and left to brew a pot of coffee.

Hours later they finally fell asleep, closed off from the world. The next day all Monica could think was the world might be embarking on a new day, but she was taking on a whole new life.

Epilogue

Two months later

"Do you love me?" Trent asked her as they stood in front of one of the company helicopters he'd had Glen fly in from the airport in Houston.

It was the week before Thanksgiving and the Morrisons had invited Trent and his brothers to join them for the holiday. Somewhere, someone heard Monica talk about Trent's bucket list desire of doing the whole cattle run with his brothers. Funny how if you told a Texan you want to ride a horse and live on the range, they'd make it happen even if winter was fast approaching. Not that Monica worried about Trent having any issues with hypothermia. It was Texas, after all. The weather didn't get that bad.

Trent, his brothers, Dean, Jack, even Gaylord were leaving in the morning for four days of camping, riding, and otherwise living off the land.

That was tomorrow. Today, Trent stood in front of a helicopter that represented one of her greatest fears, and if she was reading him right, she knew what he wanted them to do.

"You know I love you. I moved all the way across the country and now live in the snow a good four months of the year. Four months!" And she wouldn't change it for anything. The suit against the hospital ended in her favor to the tune of many zeros. She enrolled in an NP program close to the Fairchild home office and the two of them picked out a ranch-style home that sat on top of a hill facing east. They watched the sunrise together almost every day.

Ginger now had Gilligan, their new dog, to play with during the day when the two of them were gone. Poor Gilligan tried to be the man, but Ginger ran over him every chance she could.

Trent grasped her waist and teased her with a kiss. "Come with me."

Although the thought of climbing in the chopper made her heart rate race, she knew she trusted Trent.

She twisted out of his arms and swung open the door of the helicopter before she lost her nerve. "Oh, OK, fine. Let's go."

Trent didn't give her time to change her mind. He sat behind the controls in seconds and soon the now familiar headphones covered her ears, and the propeller started to spin.

"You do know that most women don't have to prove their love by riding in one of these things?"

"Most women don't sleep with the pilot."

"Do we sleep?" she teased.

He winked at her before lowering the sunglasses on his nose.

The day was clear, the Texan sun was high above, giving the day a feel of spring.

Instead of focusing on the ground, or the sky, Monica watched the joy wash over Trent as he lifted the bird off the skids and into the sky. Once in the air, he pivoted the helicopter toward the direction he wanted to go.

"You really love it," she said.

He glanced over at her, removed a hand from the controls, and squeezed her knee.

As much as Monica liked the gesture, she felt much better with both his hands on the "wheel." She returned his hand and gave it a good pat. "You fly, I'll try to keep my lunch in."

Only when she removed her eyes from him, she didn't feel the familiar twist in her gut as she had in the past. The ground was way the hell down there, but something about it had changed.

They moved over a hill and a herd of cattle started to run away from the noise. "Look," she said pointing to the ground.

Trent's voice sounded high-pitched through the intercom system muffling their ears.

"Up here, you can see them but not smell them."

"Might wanna get used to it, cowboy." They laughed, knowing full well that Trent wasn't a hat-wearing cowboy. Though Monica did have a hat ready to give him when he left in the morning.

They circled the cattle again, then flew farther from Gaylord's property and closer to Jack and Jessie's ranch, which wasn't far away. From their height, it looked much smaller than it was in person. "That's Jack and Jessie's place," she said when it appeared Trent would fly past it.

"It is?"

She couldn't imagine that Trent didn't recognize it, even from the air. "Yeah, the red barn and corral beside the hill."

"Oh, yeah."

He twisted the helicopter around and flew over. Surprisingly, her stomach didn't wobble with the helicopter movement. She removed her cell phone from her pocket to get a picture for Jessie.

Something on the hill beside the barn grabbed her attention. "What's that?"

"Not sure," Trent said as he moved closer. Long strips of yellow tarp flapped in the wind. It wasn't natural, and it didn't look like some kind of giant tent or anything. As they moved closer it appeared as if there were words written on the tarp.

"Something for Danny?"

Monica was peering at the ground, concentrating so hard on reading the words she'd all but forgotten she was staring at the ground from a hundred or more feet.

"Let's get closer," Trent said.

She squinted. Trent hovered over the tarp while she read aloud.

"Will you . . ." her jaw dropped. Her attention snapped to her pilot. ". . . marry me?" she whispered the last words.

Trent was smiling, waiting. "I love you, Monica. I want you forever."

Even with headgear and a microphone covering his mouth, she couldn't help but lean forward and find his lips. "You're crazy," she yelled, as she knocked the ear protection off of him.

"Is that a yes?"

She couldn't think of a better way for him to ask. "Yes, Barefoot. I'll marry you."

He kissed her and still managed to keep the helicopter in the air.

He placed her hands on the controls. "Hold this."

Some of the joy of the moment shifted to terror. "Trent! I can't fly this thing."

He reached into his pocket and removed a box and opened it. Inside, was a spectacular round diamond that rivaled her sister's in a cluster of similar stones set in platinum. Monica let go of the controls and squealed.

Trent grabbed the controls and nearly dropped the ring.

"Ah!" Only instead of worry, excitement filled her. With one hand, Trent managed to get the ring on her finger, kiss her, and promise forever.

Feeling like a giddy teenage girl after her first kiss, the smile on her face actually hurt. She held her hand out and admired the ring he bought with her in mind. "You have class, Barefoot. Serious class."

He was laughing.

Through her headset she heard Jason's voice through the microphone. "Trent, your ground crew is dying here. Do we have a Yankee Echo Sierra or November Oscar?"

Living with a pilot, Monica had managed to look up some of their lingo and knew what Jason was asking.

They were back over Gaylord's property and a crowd had gathered outside to watch them.

"Should you tell them or I?" Monica asked.

The cocky smile on his face never left. "I got it." Trent pressed a button, and from the helicopter streamers fell in long sheets.

"What's that?"

"Giant confetti with the word *yes* printed on it."

Out the window, she noticed the pieces of paper hit the ground and the crowd pick them up. Jessie, with her hugely pregnant belly, and Katie hugged. The kids were running in circles with the excitement. Jason and Glen lifted their thumbs in the air.

Monica moved as close as she could to her future husband and kissed his cheek. "What would you have done if I said no?" Not that he could have had any doubt of her answer. Once she let herself believe in her love for him, there was no looking back.

"We are in a helicopter. I thought I'd keep you up here until you said yes."

She gave him a playful punch to his arm. "You don't scare me, Trent Fairchild."

He leaned close and kissed her.

Acknowledgments

In my years as an ER nurse I've had the privilege to work beside, and with, some of the best doctors and nurses in the world. I wouldn't take back my years of nursing for anything … the things I've learned, the things I've seen, are unsurpassed and not something many would believe.

I've often said that I can't make up the shit I've seen in real life and make it believable in the pages of fiction.

Heroes come in many categories, but those who willingly walk into a war zone without the glory of a paycheck, or even assurance of their own safety … those are true heroes.

This book is dedicated to those who give of themselves daily for others.

Nurse Kimberly, Nurse Anna, Nurse Valerie, Nurse Ray, Nurse Tanya, Nurse Tatiana, Nurse Kathy, Dr. Schmit, Dr. Hook, Dr. Henry, Dr. Noll, Dr. Sam, Dr. Shultz, Dr. Ziemba …

I cannot list enough names.

Thank you!

About the Author

New York Times best-selling author Catherine Bybee was raised in Washington State, but after graduating high school, she moved to Southern California in hopes of becoming a movie star. After growing bored with waiting tables, she returned to school and became a registered nurse, spending most of her career in urban emergency rooms. She now writes full-time and has penned the novels *Wife by Wednesday*, *Married by Monday*, and *Fiancé by Friday* in her Weekday Brides series and *Not Quite Dating* and *Not Quite Mine* in her Not Quite series. Bybee lives with her husband and two teenage sons in Southern California.

Can a sexy pilot's dazzling smile melt the Ice Queen?

Monica Mann has made it her life's work to save lives. After an earthquake and tsunami hit the shores of Jamaica, she volunteers her trauma skills with Borderless Nurses. Calculating and methodical, she creates order out of whatever chaos she finds . . .

Until she finds the perpetually barefoot, impossibly masculine Trent Fairchild. No one can pin him down. No, really. He's a pilot and manages a small fleet of choppers on his adopted island home. Hopelessly drawn to one another, they manage to slip away from the wreckage of the storms to get a little closer. And they get a lot closer than expected when aftershocks from the earthquake trap them in their own life-or-death scenario. Paradise has brought them together. Now will it tear them apart?

ISBN-13: 978-1477809594

51295 >

9 781477 809594

Montlake
Romance